D09753577

N. D. WILSON

OUTLAWS OF TIME

The LEGEND of SAM MIRACLE

Illustrations by
FORREST DICKISON

KATHERINE TEGEN BOOKS
An Imprint of HarperCollins Publishers

Katherine Tegen Books is an imprint of HarperCollins Publishers.

Outlaws of Time: The Legend of Sam Miracle
Text copyright © 2016 by N. D. Wilson
Illustrations copyright © 2016 by Forrest Dickison

Library of Congress Control Number: 2015948280
ISBN 978-0-06-232726-0

Typography by Carla Weise
16 17 18 19 20   CG/RRDH   10 9 8 7 6 5 4 3 2 1
❖
First Edition

For mi padre,
from a grateful son

PROLOGUE

I<small>F YOU COULD STAND STILL IN TIME, YOU WOULD FEEL IT</small> hissing around you like wind made of sand. If you had wings made for that wind, you could soar above the swirl of history as easily as a crow circles a hayfield. You could float just beyond the edge of every *now*; you could spread your time-gliding wings like two cold shadows over *always*. Priests would shiver when you passed. Dreams would scatter. Dogs would howl. Slow ghosts would trail behind as you peered down into moment after moment, searching for your prey, searching for the one boy you had lost, for the boy who had been hidden in *sometime*.

If you had those wings, if you did those things, you would have a name to match your evil.

Are you the Vulture? El Buitre?

No. Nor am I. But I have seen him. Seeking.

1

Sam

THERE'S A KIND OF HEAT THAT CAN PEEL LIZARDS, EVEN IN the shade. Heat that sends every creeping thing slithering under rocks and into graves, heat that floats the crows up and away to find whatever cool whispers of mountain air might be trickling in over the painted mesas.

If you've ever felt heat like that, you already know that the only thing a person can do is go looking for a basement and a cold drink or an air conditioner with enough courage to rattle and hum and battle the sun without so much as a minute to rest.

On those days, days like today, when even the cacti

would be crying in pain if it didn't mean losing their water, the boys of St. Anthony of the Desert Destitute Youth Ranch were actually happy. Because when the sun was in a killing mood, there could be no chores. And when there were a dozen boys and no chores, they would pour into the Commons—the mostly empty concrete-and-cinder-block building where they did their reading and resting and recreating when the sun was down or deadly. Then Mr. Spalding would unlock the Ping-Pong table and turn on the old pinball machine and fill two coolers with ice and Cokes and open the little library of paperback westerns and science fiction comics. And if Mrs. Spalding was feeling pleasant, they would even allow a little music on the old record player.

At SADDYR, those boys hoped for 115 degrees in the shade like most kids hope for Christmas. And if you lived there, you would, too.

Twelve-year-old Sam Miracle was tipped back in an orange plastic chair, perched as still as a stone. His desert-blond hair had been chopped short, but it was fighting back. He had a colony of freckles scattered across his lean sun-dirty cheeks that looked like little brown ants who had finally given up trying to keep his face clean. Stare at Sam for longer than a few moments and you'll see that he might be young, and his skin might be smooth, and his teeth even whiter than the sun could make them, but he didn't seem young. Sam was more like something new made from very old things. Timber fence posts sunbaked to rot. Tangles of barbed wire more rust than steel. Boots cracked and dry and missing soles. Things once useful now with usefulness lost. He didn't look like those things . . . he felt like them.

"SAM!" THE NAME HAD BOUNCED ALL AROUND THE ROCKS, thrown by the voices of eleven different boys searching eleven distant places.

Sam hadn't felt himself fall in the heat. But his head had ached when he'd finally opened his eyes and the bright sky above him had come into focus. And in the sky, dark wings, descending in a circle. Three pairs. Black.

Vultures.

The scabby bald birds had shrieked and hopped as they'd touched down on the boulders around him, assessing his weakness.

A flying stone had sent the biggest bird tumbling in a squalling, flapping cloud of feathers. And then a long boy with broken glasses had hurled a boulder and kicked the next bird all the way out of Sam's range of vision.

"Here!" he had shouted. "He's here!"

Ten more boys had followed, urgent and angry and lofting stones after the disappointed vultures. Sam had been lifted and carried back to the ranch, where he'd been propped in his orange chair and filled with fluids. And after much scowling and irritation, Mr. Spalding had declared the workday over due to heat.

Sam rolled his neck. There was a little patch of dried blood in his hair from today's collapse out on SADDYR land. And it itched. Like crazy.

Sam's plastic chair was just beneath a badly painted mural made up of St. Anthony of the Desert—a bald man with a beard that looked more like a waterfall of noodles—alongside the giant words that Mr. Spalding thought were inspirational.

BE SADDYR!
S *is for* **SAINTLY!**
A *is for* **ACTIVE!**
D *is for* **DILIGENT!**
D *is also for* **DETERMINED!**
Y *is for* **YESNESS!**
R *is for* **RESPONSIBLE!**

Sam turned his head to the side and ground the itchy scab spot against "R is for RESPONSIBLE!"

All around Sam, the little rectangular Commons echoed with the violence of Ping-Pong, laughter, and the *bloop* and ring of the pinball machine. Two of the boys were rotating through Mr. Spalding's antique disco

4

records—squeaking one quick beat to a stop only to start up another nearly identical one.

"Sam?" Peter Eagle, the tallest and toughest of all the Ranch Brothers, pointed his Ping-Pong paddle at Sam from across the room. His dark hair looked like midnight polished into glass, and his eyes were volcanic even when he was happy. "Need a drink? More water? A Coke?"

Sam shook his head just as Peter spun away, smacking his opponent's stealth serve back across the net without looking.

"Ha!" Peter slapped his chest with his paddle. "Nothing sneaks past this! Nothing!"

Barto, long and lean, set a stack of tattered comics on the floor beside Sam and adjusted his broken and rewired glasses.

"You okay?" he asked. "Need anything else?"

"I'm good," Sam said. "And thanks for today." He managed a smile. "I've never seen anybody kick a vulture."

"Yeah, you have," Barto said. "But those birds were bold today. Glad they didn't tear out any chunks before we found you." Barto sniffed. He was always serious, his lips too tightly pursed for smiles. But he had helped Sam out of trouble more than anybody. He picked two comic books for himself, patted Sam's shoulder awkwardly, and drifted off into a corner.

Sam looked down at the comics. He had already read every one of them a dozen times—mostly retellings of classic novels. And his favorite fat paperback was already spread wide on his knee. Sam knew the adventures of its misunderstood outlaw hero well enough to flip to his favorite sections by feel, and most of his daydreams echoed scenes in the book, but he couldn't read anything right now. His mind was slipping away. Slowly and gently at first, and then, once it was free of the ranch and the Commons and the moment . . . it raced.

Sam's eyes trembled, wide and unblinking, leaking water down his freckles. Most boys who let their minds wander end up looking even dumber than they did moments before—limp faces and sagging jaws, droopy eyes and droopy lips always in danger of drooling. But Sam's face didn't go slack. His jaw tightened. His freckle-stained cheeks shivered just enough to worry anyone who might be paying mind. He might still be sitting right there in the Commons, but Sam Miracle was lost all over again.

OVER THE COURSE OF ITS SEVENTY-YEAR HISTORY, SADDYR had been home to a total of 144 Destitute Youth. Of those, fully a third had grown up and gone to prison or had died while committing some kind of crime. Of the twelve current residents, only Peter was truly bad—already having burned down a gas station. His best friend, Drew, was mostly bad—already having wished that he could burn something down, too. But all the boys were . . . *difficult*.

If you asked the Spaldings, they'd tell you that Sam Miracle was the most difficult of all. The most difficult *ever*. Yes, skinny Sam Miracle. He never fought. He wasn't loud. He was young. But he was still the worst boy they had ever agreed to guardian in nineteen years of agreeing to guardian absolutely any boy the state of Arizona might be willing to send them (along with a check).

And when they said Sam was the worst, they weren't wrong.

For starters, Sam's mind was off. Away. Lost. Often. He'd forget to drink water while he was working. He'd forget to blink in the sun. He had to be fenced like a cow or he'd wander off into nowhere and helicopters would have to be called. Sam Miracle had daydreams so powerful, and they carried him so far around the world, that when his mind finally wandered home again from the other direction, he didn't always recognize himself. And his body wasn't always where he'd left it.

Not only that, but he had trouble digesting any food that hadn't been canned and he tended to throw up when people made him eat it anyway.

But worst of all, the bones in Sam's arms had been shattered and fused again so tight at the elbows that he couldn't even touch his own chest, let alone button a shirt

7

or brush his matted light hair. Sam was used to pain, so he was hard to scare. Threats and punishments were no use at all. And he never complained, which made Mrs. Spalding sure that Sam thought he was better than everyone else, especially when he'd laugh or smile his crooked dimply smile for no reason at all.

And then there were the extra state inspections.

And the extra visits from the therapists.

And the reprimands every time the Spaldings lost him.

And the way the other boys all cared for him. Yell at Sam and eleven others would stop everything and become very difficult indeed.

Beyond all that, Sam Miracle wasn't much different from you or me or any kid his age. Take away your family, your memories, your bendy elbows, and then pop you in the desert for a couple of years, and your daydreams might become just as powerful and important to you as his were to him.

Leaning back in his orange chair with a paperback on his knee and rigid arms hanging at his sides, Sam stared across the noisy Commons and out through the rippling heat beyond the sliding glass door. His eyelids fluttered, and his breath quickened. The veins in his neck jumped with his heart, like twin snakes beneath his skin. And just like that, he was gone.

SAM WAS RACING LOW THROUGH A DITCH BESIDE A HIGH road. He was inches taller and a layer of muscle heavier, and a heavy revolver slapped against his thigh with each stride. His leather jacket flapped loose behind him, and his pumping, fully flexible arms were painless in the sleeves—as cool and smooth as liquid. He puffed sweat off his upper lip. Tall grass lashed his hands. He shot over a cactus carcass and dry stones rolled beneath his weight as he landed, but he was too quick to slip. And he was too quick for the big truck bouncing along the rough road above and ahead of him. Too quick and too low to be seen by the guards with rifles in the back.

At a crossroads up ahead, the ditch ran into the gaping dark mouth of a culvert, wide enough to channel flash floods beneath the roads, but dry for the moment.

Sam drew his weapon. Leaping sage and dodging boulders, he aimed up at the truck's rear tire, and he fired. Rubber exploded. The truck swerved. The two guards braced themselves. Unseen, Sam disappeared into the dark tunnel below. And he accelerated.

In the dark, rattlesnakes buzzed surprise, but Sam was already past them. Gritting teeth and dripping sweat, Sam erupted back into the light and scrambled up out of the ditch just as the truck . . . no, the truck was gone . . . just as a stagecoach pulled by a team of black foam-flecked horses thundered past.

The desert was gone. Redwoods towered above one side of the road; a cliff fell away on the other, stretching its bony slope down hundreds of feet to the sea.

Sam had changed, too. He was smaller, he was wearing a scratchy old poncho, and he was straddling an old motorcycle with a rickety sidecar. The motorcycle roared, spewing up a plume of dust and gravel, and Sam shot forward after the stagecoach.

When he was beside the rocking stage, Sam hopped up on the motorcycle seat, balanced for one terrifying moment, and then jumped.

The motorcycle wobbled, rolled, and flipped off the cliff.

Sam slammed against the side of the stage, slowly pulling himself up by the door handle. Inside, a girl with long straight blond hair was bound and gagged and hanging from a hook like meat.

Millie.

Anger pulsed through Sam's whole body when he saw his sister. But Millie didn't look afraid. She looked angry, too. Angry at Sam. But why? She shook her head. She yelled into her gag. And then she slid her feet toward the door and kicked. The door swung open, whipping Sam out over the cliff, over the tiny explosion of his motorcycle impacting far below him and the lines of tiny waves waiting to eat it, and then slamming Sam back against the stage. He didn't fall. Gasping, he grabbed onto the luggage rack on the roof, and then pulled himself up on top of the rocking stagecoach.

A cowboy with a big white mustache stained mostly yellow was already twisted around beside the driver. He was holding a short shotgun with two barrels, and it was pointed right at Sam's middle.

"Darn it," Sam said.

The cowboy smiled. And then he fired.

SAM JERKED AND HIS ORANGE CHAIR ALMOST SLIPPED OUT from under him. He blinked quickly, exhaled slowly to steady his breathing, and then forced a long yawn until his frantically beating heart began to normalize. Finally, he shrugged up his shoulders one at a time to grind his cheeks dry.

Just one more thing about Sam. Your daydreams probably end well. Sam's never did. But he didn't really mind. After all, one moment ago, his arms had been working great.

Sam swallowed and looked around the room.

Things had quieted down a lot while he had been stage chasing, and his overheated Ranch Brothers had settled down onto the cool concrete floor all around the room. The music was off. No ping. No pong.

"Hey," Sam said. He looked around. The boys all looked back.

"Anything interesting?" The boy asking had long legs crossed tight beneath him, sharp eyes, a tangle of curly dust-colored hair on the top of his head, and hands criss-crossed with ugly scars. His name was Jude, and when he wasn't competing with Sam for comic books, he was writing. He had a thick rumpled stack of pages in his scarred hands now, and given the tone of the room, Sam knew that Jude had just been reading one of his stories to the group.

"Anything?" Jude asked again. He dug a pencil stub out of his pocket.

Sam shook his head. "Just . . . stuff. Are you reading a new story? Did anyone try to wake me up?" Sam looked at Peter. The burner of gas stations had his veined arms crossed and his eyes shut. Drew Dill, the number two villain on the ranch, was seated beside Peter. He was only slightly shorter than Peter, but he was darker and broader and his head was shaved.

"You know you don't just wake up, bro," Drew said. He might not have burned down any gas stations, but Drew had chopped off his own pinkie finger on a dare, and the little stump on his left hand was a grisly reminder to the boys never to dare Drew to do anything.

"I'm sorry, Sam," Jude said, shuffling papers. "Let me catch you up."

"No," said Peter. He didn't even open his eyes. "The rest of us are waiting."

Jude looked from Peter to Sam.

Sam shrugged. "Just keep going. I'll figure it out."

"It's about our redheaded fools," Peter said. "That's all you need to know."

Jimmy Z and Johnny Z both grinned. They were twins, redheaded, almost always sunburnt, and just one year older than Sam.

Jude cleared his throat, tapped his papers together on the floor, and commenced reading.

"Jimmy and Johnny Z had always been the quietest of the Ranch Brothers, at least until a fight broke out. In a fight, they became two wild, roaring redheaded storms—true sons of thunder—flurries of feet and fists and teeth. But how could an average outlaw know that just by looking at them? And Peanut McGee was definitely a below-average outlaw . . ."

Jude continued, but Sam drifted away, looking around the room at all the listening boys who were leaning back against the walls or sitting cross-legged on the floor. Jude had written stories for all of them. All but Sam.

Flip the Lip was leaning against the pinball machine. He was stocky, and when he wasn't mouthing off, he was chewing his lower lip. There was blood on it now. He said he started doing it to stop himself from grinding his teeth. In Jude's stories, he was the fast-talking, knife-throwing, futuristic son of a sewer pirate. Barto was tall and bent, and the only boy with glasses—broken and wired together again more times than anyone could count. Jude called him Bartholomew Whig in his stories, an inventor of magical machines. Barto pretended to hate it. His long fingers were never still, and he was braiding wire into some kind of wreath while he listened to Jude.

Two scrawny blond boys were quietly playing a bizarre card game behind Jude as he read. Both boys had cards tucked behind their ears, cards pinned down to their necks with their chins, and they'd stripped off their shoes and socks to hold fans of cards between their toes. And they were taunting each other with silent snarls and exaggerated goon faces. Matt Cat and Sir Thomas. Matt had a face like a lumpy biscuit, but Sir T had features as sharp as creased paper. The two of them were completely ridiculous, but even they had gotten their own stories from Jude. Even worse, he had officially named them the smartest boys on the ranch. They argued constantly, even in Jude's stories, but they also solved every puzzle, unraveled every mystery, and invented complicated and impossible games that none of the other boys found interesting.

Matt and Sir T saw Sam watching them, and both

focused their attention on him—eyes wide, tongues out, nostrils flared. Sam looked away quickly before he could laugh and disrupt the story all over again. Jude had Jimmy and Johnny defending a wagon train full of beautiful pioneer girls, and that kind of thing should not be interrupted.

Just off to Sam's left, Tiago Lopez and Simon Zeal both leaned against the cinder-block wall with their legs stretched out. They were motionless while three blue-tailed lizards skittered over and under their legs and then darted behind their backs. The lizards had tiny leashes of red thread tied to the boys' fingers. Tiago wore a short Mohawk on the top of his head only, and Simon wore his dark hair however the bed left it until the Spaldings finally did something about it. These boys made traps whenever they could—sometimes with Barto's help— and snuck out of the dorm late at night to set them. When Jude needed heroes to tame or find some legendary beast, when he needed a monster defeated in some distant darkness, Simon and Tiago always made the trip and got the job done.

So why didn't Sam get any stories?

Sam looked down at his arms. The answer was a little bit obvious, but that didn't mean he had to like it. Jude could easily fudge his arms in a story. Sam did it in his dreams all the time.

Of course, Jude didn't write stories about Peter either. But that was probably because he was scared Peter would hate them.

"Sam!"

Mr. Spalding loomed in the doorway, a tall backlit shadow. Everything stopped. Jude dropped his pages. Barto set down his wire. Matt and Sir T both spat out cards. All eleven of Sam's Ranch Brothers were silent, staring.

"Sam," Mr. Spalding said again, quieter this time. "Got a doc here for you." He looked around the quiet room. "You boys . . . behave."

He slid the door shut and was gone.

The boys watched Sam stretch out his legs and then rock up onto his feet.

Peter pushed himself up off the floor. Drew did the same.

"Want us to come?" Peter asked. "We can."

Sam shook his head and smiled. Peter always offered. Sometimes he insisted. Even when it was just a nurse with some new cream she wanted to try on his arms.

"I'm fine," Sam said. "Finish your story. I'm sure Jimmy and Johnny both die at the end."

"Hey!" The redheads spoke in unison. "No way!"

Matt and Sir T threw a pile of cards at them.

"Kill 'em, Jude!" Matt said.

Sam tugged the sliding glass door open, ignoring the throb in his rigid elbows. Heat punched him in the face as he stepped outside. He jerked the door closed on laughter behind him.

The Youth Ranch consisted of three cinder-block buildings squatting around a gravel courtyard decorated with barrels and a rotten old wagon with no wheels. Next to the Commons, there was the Bunk House, where the boys slept and showered. Across the courtyard from Sam, the Spaldings' house shone with a fresh coat of pink paint, courtesy of a life lesson for the Destitute Youth earlier in the month. Pink or not, it still looked more like a prison than a house. The windows of both stories were dark and caged with bars, and the metal roof had grown a skin of rust decades ago.

Beyond these three buildings, there was a rickety water tank on stilts too short to be called a tower and a small shed the boys called the Blood Barn, where coyotes eventually killed and ate any livestock that the Spaldings might have recently purchased for the boys to raise. There were two goats in there now, alive but nervous.

Beyond the Blood Barn, twelve acres of boulders and cacti had been fenced off—one for each of the Destitute Youth to learn about cultivating rocks. Beyond the fences, miles of desolation rolled slowly upward toward the mountains, hiding abandoned mines and railroads, skeletal ghost towns, and eventually Mexico.

Sam paused in the courtyard. He was alone with the sun. Whoever was waiting for him could wait another minute. He bowed his head and extended his scarred brown arms straight out from his shoulders, letting the solar fire do its work. When his arms were hot, his right arm could bend at least a centimeter, and his left a full inch. The burn was worth it.

"What are you doing?"

Sam dropped his arms and looked up. A girl was leaning against the pink house, squeezed back into a thin shadow. She was wearing a baggy old SADDYR T-shirt and jeans belted with bright braided rope and cuffed up well above her boots. She was thin, but her cheekbones were wide and high and soft. Her eyes were hidden beneath a ball cap pulled low, and her long black hair fountained out the back in a ponytail. She wasn't any taller than Sam, and she couldn't be much older. Sam knew who she was. He'd seen pictures of her before, but never the real thing. And the pictures he'd seen—of a chubby-cheeked dark-haired girl in frilly dresses—clearly were years out of date.

"Most people can't stand the heat," she said. "You looked like you were trying to cook."

Sam shrugged. "My arms move a little when they're hot. I like to feel them bend."

"Doesn't the burn hurt?"

"They always hurt."

The girl considered this. "Well, you should at least wear a sweatshirt or something. Cover the skin. Why don't your arms bend?"

"I'm not sure." Sam squinted, trying to see her face. "Not exactly. The doctors say I was in a car that got hit by a train and thrown off a cliff. They say I'm lucky to have arms at all."

"Don't know if I would call that lucky," the girl said. "Do you remember any of it?"

Sam blinked slowly. Sweat ran down behind his ear. He flexed his right arm, and for once, he didn't even notice if it bent.

Sam shook his head. "I dream a train wreck lots of nights. But it isn't a real memory or anything. I'm always inside the train, and my arms are fine afterwards, but there are these gunfighters . . ." Sam stopped himself. Gunfighters? Really? He sounded eight years old. Nobody ever sounds smart when they're talking about their dreams. The girl was just staring at him. She might be thinking anything.

"It's actually a scene from the beginning of a book," Sam said. "About an outlaw with really fast hands that people can't hardly see, and he always wears this poncho . . ." He trailed off. Talking about the book wasn't helping.

19

The girl pushed off the wall and stepped into the sun, clearly assessing him. "I've never dreamed it, but I've read it. *The Legend of Poncho*. With the red cover. It's always been here. Kinda weird, but I liked the end. I'm glad he died. The bad guy was cool."

Sam's lip curled, and he shook his head. "I make up different endings every time, and all of them are way better. That's the only part of the book I really hated."

The girl crossed her arms. "Well, you should read that part again, because that's how it had to happen."

"I can't," Sam said. "I tore those pages out and flushed them down the toilet a year ago."

The girl laughed, but bottled it up quickly in a smile, and then smudged the smile down into a smirk.

"I'm Gloria Spalding. My friends call me Glo. My parents are too scared of you boys to keep me around, but I'm in between boarding schools at the moment."

"I don't think I'm going to call you Glo," said Sam. He shrugged up a shoulder and ground his sweaty cheek against his shirt.

Gloria flinched. "Nobody said you had to. You're not my friend."

"Even if I was, I still wouldn't. Glo makes me think of worms."

Above them, a fist was thumping on glass. Sam

looked up at the second-floor windows in the pink house. He could see Mr. Spalding's shape behind the bars and the reflection of the sky wobbling as the pane moved. He looked back down at his guardian's daughter.

"I'm going to call you Glory." Sam Miracle smiled. "Now I should go."

Sam moved toward the side of the house. Glory watched him go. When he reached the screen door, she spoke.

"I wouldn't go up there. The guy is a total creeper. That's why I'm out here. Just hide with the goats or something."

Sam pulled the screen door open, pushed through the heavier door inside, and shut both behind him.

The air in the entryway was cool and lifeless. The light was dim, but Sam could see the dark thickly carpeted stairs rising up in front of him. He stepped forward while his eyes were still adjusting. Paper crunched under his shoe. There was a note on the stairs. He bent and picked it up with a rigid arm.

Heavy woven paper with rough edges. Sharp large handwriting and curly exclamation marks.

RETREAT! LIFE AND DEATH! BUNK HOUSE NOW! EXPLAIN LATER!

FT

Who the heck was FT and what was he talking about? Not that it mattered. The note couldn't be for Sam. He straight-armed it into his pocket and hopped up the next two stairs. He could hear voices trickling down from the Spaldings' living room. Mrs. Spalding was laughing uncomfortably.

Paper crunched, and Sam stopped again. Another note. How had he missed it? The light paper stood out on the dark carpet like snow on asphalt.

IDIOT! BACK DOWN SLOWLY, GET OUTSIDE, THEN RUN!
    FT

Sam looked up the rest of the stairs. No more notes. He could see the old photos of frilly-dress Glory near the top. He could see the fuzzy rope dangling from the ceiling to hold Mrs. Spalding's fake plants.

Sam took another step.

Crunch.

How was this possible? Was this a joke? Sam's heart was pounding. He looked down the stairs behind him.

"Glory?" he whispered. "This isn't funny."

Nobody. He picked up the note.

I CAN'T KEEP CIRCLING BACK FOREVER WITHOUT
GOING INSANE! NITWIT! LEAVE NOW!

22

Sam didn't even move before the next note appeared. One second it was simply there and a small swirl of sand rustled off it onto the carpet. The handwriting had grown so large, Sam didn't need to pick it up to read it.

IF HE GETS YOUR HEART, THERE'S NOTHING I CAN DO

The next second, in a gust of wind, multiple notes appeared clustered on every single step all the way up, sand hissing across the loose paper.

Sam ran. Up. Not down. Slipping on the notes, kicking them into a cloud behind him, he fell onto his stiff arms and scrambled on all fours. Heart drumming, adrenaline humming, he crashed into the Spaldings' living room, kicked over a lamp, and rolled clear of the stairs.

Conversation stopped. Five eyes focused on him.

~ 2 ~

Tiempo

Mr. Spalding was standing in front of the window
with his hands behind his back. He had a head like a
speckled egg stuck in a small hair nest, his skin was loose
and sun-flaked, and his forearms were bald from years of
nervous picking. He didn't seem at all surprised that Sam
was sprawled on his floor beside a broken lamp. Sam had
done far more surprising things than this.

Mrs. Spalding was squeezed into a plush recliner and
her face needed extra skin just about everywhere. Her
hair was big, her eyebrows were made of pencil, and she
was wearing her best floral bathrobe. Even as a woman

who survived exclusively on mail-order cookie dough and who never got dressed before dinner, she still managed to aggressively judge others. She was judging Sam right now.

"Samuel Miracle! You wouldn't think it, but of all the boys we've ever found it in our hearts to foster, he's the most trouble per inch." She wasn't looking at Sam. Her eyes were focused on someone behind him.

Sam jumped to his feet and spun around, nearly falling all over again.

"I don't doubt."

The man who spoke was thinner and taller than Mr. Spalding and bent like a fingernail moon. He was wearing a tweed three-piece suit much too small for his bony frame with the trousers tucked into high black motorcycle boots with big silver buckles. The sleeves of his jacket stopped inches short of his knobby wrists, revealing two thick tangles of string bracelets. His long-fingered hands were webbed together around a battered old coffee cup.

Sam stared. He'd seen this man before, or . . . some version of this man. A shorter and thicker and unbent version. And the experience hadn't been pleasant. Sam might not be able to remember, but his body could. His already pounding heart was kicking harder. His throat was tightening.

The man's eyes were hidden behind dark sunglasses,

but a deep scar ran down his forehead and dove behind the glasses onto his cheekbone before veering sideways and almost completely halving his nose. His dark hair was parted hard and oiled back, and he was grinning above a small pointed beard much too delicate for his face.

"Sam," said Mr. Spalding. "This is Professor Tiny. He's from England."

"Professor?" The man laughed. His voice was deep. "Naw. That was just a posh tone to shine you. Sam knows me. We've been mates for ages. We've bled together." He took a long wobbly step forward. "You remember Tiny, don't you Sam? Don't hurt my feelings."

Sam coughed and stepped back. "I . . . don't remember." He heard the door open downstairs. "Sorry. I don't remember lots of things."

"Oh, but I do," Tiny said. "This flesh has stretched out a bit with all the laps I've run from *then* to *now*, but my mind's as fit as fit gets. Not like yours." He took another step forward, long fingers gripping his coffee cup. His smile grew and his voice hardened. "I remember your sweet mother. I remember her funeral and your pretty sis taking you on that slow train. Because I've seen it all over and over again searching for you. And I remember a boy named Sam Miracle carving my perfect face in two." The lengthy man sneered and the mug shattered in his hands.

26

Coffee and ceramic shards rained down on the carpet between his boots.

"Greg," Mrs. Spalding said. She slipped out of her recliner and backed toward the kitchen. "Greg! Do something!"

Mr. Spalding inched forward, resting a hand on Sam's shoulder.

"Mr. Tiny, it appears you have no real medical interest in Sam, so I'm going to need you to leave."

Tiny laughed.

Sam could feel his guardian's hand shaking on his shoulder. But his own fear had evaporated. His mind was wandering, searching, racing through dreams and memories for something that he had to find. His mother? A sister?

He could see the old wooden train platform. He could hear the same chuff and puff of the engine that he heard in all his dreams. He could see long blond hair moving down the aisle of a train car in front of him. And then he saw the hair begin to float toward the roof. He was floating, too. Rising among suitcases and hats. And then metal began to scream and glass began to shatter.

Glory stepped out of the stairwell into the living room. Sam didn't even look at her.

Groaning. Crying. Fire. Laughter. Gunshots.

Sam was pinned between a broken bench and a bent slab of floor. He braced his feet against the bench. Sputtering blood, he pressed it away and rolled free.

A man stood above him with a revolver in his hand. He wasn't tall. He had a pointed beard. And his dark hair was parted hard and oiled back. His eyes were vivid blue. And then he grinned.

"Guv! Over here!"

The man pointed his gun straight down at Sam, cocking it with his thumb. Sam's hand closed around a long jagged shard of metal, and he knew that his arms could still bend.

Sam Miracle blinked. And blinked. He twitched his head from side to side, trying to focus. Mr. Spalding's hand was still on his shoulder. Glory was looking at him from the side, dark eyes worried.

"Sam?" Glory asked. "Are you okay?"

Tiny was amused. His scarred face as curious as it was threatening.

"Black out often, do you?" he said. "See anything worth sharing?"

Sam lunged forward, his stiff arm swinging. Tiny flinched back too late, and Sam's hand slammed into his face. The sunglasses snapped and spun free.

Tiny snarled. His right eye was completely missing. His left was vivid blue and on fire with hate.

"I remember," Sam said. He pointed up at Tiny. "I remember you taking my sister. I remember when you had both your eyes."

"Your sister?" Tiny snorted. "How much do you even remember? What was her name, Sam? You remember my eyes, what color were hers?" He laughed. "She's been erased from her own brother's memory. She's forgotten. That's even crueler than killing. Thank the priest for that. We only snatched her."

"*Millie*," Sam said, and the name practically choked him coming up. It lived inside him somewhere deep. Deeper than memory. It was written in his blood. Rooted in his heart. "I see her every day. In every dream."

Tiny laughed and his torso rippled. "And in these dreams, does your sweet sister survive, Sam? Because if she does, then you're playing make-believe."

Sam's fists were clenched, and he leaned forward against Mr. Spalding's grip. But his guardian backed him away. Glory was rooted to the carpet, her mouth frozen open. Somewhere behind Sam, he could hear Mrs. Spalding sobbing.

The windows in the living room began to chatter. Sand hissed hard against the glass. The fake plants swung on their fuzzy ropes.

29

Tiny glanced up and smiled. "Speak of the devil and he's soon at your elbow." He pulled a worn old-fashioned revolver from inside his coat and pointed it at Sam. "You're coming with me, laddo."

Sam heard the door bang open downstairs. Boys were shouting.

"No way!" Glory jumped in front of Sam. "Mom, call the cops!"

"Yes, give them a ring," Tiny said. "Tell them that Samuel Miracle has gone missing for the last time."

Mr. Spalding exploded. With one hand, he threw Sam to the floor. The other tossed Glory down after him. Roaring, he jumped at Tiny, grabbing for the gun.

Sam landed on his back with a gasp, and his breath was gone. Dazed, he watched the world slow down. Glory floated on top of him, flailing before she slammed onto his chest. He saw Mr. Spalding swimming through the air toward his enemy, and he thought that Mr. Spalding wasn't very boring after all. He saw Tiny's gun barrel thump Mr. Spalding on the head, and he watched his guardian crumple. He saw sand streaming into the room and he watched the fake plants fall as the sand raced across the ceiling.

He watched Tiny step forward and point his gun straight down at him. If his arms had been bendy, he would have been able to push Glory off him in time.

There was a stampede on the stairs. A Ping-Pong paddle spun through the air, crashing into Tiny's cheek. Drew Dill dove out of the stairwell and put his wide shoulder into Tiny's ribs.

Sam saw the flash from the barrel and felt something punch him clean through the gut. Boys erupted up the stairs. Two roaring redheads. A boy with a Mohawk and a knife. Tiny fought to keep his feet. But hissing sand swept across the room, swallowing them all, swallowing the world. And then there was nothing.

"Idiot! What did that fool hope to accomplish? Oh, I added inches more to that awkward frame. Tiny, indeed! Ha. And what did he gain? A chance to ruin some poor girl's life? She had nothing to do with this. Nothing!"

Sam opened his eyes. His breath was still gone. He was still on the Spaldings' living room carpet, still staring at the ceiling, but the lights were all off. Moonlight flowed down on him through the windows.

And he was in pain. More than usual. A lot more. He fought to breathe and barely managed a burble. A man in a black robe stepped into view and dropped into a crouch beside him. His jet hair was wild and uneven but contained by a rag strip tied tight across his forehead. His skin was dark and smooth except for two deep creases high on his cheeks. His teeth were wide and white in the

31

moonlight, and his black eyes were overflowing with irritation. He was wearing the black shirt and white collar of a priest.

"How's the pain?" he asked. "Manageable? I need time to think."

Sam shook his head. Very much *no*. His lips sputtered.

"Where . . . Glo . . ."

"Right here," the priest said. "Slightly better off than you are." With a cool hand the priest turned Sam's head. Glory was lying on her side next to him. Her cap had fallen off and her face was slick with sweat. Her eyes were wild, searching the room.

"Breathe," the priest said. "Stay calm. Try not to wake the Spaldings. Things can always get worse. Always."

"I don't—" Sam began to cough.

"Understand?" the priest asked. "Right. Well, you never do and you don't need to. Not yet, at any rate. We've only hopped into tomorrow night till I can settle on my next move. It isn't speed chess but sometimes it feels like it."

Sam shut his eyes. Now would be a lovely time for a daydream. But he was probably daydreaming already. This couldn't be real. He opened his eyes again and they locked into Glory's.

"Who . . . ," she said. "Who . . ."

The priest was pacing. "If I reset you two in the moment before the shooting, there's no surety that you'll remember this, and Tiny might be expecting it and be waiting. And if Sam has proven anything, it's that he's incapable of following instruction. If I reset earlier, your memories will be even worse and the whole thing liable to repeat. You'll be in as much pain . . ." He stopped. "Pain." The priest dropped back into a crouch, squatting flat-footed between Glory and Sam. "Hang onto this pain. Promise me. Feel it. Remember the agony of this moment or you will be doomed to forget and repeat it. Can you do that? Both of you get to the Bunk House. *The Bunk House.* Lock the door and wait for me."

Panting, Glory eyeballed the priest like he was a nightmare.

"Who . . . ," she said again. "Who . . ."

"Father Atsa Tiempo," the priest said. "We've never met, but you'll have to trust me. I've known Sam for more than a century. He'd vouch for me if he could remember any of it."

Father Tiempo crossed his arms, placing his right hand on Sam's head and his left on Glory's. Then the priest shut his eyes and began to whisper. His quiet voice was like an unbending wind from another world. Sam felt like he was flying apart. Racing sand peeled him away layer by layer.

The pain in his stomach vanished first. And then the rest of everything.

❖ ❖ ❖

Sᴀᴍ ʜᴀᴅ ɴᴏ ɪᴅᴇᴀ ʜᴏᴡ ʟᴏɴɢ ʜᴇ'ᴅ ʙᴇᴇɴ sᴛᴀɴᴅɪɴɢ ɪɴ ᴛʜᴇ
sun. Had he dozed off on his feet? It wouldn't be the first
time. His eyes were still shut. A moment ago he'd been in
total darkness, but now sunlight was filtering bright and
bloody red through his eyelids.

"Sam!"

He opened his eyes, immediately throwing a stiff arm
up in front of his face to shield a squint. A girl was standing beside the Spaldings' house in a baggy old SADDYR
T-shirt. She was poking and prodding herself like something was missing. She looked up.

"Sam!" Her eyes were wide. "This is insane. That was
for real, right? Who was that guy? How did he do that?"
She moved out into the sun, pointing at Sam's stomach.
"You're fine. You should be a dead bloody mess, but you're
fine. Where is he?"

"I'm sorry," Sam said. "You're Gloria, right? I've seen
your picture before."

Glory froze. "Not funny."

A fist pounded on glass and Sam looked up at the
second-story windows of the pink house.

"I should go," Sam said. "Your dad has someone waiting for me."

"No!" Glory stepped directly in front of Sam. "Are
you nuts?" She glanced up at the house and then grabbed

34

Sam by the arms to pull him away.

Sam jerked his arms free and glared at the girl. "Don't touch me again."

Glory's eyebrows jumped. "Really? You're just gonna walk right up there and get shot all over again? We were just here, Sam. We talked, you went in, I went in, we both got shot. Shot! Wait . . . when we were here last time, you told me that you flushed the last pages of *Poncho*. Now how would I know that?" She leaned all the way into Sam's face, searching his eyes with hers.

Sam licked his lips. Nothing made sense. He was lost. He was always lost. His head was spinning, his vision was blurring, and the girl he didn't know was talking to him like he was doing something very wrong. And every part of him said she was right. Every part of him except his brain.

"I was shot?" he asked. "When?"

"In about two minutes," Glory said. "The priest said he'd meet us in the Bunk House. Dad can handle that freak on his own. We have to go now!"

"The priest?" Sam shook his head. "No. No." He shut his eyes and shook his head harder. "The priest isn't real. I'm supposed to be doing something else right now. Life lessons. I'm going to get in trouble."

Glory made a fist and punched Sam in the stomach as hard as she could.

35

Sam doubled over and fell onto the hot rough ground. Pain. Fighting for breath, he looked up at Glory standing over him.

"Does that hurt enough?" she asked. "Remember now? Think about the pain."

Sam spat. Tiny had stood over him and pulled the trigger. He'd fired right through Glory's back and into his stomach. It didn't make sense, but it had happened. And the priest . . . the priest was real.

He looked into Glory's eyes and he nodded. She grabbed his hands and pulled him to his feet. A tall shape moved behind the glass in the upper window.

Somehow, Sam knew what was coming. He jerked Glory to the side and dragged her into a run.

Tiny had guessed right. Sam would have walked right back into the same trap. But not Glory.

A gun fired behind them as they ran. Shards of window spun down through sunlight.

3

The Legend of Poncho

SAM BANGED THROUGH THE BUNK HOUSE ENTRANCE AND staggered along between the two rows of metal bunks. Glory slammed the door shut and leaned her back against it. Both of them were breathing hard. An air conditioner was whispering through ducts in the stained ceiling. Every window had been curtained, but sunlight the color of custard still oozed through them.

"Why am I so stupid?" Sam jogged between the beds to another door at the far end of the Bunk House. When he had checked the lock he turned around. "I never understand anything. I think something is real and it isn't. I think something is fake and it's actually real."

Sam thumped his head against the wall and then blinked hard like he was trying to clear his vision. He looked back at Glory. "You might think I'm crazy, but this isn't the first time stuff like this has happened. I've had the longest dreams you could imagine—like living a whole life—until I completely forget this place or that I was ever here, and then I wake up in the desert with a helicopter landing next to me and some fat man-nurse starts sticking needles in my arms and they bring me back here and your parents tell me that I was working on a fence and was only lost for one night."

Glory slumped down until she was sitting on the floor. She buried her head in her hands.

"Something is seriously wrong with me," Sam said. "I mean that for real. I feel totally crazy." He pointed a stiff arm at Glory. "If I had to bet right now, I would say that you're probably not even here, that the Spaldings don't even have a daughter, and that I'm making all of this up. All of it. In a second, I'll think I'm chasing a stagecoach or a train or a truck and then I'll get shot or trampled by a horse or thrown off a cliff and I'll wake up . . . somewhere. Could be the helicopter and the fat nurse all over again."

"Stop talking." Glory's voice was muffled by her hands.

"I'm useless," Sam said. "The crazy kid with brain problems. Talking to some imaginary girl."

"Stop it!" Glory looked up. Her eyes were wet and her skin had gone gray. "You might not know if I'm real, but I do. I know I'm real, so shut up about it already. I just got shot, and then a priest moved me through time!" She held up her hands. Her fingers were trembling. "That was real, Sam! *Real!* I'm freaking out right now. I think . . . I'm going . . ." She leaned over sideways, fighting a gag.

"Oh, don't puke," Sam said. "If you do, I will, too. Even if this is a dream."

Bedsprings squealed beside Sam and he jumped away, startled. Father Tiempo yawned and sat up on a top bunk, stretching. Sand streamed down off his lap. He'd changed. His hair was pure white and deep hard canyons lined his dark face. His eyebrows had thickened, and his hands were gnarled and scarred.

"Hello, Samuel." The priest yawned. And then smiled. "So glad you made it. Glad I made it. There were a few decades there that were too close to call. And I will be dying soon. You are ready for the journey? Come. Time may be endless, but this moment is not."

The priest hopped lightly off the bed, his movements younger than his looks.

Glory scrambled to her feet, tossing back her hair and eyeing the priest. She held up a finger. "Hold on! We're not going anywhere until you explain what just happened. We just saw you five minutes ago, and you were a lot younger."

Father Tiempo smiled. "I was younger and you were older, though only by one twist of the earth. It was a pleasure to meet you, Miss Spalding, but you aren't going anywhere at all. From this moment, you will continue to live your life at the normal rate and in the normal way, passing into the future at approximately one second per second. And please accept my apologies for the disruption. Your involvement was the result of villainy now corrected, and is no longer required. Tiny has retreated to another time, where you will never see him again. But Sam is coming with me, back to where the pain and failure in his story began."

"Gloria," Sam said. "Gloria . . . is this him?"

"Don't call me that," Glory said.

"Sorry," said Sam. "I thought you were Gloria."

"You call me Glory." She slid closer to Sam, gripping his forearm protectively. "I don't think you should take him anywhere. It messes his memories up and he hates it."

Sam looked at Glory and then at the priest. He didn't want to go anywhere, especially if it meant more confusion. He had plenty of that already.

Father Tiempo scratched his thick eyebrows. His old

eyes were completely focused on Glory.

"It's regrettable, yes, but Sam's memory troubles are to be expected, and he recovers. Somewhat. You are more unexpected. What do you remember from when you were shot tomorrow night? How much from our first meeting?"

"Everything," Glory said. "You talk a lot even when you think people aren't listening. You were deciding where to move us so the killer wouldn't be waiting. You said it was like speed chess. You said you added inches to Tiny's frame, which made me wonder how. You can stretch people? You said you had known Sam for a century and you told us to focus on the pain and meet you in the Bunk House. You crossed your arms to touch our heads and then everything was all wind and sand. Oh, and you said your name was Atsa Tiempo. I was thinking about that after everything went dark but before we were back in the courtyard. I knew a boy named Atsa, and it's Navajo for 'eagle,' but *tiempo* is Spanish. Are you one or the other or both or neither?"

Father Tiempo's old lips tightened. "You were thinking in the darkness between times?"

Glory shrugged. "If that's what it was, yeah. My brain doesn't really turn off. I can even study for tests while I'm asleep. If I am sleeping. Either way, it gets tiring."

Sam shuffled his feet and slipped his stiff arm out of Glory's grip. He didn't like feeling inadequate. And he

41

didn't need a girl—especially a girl he barely knew—protecting him from an old man.

"I'm fine," he said. "I'll go anywhere. Let's go."

The priest didn't even look at him. His eyes were alive with light and searching Glory's.

"I do remember stuff," Sam said. "I'm not always an idiot. I remember all sorts of things." He stepped further back and leaned against a bed. "It's just that some of the things I remember aren't real." Glory and the priest weren't listening. He could walk back to the Commons and start playing Ping-Pong and they wouldn't even notice. They were focused on each other. Sam began grinding an itch on his back against the bed. "See? I remembered the Ping-Pong! I even know which comic books I was reading, and I can tell you anything you want to know about *The Legend of Poncho*."

Father Tiempo finally looked at him. "Good," he said. "Very good." He stood up tall and raised both hands toward the ceiling.

"Gloria Spalding, I, Father Atsa Tiempo, am going to tell you a story. And when I have, you will choose which wing of Time's library will include the story of your life."

Tiempo's hands fell, and the walls of the Bunk House collapsed into sand. The sun and its heat vanished, the buildings of SADDYR vanished, and a moon rose over cacti and rugged stone.

The air was cool. Distant coyotes were calling to one another. The embers of a small campfire were spitting themselves to sleep. A kettle and pot hung on hooks above it.

Father Tiempo sighed happily. "Thoughtful of me to have remembered. I am quite hungry." He picked up a tin cup and poured himself coffee from the kettle before plucking a fat sausage from the pot with his fingers. He looked up at Sam and Glory. "Encouraging, too. Apparently I live long enough to have remembered to provide myself refreshment." He lowered himself onto a boulder and nodded at the pot.

"Eat if you're hungry. Then sit. Listen. And remember what I say always." He focused on Glory. "Even in the darkness between times."

Glory turned in a slow circle, taking in as much of the moonlit desert as she could. Sam crouched over the campfire pot and sniffed at the sausages.

"They're excellent," the priest said, chewing. "Try one."

Sam pinched a sausage between his thumb and forefinger, and his stomach rumbled. It smelled amazing, but he knew he shouldn't. Canned and blended foods only for Sam Miracle. There wasn't a bathroom anywhere near, and he didn't want to throw up in the rocks. Of course, with his rigid arms he didn't have any way to get the food to his face, either—his special silverware was back wherever they used to be—and he wasn't hungry enough to drop a sausage on a rock and chase it around with his mouth like a dog. Not yet, at least.

Father Tiempo pointed at him. "Don't worry about your stomach, it won't upset you here. You're incredibly distant from what was disturbing it."

"What was disturbing my stomach?" Sam asked.

"The primitive technologies of the post-nuclear era," the priest said. "But none of that matters at the moment. Eat."

"Where are we?" Glory asked.

"Just where we were," Father Tiempo said. "Why would we be anywhere else?"

Sam poked the sausage again.

"Oh, right!" Father Tiempo jumped to his feet and looked around. "Surely . . . yes!" He picked up a long metal prong with a wooden handle, stabbed a sausage out of the pot, and then pressed the handle into Sam's hand before sitting back down.

The process was hardly new for Sam, but the prong was much heavier than he had grown used to at SADDYR. He could hear the priest talking and Glory spitting out questions, but he concentrated on holding the prong with both hands below his waist and using his fingers to rock and sway the meat toward his face.

Catching the sausage in his mouth, he nibbled off a crusty end. The taste was . . . emotional. Like a solid memory long lost but found again. He took a much bigger bite and let the grease burn his tongue. As he chewed, he looked into Glory's eyes. She was staring at him. Her arms were crossed like she was bothered, but her face was soft. Sad, even.

"That looks . . . hard. But you should try to pay attention."

Sam blinked. He didn't know what she meant.

"I'm just eating."

"I know. But you said you don't like being confused, and the whole ranch just disappeared, and *he's* actually answering questions. Maybe the hot dog could wait?"

Sam tore the rest of the meat off the prong, quickly cheeking as much as he could. "Sausage," he mumbled. "Not a hot dog." He dropped the prong and pointed at the priest. "He said to eat. So I'm eating."

Grease dribbled onto his chin and Glory stepped forward, raising her hand, but hesitating.

"Do you need me to . . ."

Sam quickly ground his chin against his shoulder. His face was burning hotter than his tongue.

"I'm fine," Sam said. "Fine. Just . . . don't worry about me."

Did Glory think he was a baby? Did she want to be

his mom? He wanted to snarl and spit and say something mean. He wanted his words to scratch. But the priest was watching him, waiting with unblinking firelit eyes. Sam swallowed and let the anger drain out of him, and some of his shame went with it. Stiff arms could make him messy—they had hundreds of times. But they didn't have to make him nasty.

"Sorry," Sam said.

"For what?" Glory smiled at him.

Sam didn't answer.

"Right," said the priest, after a moment. "Well, I didn't mean to be confusing. We *are* in the same place because we haven't moved any distance. This is the location of the Bunk House, but seven hundred and seventy-seven years after our previous moment. When moving through larger blocks of time, increments of sevens are the easiest to work with. And moving into the future is always easier, because that is what all of humanity is always doing anyhow. The ranch did not simply disappear. It was erased over centuries."

Glory perched on the edge of a boulder, flattened her palms, and exhaled slowly, focusing her attention entirely on the priest. Sam chose his own rock, lowered himself onto it, and for the first time—at least that he could remember—he forced every last ounce of his attention at another human. He didn't want to forget a single word that might be said.

"Just start at the beginning," said Glory. "But get to everything."

Sam didn't even nod. It might have distracted him.

For a long moment, the priest looked at the fire. Sand rustled across the ground, sifting and sorting itself around the old man's feet.

"I do not live stories as you do," Father Tiempo said. "And yet, I live as all mortals do, from the first page to the final page. From the first moment when a man became my father through the warmth and safety of my mother's womb to my many days under the sun, I march, as we are all meant to, toward my own grave and the stars beyond. I have lived a past, I live a present, I live into my future. Looking out of *my* eyes, life runs in a straight line. But my past may be in your future. My future will hold moments previous to this one by your reckoning."

The priest looked up. "In history's tapestry, I am a red swirling thread among the blue, woven on my own course and given my own tasks. You, Sam, were one of those tasks, and my greatest failure."

"Wait," Glory said. "So you are a regular person? A mortal. Not an angel or something."

Sam was thinking about threads and colors. He

pushed those thoughts away and refocused.

"An angel?" The priest laughed. "No. Not in the way that you mean. And yes"—the priest slapped his knee—"this flesh will end. But I am an angel in another sense, because I am sent and I go. I am charged and I obey, and the darkness between times obeys me, but not for my sake. It too has been charged and it obeys. But none of that will help you understand. Know only that I walk the secret paths between times, not the main road. And Sam has often walked with me."

Sam cleared his throat. "Could we get to that part?"

Father Tiempo smiled. "I promised a story. A long time ago a bloodthirsty man, consorting with powers beyond his imagination, learned how to wander the *elsewhens* of this world."

"But how does that even work?" Glory asked. "I mean, is it magic? It seems that way when you do it. Is it some kind of trick that anyone could learn? Or is there some kind of machine or rings or anything?"

The priest smiled at her. "You will never find a corner of this world where there is not magic. But that word will distract you. Think of it as power. Ability. To some it is given, even without their asking—like a bird is given wings. Others seek to steal it. With forces beyond the natural, or with machines, it does not matter to them, so long as it works."

Sam's eyes wandered back to the sausages, but he refocused quickly. This was important.

"This man was a very effective thief indeed." The priest grimaced, deepening the caverns on his face in the firelight. "Young, he was merely a killer and a gangster, the type normally devoured by history by the thousand. He killed whom he wanted and took what he wanted. But what he wanted was forbidden knowledge. The great secrets. The hidden powers. He lived in a grim, soulless, and mechanical age, and he believed that if he could just find the levers and gears of time and learn their secrets, then he could reshape all of history to his own tastes and bind it to his own bloody pleasures. He could fly between times, feeding where he willed."

Sam shifted on his stone as the embers spat. The priest stared at him. Glory was silent.

"He succeeded," the priest said quietly. "Time is more wind and river than any machine, but even wind can be bridled. Rivers can be dammed. He communed with the dark keepers of dark secrets, allied himself to the most ancient of all thieves, and set out to steal the story of the world."

The priest stopped and stared at the fire. Sam licked his chapped lips and waited. After a moment, Glory leaned forward.

"So what happened to him?" she asked. "That kind

of thing has to go really, really wrong. It has to."

The priest smiled. "So I pray, so I hope, so I must believe. As he labored to lay foundations for his new eras and new histories, he constantly feared his own end. In all time's byways, in all the in-betweens, he consulted with spirits and bodiless reeks until he was finally given a vision of his own death—learning what I already knew. In the old west, when the city of San Francisco was still young, the great thief and killer called El Buitre—the Vulture—would fall in the street to a young gunfighter out to avenge his sister. The gunfighter was known only as—"

"Poncho," Glory blurted. "You've got to be kidding me." She laughed, uncomfortably, and looked at Sam. He wasn't laughing. "El Buitre? I've read *The Legend of Poncho* enough times to know where you're getting this stuff. Man, I feel like an idiot. I was actually believing you." She stood up and looked around like she expected the world to vanish, like some trick had been revealed. "I don't know how you did the sand-whooshing thing, or what your point was, but we should get back. Are you a hypnotist or something? Come on, Sam."

Sam shook his head. It might be one of his dreams, but he knew it wasn't a trick.

The priest just stared at Glory. She shifted in place and then crossed her arms, nervous. The world around her was still very real. The fire popped. Coyotes barked, and the moon slid slowly through a ragged slice of cloud.

"You got the ending wrong," Glory muttered. "Poncho doesn't kill the Vulture. The Vulture kills him."

"That," said the priest, "is the problem. The story is no longer as it should have been."

Sam shut his eyes. He'd read *The Legend of Poncho* a dozen times, and he'd imagined its sweeping scenes of blood and loss and gunfights at least daily since his first time through. And he knew that it had shaped his dreams. But he'd never once thought the story might have been real. Father Tiempo continued speaking, and in his mind, Sam saw the scene, but not because of the priest's description.

Horse-drawn wagons plowed slowly down a muddy street in San Francisco. A boy with hard eyes and sunken cheeks slid off a bedraggled horse and looked around. Two revolvers were hidden beneath his fraying poncho. Every building on the block was owned by the same man. A giant hotel and tower built with brick and glass and black iron. An opera house with a massive tarnished copper planetary mobile slowly swirling around a tall spire crowned with a smoking copper sun. And a strange tall building without windows that was "capped with a tangled crown of chimneys breathing steam." That was how the book described it, and Sam thought it was perfect. In front of this building, El Buitre himself was standing on the wide wooden sidewalk, surrounded by the kind of gunslinging killers who wore suits and bowler hats and oiled their mustaches.

Sam opened his eyes refocused on Father Tiempo's face, lit warm from the fire below and cold from the moon above.

"Poncho didn't look like much," Tiempo said. "Just another poor boy drifting through the west. But to quote the book, 'his hands were faster than a spark jumping between fingertips.' Poncho called out to his enemy and the Vulture was proud enough to face him. The outlaw drew first, but he couldn't even fire before both of Poncho's guns had been emptied. This was El Buitre's dark vision of his own end. The great outlaw watched himself die, and from the moment of his waking, he set out along the hidden paths of time, to learn the true identity of the boy called Poncho. And to kill him young."

"I like the book," Glory said. She looked at Sam. "Poncho dies at the end and meets his sister again in a sunshiney dream place that was probably supposed to be Heaven. But El Buitre just goes on getting more rotten."

"Not in my version," Sam said. "Not in any of my versions."

"The story has been lived many times now," Father Tiempo said. "And in all of them, El Buitre has triumphed.

Only in that first stolen vision of the future did the boy called Poncho defeat him. Then the train of history was derailed, the real boy was killed in his youth, and El Buitre became the arch-outlaw he still is, ruling his own time like a nightmare with no fear of morning, continually reliving the years of his choosing over and over again, growing his knowledge and strength and dominance and efficiency as he repeats them, creeping further into the future with each of his demented cycles. Eventually, he will choose to no longer double back. He will release a reservoir of changes on the world. He and they will flow into the future, toppling this reality at the foundation." Father Tiempo splayed his fingers at the fire, and then clenched both hands into fists, pressing them down into his knees.

Glory and Sam were silent, waiting for more. The priest looked up at the moon, and he spoke toward the stars.

"Since that first moment of his triumph, I have labored to repair the damage he has done. To find some way to right the train, to sort through the wreckage and make repairs. But it is easy to smash and hard to build. Easy to poison a stream, difficult to purify it. And thus far, I have failed. In all of my adjustments, after hundreds of lived versions, the boy has been killed in every one but the last."

"What happened in the last one?" Glory asked.

Father Tiempo grimaced and looked back down at the fire.

"He was brutally maimed, and his arms were made useless." Father Tiempo looked at Sam. "But his mere survival was enough to worry the Vulture, and his villains did not stop hunting for the boy. Hoping for a chance at healing, and time to heal in, I hid the boy in a future moment as safe as any I could find. But I failed you again, Sam. You have not healed, they have found you once more, and my only remaining plan is more desperate than you could possibly imagine."

Sam was feeling dizzy. He flexed both arms against his bone-fused elbows. Glory was staring at him with her eyes wide and her mouth slack. His tongue was sandy dry and thickening quickly. He practically choked trying to swallow.

Throwing up was one option.

So was crying.

Sam scrambled up to his feet, breathing hard, sweat beading on his face.

"The daydreams," he said. "The things I see . . . when I don't know where I am?"

"Memories," Father Tiempo said. "Glimpses of our other attempts at *now*. With everything your mind has been through, it struggles. We've actually had this entire conversation many times before. And memory is essential. I placed Jude's book here to help keep some of your memory from other times awake, but Glory will be more helpful than anything. If she's willing."

Sam was rocking in place. Blinking. Head twitching. So many images flickering through his mind. So many things he'd been told to push away.

Wait. *Jude's book?*

"Jude?" Sam asked. "He wrote *The Legend of Poncho?*"

Father Tiempo nodded. "He will. It is the last story he will ever write. Assembled in his old age when the dust has settled on all your adventures and your life is fully known."

"I have a story," Sam said. His face felt heavy. Numb. His ears were ringing. "But I die. I'm the one who dies."

"You have died more times than I care to count," Father Tiempo said. "Shot. Poisoned. Crushed. Stabbed. Drowned. Burned. Most people cross that cold river only once. But most people also only have one chance to get their living right."

Sam stumbled forward, almost falling onto the fire.

Glory jumped up, grabbing his shoulders. "Sam! Sam! I was wrong," she said. "You were totally right. The ending was terrible. New ending for sure, okay? Totally new ending. I'll help you."

Sam nodded. Then he looked down at his hands, at his stiff arms. They looked like bad art—scrawny except where they were lumpy with scars, slightly crooked and unmuscled. They could never be fast enough to change the ending.

Glory tapped his chin back up, catching Sam's eyes with hers.

"Let's change the title, too. I never liked it." She smiled. "*The Legend of Sam Miracle* sounds way cooler."

"Sam," the priest said. He stood up behind Glory. "I need you. You've been through so much already, and you're badly broken. But your work here isn't done."

Sam closed his eyes. He didn't want to see the priest. He didn't want to think about being broken. It was easy to recall the scenes he had read in *Poncho*. Harder to think of those scenes as real. As his.

A girl with long straight blond hair stood on a front porch looking down at him. Her blue eyes were wide and worried, and seven long golden watch chains bound her to the porch posts. The house behind her heaved flames up into the night sky, but his sister held a pie in her chained hands.

Millie.

Sam wanted to cry. Millie would burn. Millie, who had cared for him when everyone else was gone, who had fed him and sung to him and told him stories about old and new lands, about brave hearts and faithful loves and bold heroes who had both. Sam tried to lunge forward, but his dream feet wouldn't budge. He tried to reach for his sister, but he had no hands.

"I can't!" Sam yelled.

"Bet my life you can," Millie said. "Breathe, brother. Be calm. You have been lost for so long. But now you are found. And you must fight." She smiled while the flames grew behind her. "I made you pie."

Her voice was soothing, and Sam quieted.

"Is he okay?" The voice was Glory's.

"Apple?" Sam asked.

"Strawberry," Millie said. The flames behind her were growing. "And rhubarb. Like Mama used to make."

Sam opened his eyes, suddenly back in the desert night. Glory was holding him up while the priest watched.

"Where is my sister?" Sam asked. His heart felt like hot stone, heavy in his chest, heavy and unbreakable. "Tell me."

"You'll see." The priest smiled, but sadly. "Tomorrow we will begin the first day of your final reliving."

Reliving

Sam was sleeping. His only dream was dreamlessness. Dark, cool, and calm. He wanted more. His bedsprings squealed as he rolled over.

And then the loudspeaker in the courtyard began to blare.

"Good morning, sun!" Mr. Spalding's prerecorded voice rattled the windows. "Good morning, boys! Welcome to another day in which to excel!"

Beds rocked and shifted all through the Bunk House as the boys rose. Feet dropped off the top bunk above Sam, and Peter landed heavily in front of his face.

Peter stretched. "How you feeling, Sam?"

Sam groaned and shut his eyes.

Jude crossed the bunk room on bare feet. He had loose pages in his hand and a pencil stuck in his curly hair.

"Any dreams?" Jude asked. "Anything strange? Yesterday was a little crazy." He pulled the pencil out of his hair and dropped into a crouch, propping the pages on his bare knobby knee, ready to write.

Barto leaned against his bed across the way, examining his patched-together glasses with his long hands.

"Leave him be, Jude," Barto said. "We chased that guy off."

Sam looked around. All the boys were out of bed, most in boxers and undershirts, all were watching him. Tiago and Simon were missing—most likely out before the sunrise, checking traps.

Broad-shouldered Drew moved between the rows of bunks, pulling on a fresh shirt as he walked, finally stopping beside Peter.

"Think that guy will come back?" Drew asked quietly. "Will Sam need to hide?"

Peter's face was hard, but his voice was low. "They all come back. They never stop coming back."

Sam didn't sit up. His pillow was too comfortable, and he was tired. "What guy?" he asked.

"Tall," Jude said from his crouch. "One eye and a big

scar. Motorcycle boots. Nickname: Tiny."

"He didn't hang around long," Drew said. "Shot out a window before he left. Mama Spalding won't recover for . . . I don't know."

"Ever," Barto said. He slid his glasses on and blinked down at Sam.

"That was yesterday?" Sam yawned and shut his eyes. His memory of Tiny was blurry, but he could remember the campfire sausage perfectly. Probably because the taste still lingered in his mouth.

"Right," Peter said. "Everybody out. Let him sleep. I'll tell Mr. S. he's sick."

"Someone should stay with him." The voice was Jude's.

"Not this time," Peter said. "New plan this—"

Sam didn't hear the rest. He had burrowed back into the perfect stillness of sleep. And he stayed there until a cold hand slapped his face.

Sam jerked into full consciousness. Glory was leaning over him. The boys were gone. Her dark hair was in a ponytail and she was wearing a backpack.

"Do you ever remember anything?" she asked.

Sam pushed her away and sat up. The Bunk House was completely empty. "I was asleep! What am I supposed to be remembering?"

"Sam Miracle!" The loudspeaker outside sounded upset. "Samuel Miracle, report to the Commons!"

"Do you remember who I am?" Glory asked.

Sam snorted. "Why wouldn't I? Can you leave? I need to get dressed."

"Yeah, you do." Glory turned around, but she didn't leave. "We're twenty minutes late already."

Sam threw his blankets off and then dug a pair of jeans out of a drawer below his bed.

"Do you remember what we're doing today?" Glory glanced back over her shoulder. Sam snarled and she quickly looked away. "Sorry. But today is huge. Today is the most insane, most exciting, most *dangerous* day of my life. I know you've had lots of dangerous days, but I haven't. This is new for me. I'm actually pretty nervous."

Sam was concentrating on putting on his socks. He was nervous, too, but there was no way he would admit that.

"So what is it that we're doing?"

Glory spun around. Eyebrows down. Serious face.

"I'm not joking," Sam said. "I'm not even sure what day it is."

"Father Tiempo," Glory said. "Today. He called it the day of reliving."

Sam reached for his shoes.

"It's been one night." Glory shook her head. "How could you forget when absolutely nothing else happened since then?"

Sam smiled. With Glory flustered, he felt less nervous. A little.

"I just wanted you to feel useful," he said. "You're supposed to be the one who remembers everything. I just have to go back in time and—"

"Survive," Glory finished.

"Right," said Sam. He began slowly tying his shoes with his rigid arms. Glory watched. Impatient, she dropped onto one knee and swatted his hands away.

"I'll do it. I need to feel useful."

Sam never would have accepted help like that from one of the other boys. But he didn't feel up to fighting Glory.

She jerked the laces into a hard double knot and moved on to the next foot. "I know you can do this," she said. "It's just . . ."

"It's hard," Sam said. "Thanks." He smiled, but the expression didn't feel real. Nothing did. He had a sandbag in his stomach and fear whispering in his head. The priest had made his whole plan sound pretty awful.

"Remind me why I'm doing this," Sam said. "Why can't I just stay here?"

"Because you don't want to stay here," said Glory. She stood up, adjusted her backpack, and put her hands on her hips. "Because somewhere else, you matter. A lot. And here you don't. At all. And you never will."

Sam shrugged. "You don't know that. Maybe I'll invent a new kind of barbed wire or discover how to talk to cactuses."

"Cacti," said Glory. "And if you stay here, they will kill you. Like they killed your sister."

Sam inflated his cheeks.

"You might not remember it, but it happened. To *your* sister. And if you don't go back, you're letting it stay that way forever. It's like you want it to."

"Shut up." Sam bounced himself up onto his feet. "You didn't even know her. I don't even know how much I remember her and how much I just made up."

"You've read the book," Glory said. She slung off her bag, pulled out the old paperback copy of *The Legend of Poncho*, and held it up. The pages were yellow and splayed with use, and the cover was creased, but it still shone like blood on old silver. The hero stood in a graveyard at sunset, surrounded by enemies. His head was down, and his tough hands were just visible beneath his poncho, ready to draw his weapons.

"She's in here," Glory said. "I totally know her. She's my favorite character. Want to know why I was glad you died at the end? Because you ran and hid when she faced the outlaws alone. Because you made your choice and your sister died and that was your fault, and no matter how much you wanted to blame El Buitre, you were the one who needed to die."

"Don't. That wasn't me," Sam said. "Not *this* me. I remember reading it, but I don't remember doing it."

"Then who was it?" Glory sniffed. "I'm pretty sure there's only one of you even if that you has tried living the same thing a whole bunch of different ways." She tucked *Poncho* back into her bag. "Or maybe you make the same mistake and leave her every single time. Seems like you're thinking about doing that again right now."

Sam took a step toward Glory. He didn't care if she was a girl—he was ready to fight.

The Bunk House door flew open and Mr. Spalding stepped inside, looking angry.

"Gloria?" Mr. Spalding froze. "What are you doing here? I dropped you at the bus station two hours ago."

Glory shrugged. "I came back."

"We talked about this. You can come back for Christmas. Right now, you should be on your way to St. Angela's."

"I'll go," Glory said. "Don't worry."

Mr. Spalding stepped forward. "As for you, Sam, Peter has been lying for you again. It has to stop. Why did you skip roll call this morning?"

Sam blinked in surprised. If he wanted Mr. Spalding to leave him alone, he had to seem delusional. Which would be easy, even without lying. He gave his guardian his widest and most ominous smile. "I'm going on an adventure today, Mr. Spalding. A big one."

Mr. Spalding shook his speckled head. "Absolutely not. No. You are doing your schoolwork as per usual and then you will attend to your regularly scheduled chores."

Sam flexed his stiff arms. "I'm going to meet a priest in the desert and he's going to take me back in time to when my arms got wrecked. This time, maybe I'll live it better and they'll keep bending."

"Right. Okay." Mr. Spalding looked concerned. "Sam, I want you to go back to bed. Lie down and shut your eyes and go wherever you want in your head. And I hope your arms bend. I do. May you have the bendiest arms in the whole wide dream-world." He backed toward the door. "Gloria, you're coming with me."

An alarm bell began to clatter in the courtyard. A flood of shouts followed. Mr. Spalding sniffed at the air. Sam could smell it, too. Smoke. And a lot of it.

"Peter," Mr. Spalding said, his eyes widening. "Peter!" And he sprinted out the door.

Peter's voice roared above the sound of the alarm. Jimmy and Johnny Z were whooping. A gun fired.

Glory and Sam looked at each other. And then they began to run.

Beyond the Bunk House, beyond the Blood Barn and its nervous goats, Sam and Glory hopped rocks, ducked through fences, and raced along the narrow paths through the saguaro groves. Behind them smoke seethed slowly up into the sky, eclipsing the low sun and throwing a long shadow deep into the desert.

The Commons was engulfed in flames. The shouting had died. The gunshots had dwindled.

"We should go back," Sam said, looking over his shoulder. "They might need help."

Glory didn't even give the smoke a glance. "Whoever is doing this will leave them alone as soon as they're sure you're not there."

"I hope they're okay."

Glory hopped a boulder and Sam followed.

"They'll be fine. Dad is tough if you push him. And I feel bad for anyone who messes with SADDYR boys."

The two of them reached the top of a small hill and paused beneath the sprawling arms of an enormous cactus. An owl peered down at them from a small hole wedged between the rows of needles. A snake tail vanished beneath a stone by Sam's feet.

Sam hooded his eyes with a rigid arm and looked back into the smoke-filtered sun. The twelve fenced acres were empty. Thirteen shapes were scurrying around the courtyard—one tall, one female and in a bathrobe. Eleven boys.

"They're okay," Sam said. He felt lighter just saying it.

But SADDYR was definitely not okay. The flames had moved from the Commons to the Spaldings' house.

"Why would they do that?" Sam asked.

"To flush you out," Glory said. "That's where you were supposed to be. Remember the book. When the Tinman was looking for you in a hotel, he didn't go room to room, he just set a fire and waited by the exit with his gun ready."

"That wasn't me," Sam said. "Stop talking about that stuff like it was me."

Glory scrunched her lips. "Fine. But it's more you than anyone else."

Sam turned away from the smoke. Glory didn't. She had her hands cupped around her eyes.

"Why are you doing this?" Sam asked. "I've known you for, like, not long at all."

Glory didn't look at him.

"Your mom and dad are down there. Your whole life. Maybe it's not a normal life, but a not-too-bad one. If you come with me . . ." Sam thought about the possibilities. If even half of his scattered daydreams were real *memories*, the story Glory was stepping into could go very painfully wrong for her. Sam cleared his throat. "Seriously," he said. "I have to do this. I even almost want to do this. But you don't. Anything could happen. Think about my sister. Or me. It won't be safe."

"I know." Glory turned and faced him. "But I only get one life story. I don't want mine to be safe. I want it to be worth writing a book about." She smiled. "Like yours."

Sam scrunched up his face, looking back down at SADDYR. "I don't know. Safe sounds kinda awesome. I loved most of my book when I thought it wasn't real. But now . . ."

"My mom ran off when I was born," Glory said. "The Spaldings fostered me and my older brother. Eventually, he ran away and ditched me, too. That was four years ago. The Spaldings were nice enough to adopt me when he left, but they keep shipping me off to the most boring schools in the entire history of the planet Earth. So what's to miss? I have nothing."

Sam stared at her. "I'm sorry," he said. "I didn't know."

"Don't be sorry," Glory said. "I might not have had adventures, and my arms might not have been wrecked or my brains scrambled, but I've lived through hard things." She hooked her thumbs in her backpack straps. "And I'm ready for more."

Sam snorted. "My brains are fine."

"Sure they are." Glory smiled. "That's why I'm here, because your brains don't need any help at all."

A long whistle rattled up the rocks behind them. In the distance, Father Tiempo and three fat burros were standing in a dry creek bed.

Father Tiempo was younger. His uneven black hair was tied down with a red rag across his forehead, but his face was smooth and hairless. If not for his bright eyes and the priest's collar, Sam would never have believed that he could have been the tired white-haired man who'd told the story of Poncho.

When Sam and Glory jogged to a stop, Father Tiempo swung easily up onto the largest burro, but his eyes didn't leave Glory. She dug a piece of paper out of her pocket and handed it up to him.

"Old *you* wrote this about me last night." Glory shrugged. "Just in case you didn't know who I was or something."

He glanced at the paper and then flicked it away into the rocks with a sneer.

"I know who you are. If I write something at any time, I know it in all times. That is why the old man wrote the note, not that I need his instruction." He looked at Sam and Glory both, and his burro stamped in place.

"You have more attitude than the old priest," Sam said.

"If I have more attitude," the priest said, "maybe it is because I am not yet old and weary and near giving up." He wrapped his hand tight in the burro's reins. "I can smell the desperation on myself even across centuries. It angers me. That I have been sent here, guiding you as a favor to my oldest self, tells me that I have still failed to remedy your situation even at the end of my life. One mistake in my youth, and here you are, the certain assurance that yes, that mistake will haunt me forever." He inhaled sharply, like he was sniffing at something dead and dubious. "Thus, attitude. A great deal of it. But don't worry, on the other side, an older, gentler, less angry me will be waiting for you. Come." His kicked his burro into a trot, leaving Sam and Glory still standing.

Sam looked at his burro. The animal seemed half-asleep in the sun. Its wide barrel body was mostly rump, and even though its legs were short and its back was low, Sam wasn't sure if he'd be able to swing himself up into the saddle. Not with his stiff arms. He stepped closer and was surrounded by the warm sun-cooked smell of barn. Glory was already up on her burro and waiting.

Sam scrambled up onto a boulder six feet away and prepared to jump.

"You know," Glory said. "You could just—"

Sam dove, slamming belly first onto the burro's back. The animal blared surprise like an accordion, skittered in a tight circle in the creek bed, and then took off after the priest, flapping Sam like a pair of fat wings.

" . . . lead it closer first," Glory finished. She stifled

a laugh while Sam fought to stop the animal and right himself. When Sam sat up, embarrassed and frustrated, Glory gave him a thumbs-up. He turned his animal quickly away. Then she leaned over her burro's neck to whisper in its ear.

"Shall we proceed like ladies?"

The burro threw back its head, butting Glory between the eyes, and then broke into a bouncy gallop.

THREE HOURS. OF BURRO. AND ROCKS. AND SUN. SAM HAD seen two lizards skitter and a few birds circling high like small black cracks in the sky. But the rest of the natural world was still. Gone. Hiding as far out of the sun as possible.

They were deep in the hills now. Solid rock rose up high around them, the dry creek had widened, and the banks had grown almost to cliffs.

Hooves cracked on stones and crunched on gravel. Burros chewed on their bits, clacking the metal on their molars and dripping mealy saliva out the sides of their mouths.

Glory had pulled a hat out of her bag. Father Tiempo's skin was slick and polished, but he didn't seem bothered by the heat. Or the sun. Sam was bothered by both. His scalp was burning beneath his hair. Salt had crusted above and below his eyes where his sweat had evaporated. He was wearing short sleeves and no hat, and the skin on his arms, his nose, and the tips of his ears felt ready to blister.

Glory's burro clattered up beside Sam's.

"Are you okay?"

Sam nodded. His tongue was a little too dry for words.

"Here." Glory dug a water bottle out of her pack. "You didn't eat or drink anything this morning. Have some."

The priest squinted back at Sam and Glory.

"No. Do not waste the water. You will need it."

"He needs it now," Glory said. "The whole point of what we're doing is to fix him, not to help him die from dehydration."

"He will be fine. I know his constitution. You are the heat's more likely casualty." The priest slowed his burro to a stop at a sharp bend in the creek bed.

Glory extended the water bottle to Sam anyway. He licked his cracking lips, but shook his head.

"It's okay," said Sam. "I wouldn't argue with someone who can walk into the future."

Father Tiempo watched their burros approach his. For the first time, his hard young face split into creases around a smile.

"Wise boy," he said. "But still a fool. All men walk into the future. They cannot stop themselves. The moments carry them along like bubbles on a river. A very few can fly into the future. Fewer still can return again."

Sam slowed his burro to a stop; the priest pointed up ahead.

The creek banks had grown even taller. Sheer stone and loose slides of rubble struggled up and away from each other, ending in rough lips on both sides of the canyon. The jagged and shattered skeleton of an old railroad bridge clung to one side. The rest of the bridge was heaped up in the creek bed, with timbers tangled and splintered, occasionally jutting out of the old carnage like badly broken bones.

"I've been here," Sam said. He looked up. And then down. He could picture the bridge. He could hear the river running fast, the train . . .

"I should say so," the priest said. "You've died here often. More than any other place."

"Right here?" Sam asked. "Exactly here?" He had forgotten the heat, the sun, and everything else. "How? And why don't I remember the dying part? Seems like it would be pretty memorable."

Father Tiempo scanned the bottom of the creek bed. And then he pointed. "Right there," he said. "Skull fracture from falling. Too many falls to tally. There, a bullet fired from above. And there, drowning." His finger moved again with each cause of death. "There, crushed by a train car. There, you burned." He pointed up out of the canyon. "Thrown by a horse, crushed by a train, and,

73

of course, bullets. You get the idea."

Father Tiempo kicked his burro toward a narrow winding track that clung to the canyon wall. "Let your animals do the guiding here. They'll find their own footing. Let's postpone your next death for as long as possible."

To Sam, the track up from the creek bed looked more like a thin scratch on the cliff face, but his burro managed to waddle along it without too much difficulty. Behind him, Glory spoke up.

"You know, I always thought time travel was impossible."

"Most of it is," Father Tiempo said.

"But you can do it," Glory said. "Obviously."

"I go where I am sent," the priest said. "As do you."

Between breaths, Sam was suddenly elsewhere. Somehow, he could still feel the burro moving beneath him, but he couldn't see it. And then even that feeling was gone.

Sam was in total darkness, and he was lying on his back. In a box. He could feel the sides pressed in tight against him. His arms could bend, because they were folded on his chest. Suddenly, the lid to the box opened and he was looking up at the shape of a man holding a lantern. Gold watch chains glinted against his black vest. The man began to laugh.

Gasping, Sam teetered on his burro, suddenly back in the desert. He blinked his sticky eyelids and looked past his burro's bulging side and down the growing cliff below him. He could have easily fallen and his final reliving would be over already, seventy-five feet down in a pile of red boulders.

"I don't like this place." He looked up at the priest's back, and his burro's swaying rump. A moment ago, he had been in a coffin with the Vulture laughing at him. Despite the sun, Sam's skin felt cold. He crossed his stiff forearms and rubbed goose bumps against each other. "Why do I see things that aren't in the book?"

"Because the book is only inspired by one version of your life—the version that Jude will eventually write after all of this is long over. The best version you have lived so far, though I pray a better one is still ahead of you. But you have memories of many attempts. And your mind can't help but blend them in your dreams."

"I die in the best version," Sam said. "That's encouraging."

The priest looked back over his shoulder, and then across the canyon at the clouds. "The same is true for all of us, Sam. The best-lived lives still end."

Sam looked up, squinting against the harsh sun. He wanted off the burro.

"So why can't you just dissolve this place into sand and reappear us where we need to go?"

"Because I am not God," the priest said quietly. Sam could barely hear him over the slow crunch of burro hooves. "I cannot make or unmake reality. Angels and men travel through physical space in the same way—they move. And they ride donkeys when they must."

"So you can't change space. But when it comes to time . . . ," Glory prompted.

Father Tiempo laughed, and his voice rattled off the canyon walls. "I'm beginning to understand why the old man liked you. Time is beyond your comprehension. Time is a wind. Time is an animal. Time is choices. Time is light woven into song. Time is the Poet speaking the next word. We are small, and so we hear and live only one word at a *time*, living in the way you would read a book. Outside of the book, where only the Author exists, there is no time at all. It is not even a book. It is one endless, ever-growing but already-grown page. Most people live in the lines, but I march in the margins. I am sent to make the edits, the notes, the corrections. You and I and all creatures are ink on the page, but I can lead you through the white space between the words, where time is thin. I can lift you off the page until only your shadow is dragging behind." The priest glanced back at Sam, smiling. "Does your head ache yet, Sam? Or are you daydreaming? You always used to

76

ask these questions, but you hated these answers."

"Not daydreaming," Sam said. "I'm listening. But I don't understand."

"Are there actual paths?" Glory asked.

Father Tiempo pointed up at a floating falcon. "As many as that falcon has through the air. But down here, even that bird must walk across the ground like you."

"So you can fly through time?" Sam asked.

"I can," the priest said. "But it is easier to glide, to rise, to hang and let time pass beneath me before landing in a new moment. A true flight through time can require tremendous exertion and even pain, especially when pursued while carrying a boy-size burden or transporting a soul."

The priest looked back at Sam, and while his mouth twitched slightly upward, his black eyes were hard and distant beneath the red rag on his brow, like they were sorting through whole libraries of nightmarish memory.

"What makes it hard?" Glory asked. "How far you're going? Is there some shortcut formula? You know, minutes divided by leap years multiplied by hours or something?"

The priest twisted around to stare past Sam at Glory.

"There has to be crazy lots of math," Glory added, eyebrows up.

"As much as the falcon is doing," the priest said. "As

for minutes, they exist only as ideas. A clock ticks only so men can map their moments. On our sphere, the beat of time is governed by the moon and her tides, by the sun who swings us, and by our own spinning through evening and morning."

"Circles," Glory said. "So stuff with pi, then?"

The priest laughed.

Sam was feeling dizzy and his throat was cracking. "Could we talk about something else? I would rather you just explain where you're sending me this time and tell me how to stay alive. And tell me when we can get a drink."

They had reached the top of the canyon wall, and the burros scrambled over a stone lip onto the edge of a flat and barren plateau. Sagebrush. Cacti. Stones rippling in the heat. And the dried and broken remains of a railroad line, stretching into the distance like a monstrous serpentine fossil. Beside them, the shattered timber bridge jutted out into the space over the canyon. In the distance, Sam could see the slumping forms of collapsing buildings huddled around the tracks. Father Tiempo scanned the plateau with squinting eyes, and then peered into the sky. Seriousness was heavy on him.

"So . . . ," Sam said. "What do I do?"

Finally, Father Tiempo pointed toward the buildings.

"Over there, your soul will abandon this body and I will return it to an earlier time and an earlier you."

Sam blinked. "What? Hold on. I'm leaving my body?"

"Yes. But only to reinhabit your flesh at an earlier moment in your story. You will board a train, and your one and only goal must be to reach the other side of this canyon alive. From the moment they discover our new attempt, El Buitre's men will be on you. If they remove your beating heart, that will be the final end of our game. If you cross the canyon, you will have matched your last attempt. But once there, you will still not be safe. You must hide. Be still. Do you understand? Every time you've died, your soul has been torn from your flesh. And every time I've moved it back into earlier life, the bond between your soul and mind and body has grown weaker." Father Tiempo leaned off his burro toward Sam until they were eye to eye. "If you die again, I cannot promise to save you. You may be nothing more than a dreaming vegetable, wandering confused memories. So, no fighting. No bravery. You find safety. If you *survive*, the fighting will come eventually. And this time, preserve your arms."

"My arms will work?" Sam couldn't hold back a smile even though his dry lips cracked wide. "Is that why I have to leave this body?"

"Yes. We need you undamaged."

"Where will you be?" Sam asked. "Are you coming?"

Father Tiempo sighed. "A soul can only be woven into the heart and breath of one self in one time. There can never be two in the same moment. My oldest self is there already. I am fighting already. And I fear that the old man is now desperate enough to risk everything on a single gamble. In the past, a retreat has always been prepared. This time, I am holding nothing in reserve . . . including myself." He paused, still eyeing Sam. "Do you understand the risk?"

"I'm nervous," Sam said. "I'm scared. Shouldn't I be?" He shrugged. "But if I die, at least it will be over."

"Over? If we fail now, Sam Miracle, there will be no other attempt. A younger you with foggy memories and strange dreams will not show up somewhere new. You will finally cease, and I will have likely ceased beside you. Your story on this earth will have finally ended while El Buitre's is still beginning. *The Legend of Poncho* will be just four short chapters with so many scribbles and scrawls and deaths that it was finally thrown away. But the goal is not simply to survive. The goal is to live for those who need you. Die, and you and your confusion will finally rest in peace, undisturbed. But those millions within El Buitre's still-growing reach will not."

"Excuse me," Glory said. "I'm here, too. Where will I be?"

"You are difficult," the priest said. "In some ways, you are the most desperate part of the old man's plan. It is one thing to return a soul to its earlier body, and quite another to transport an entirely new body and soul back into a moment in time where it never was before. And in this case, it also happens to involve a speeding train."

Father Tiempo turned his burro toward the tracks, rubbing his jaw as he spoke. "The complexities are infuriating. You must be thrown into the air above the tracks, exactly at the height of a train car. While you are still in the air, I must move you to exactly the precise moment in time when that car passed through that space. If I miss, and you end up in front of the train or beneath the train or between cars, it will end terribly for you, and I apologize. Also, I must wait for the first death to occur on the train before I can even make the attempt. A death will create a brief vacancy in the narrative into which you can be inserted. But with Sam's new actions on the train, along with any variation in behavior on the part of El Buitre's men, I cannot be sure of exactly when that will occur."

Sam shut his eyes and leaned forward in the saddle. "Can we just do this," he said quietly. "I'm starting to feel sick."

The priest didn't notice. "I can only hope that the old man remembers to write it down. If he writes it, I'll know."

Sam's ears were beginning to buzz, and someone was drumming inside his head. If they had to drum, he wished that they would have better rhythm. The beats were scattered and spastic. He wanted to hide his burning face in his hands. He wanted to cover his eyes or at least knuckle his temples. But his arms were still stiff as lumber. All he could do was shut his eyes and smash his face into his shoulder. His body rocked forward.

"I'd really rather not die before the adventure even starts," said Glory. Sam couldn't see her, but her voice was stern. "Sam?" Now she sounded concerned. "You should have let me give him some water!"

"Don't yell," Sam mumbled. And he felt his body falling.

TWO HANDS PRESSED AGAINST SAM'S FACE. THE HANDS WERE cool, but that wasn't possible. Was it? Not here. His eyelids fluttered. He wanted to learn how to have icy hands. And how to touch his face. Gentle thumbs helped his eyelids open.

Father Tiempo was bending over him. A rotten old building loomed over the priest's head.

"Say good-bye to this body, Sam." The priest smiled. "Stay alive. Cross the canyon. Hide. Do you understand me? No fighting. Protect your arms. It will be hard to remember in all the noise of your old memories, but you must."

Sam nodded. The priest's eyes were wet. Not just wet. Leaking onto the bridge of his nose.

Sam's voice crawled out of him like a crow's ghost. "Why are you crying?"

"Because you have forgotten me so many times. Because you and I have wandered through more lifetimes together than any other pair of friends in history. Because now we near the end." The priest's voice lowered to a whisper. "And I fear it." He placed one icy hand on Sam's forehead. "If we should perish, let evil perish with us. If we should fall, let it be in body, but not in spirit. If we face demons, make us angels, but make us angels of death. Good-bye, Sam."

The priest raised his arms, and the building behind him turned into sand. But it didn't fall. It flew.

Sam shut his eyes.

MILLICENT MIRACLE STOOD ON A WOODEN TRAIN PLATFORM and shut her eyes. A gust of wind, hot and dry, swirled her skirt and tickled loose blond hairs across her forehead. But Millie suddenly had chills. The skin on her arms and neck tightened into tiny hills. She swallowed, forcing cold fear down out of her throat and into her stomach.

She had felt this moment before. She was sure of it. Just like she had felt the moment of her mother's death before it had happened. And her father's. Just like she had known the smell of the loose earth inside the graves before the shovels had even pierced the turf. Just like she had known that rain would spatter on her father's coffin before there had been a cloud in the sky.

Millie shivered. The sensation of preemptive memory was unpleasant, but it wasn't a surprise. For her, memories often arrived prior to actual experiences. New moments felt old to her all the time. But sometimes how she felt was wrong.

Sometimes, Millie had the absolute sensation that something had happened when it hadn't. When it never would.

How many times had she felt the horrible loss of her brother, the sick certainty of his death, only to have him enter the room alive and laughing? How many mornings had she been sure that she was finally alone, sure that he had been shot or burned or stabbed, only to find him snoring safely under his blankets?

Millie felt his absence now. Her heart ached behind her ribs, swearing to her that her brother had been taken forever. That he was gone. Dead. Fed to vultures.

But her heart was a liar and she had learned not to trust it. At least when it came to her brother.

Millie opened her eyes and blinked against the harsh Arizona sunlight. She turned around, looking for Sam.

~ 5 ~

Train

SAM MIRACLE YAWNED LONG AND HARD, STRETCHING HIS arms above his head. His feet were hot in his boots, and his wool coat was planting itches on the back of his neck. He felt like he'd been sleeping for a very long time—and dreaming—but it all had slipped away from him quickly. He'd been riding a donkey with some girl and a priest. The girl had been funny and bossy. Like Millie. He'd liked her. Somehow, even though he was dreaming, he was still on his feet.

Why Sam was wearing a wool coat in this sun, he didn't know. He looked around the little train station for some place to rub his neck. It wasn't a big place. Too small to be a town, but close. Beyond the wooden platform where he and his sister were waiting, there was a little general store with a crooked sign. Beside it, a corral made of split rails was currently empty of cattle. There was a saloon, two houses built, and a third under way—all with wooden siding—and a squatting little adobe thing flaking off its skin. The front door and the one window were boarded up, but two tall sun-bleached signs still sat out front. On one:

St. Anthony
of the
Desert
Wishes You
Sweet Respite

On the other:

Bed
Bath
Shaves
Haircuts
Laundry
Fortune-Telling
Holy Amusements
Admonitions

Strange. Sam rolled his sweaty neck against his collar, but that made the itching worse. He sidled back toward his sister.

"Scratch my neck?" he asked.

His sister was two inches taller than he was, and wearing a buttoned-up and faded blue-checkered dress. Her blond hair was pulled back behind her ears where it fell straight down to her waist. Her eyes were blue, but uneven—like undermixed paint—with rays of dark and light stark in the bright sun. She had the same rough spray of freckles across her cheeks that Sam had on his. A large trunk was at her feet, and a ragged paper tag was pinned to her collar, with her name and destination scrawled in blotchy ink.

Millicent Miracle
San Francisco, California

She ignored Sam. He turned around, hunching his back toward her.

"Millie, please! It's killing me."

"So scratch it," she said. "You're making a spectacle of yourself already."

"I can't. My arms. And this coat!" Snarling frustration, Sam began to bounce and writhe where he stood.

"Samuel!" Millie leaned toward him. "What is going

on? Was it one of your spells?"

He froze. "One of my what?"

"Look at me." Millie's voice was firm, and Sam immediately stared into his sister's blue eyes. "Do you know who I am?"

Sam nodded. Farther down the platform, three nuns were looking at him. Two long cowboys who had been sleeping on a bench both tipped back their hats.

"Do you know where you are?"

Sam looked around the station. "Arizona," he said. "But my head feels like a cotton ball."

"It's been that way all year," Millie said. She straightened back up. "You're fine. Your arms are fine. Just take off the coat. But don't lose the tag."

For a moment, Sam forgot his itch. He looked down at his arms. Veins were standing out on the backs of his hot hands. Slowly, cautiously, he bent his elbows. Both hands moved. Two inches. Three. Four. Five, and still no pain.

"Ha!" Samuel tore off his jacket and dropped it on the ground. He swung his arms and slapped his chest and clawed his neck and touched his face and messed up his own hair. His own fingers on his face felt so strange, like he hadn't touched his own cheeks and jaw and forehead in years.

How was it possible? He remembered the pain. The

pain had been very real. And with the pain he remembered the hot grounds of SADDYR. He could almost envision his Ranch Brothers—blurry shapes and sizes, faces without features. He turned to his sister, and her eyes were far from irritated. They were concerned.

"Samuel, we need to get you into the shade."

Sam shook his head. "I'm fine! And my arms are fine. It's just that . . . I don't even know." He felt each elbow carefully and then looked back up at his sister. "Millie, I had the strangest dream." But it couldn't have been a dream. The happiness in him was too strong. It was quivering behind his ribs. It was shaking his voice. Tears were even leaking onto his cheeks.

And he could wipe them.

Laughing, Sam slapped at his cheeks and then leapt at his sister. He threw his arms around her, hugging her tight. Then he grabbed her waist and picked her up, ignoring her pounding fists and spinning in two quick circles. When he dropped her, she was fighting her own smile.

"My arms can bend!" Sam said, and he flexed them.

Millie laughed and shook her head. "Try to be sane, Samuel. I need you sane."

Sam hopped up onto the trunk, clicked his heels together, and saluted.

In the distance, he saw steam. A moment later, the

sharp blasts of the engine whistle reached the platform.

"Get down," Millie said. "And pick up your coat. If Father were here, he'd smack you."

Sam hopped down. "Well, good thing he's not, then."

The last traces of Millie's smile vanished. She stepped toward her brother with blue eyes flaring, and her hand planted a slap across his face before he even saw it coming.

"Samuel Miracle, I don't care if the sun's boiled your brain, don't you ever joke about that. Ever. Now pick up your coat."

Sam had no words. As the train chuffed and squealed to a long and steaming stop, he stood on the platform with his coat at his feet. Motionless. Strange images swirled through his mind, jarred loose by the stinging on his cheek.

People were moving around him. A cowboy was dragging the trunk into a train car for Millie. A conductor had hopped off and was yelling.

Sam looked down the length of the train, down the tracks, to where a narrow timber bridge spanned a canyon. So many memories were flying through him, they were impossible to sort out. There were gunfighters and a girl and a priest and terrible pain. But there was also Ping-Pong. And baseball hats. Had he made those up? He could see an older boy, worrying about him, and he knew the boy's name was Peter. And then all the faces came into focus, and they all had names. Jude and Barto. Matt Cat and Sir T. Jimmy Z and Johnny Z, the redheads. Drew. Flip chewing his lip . . . and it was all fading again.

"Samuel!" Millie picked up his coat and tugged on his hand. "Come. Now."

Sam looked into his sister's eyes. "Do you ever dream the future?"

"Every night," she said. "I dream a future in California on a farm with green grass and fat cows and trees that grow oranges. And I dream the past."

"I don't mean what you hope the future is," Sam said. "I mean the future for real."

"Like a prophet?" Millie asked. She raised her eyebrows. She wasn't about to admit anything about her strange relationship to future feelings. "No," she said. "And neither do you. We've talked about this. Now get on the train or I might hit you again."

Sam followed his sister to the train. He stood behind her as she handed a man with a huge beard their tickets. He helped her climb the two flip-down iron steps up onto a small platform at the end of a passenger car, and he held the little wood-and-glass door open so that she could enter first.

All the windows in the train car were open, but the place still smelled worse than the bathroom when the boys had skipped cleaning for a month. Even as he had the thought, it didn't make sense. But the smell was still familiar. The air was sour with old sweat and unwashed bodies, and the temperature wasn't helping. Wooden benches with worn rawhide and wool cushions faced each other in pairs, like restaurant booths with no table. Two cowboys were in one. A large family with sweating, moaning children filled two. An old Indian was sleeping near the front.

Millie chose her bench and Sam dropped onto the bench across from her. She had already turned her face toward the open window and was fanning herself.

"It's an oven in here," Sam said. "Is the air conditioner broken?"

Millie shot him a curious look. Sam looked around the car, flaring his nostrils in disgust.

"I could skip showering for a week and not smell this bad."

Millie leaned forward. "You're babbling. Conditioning air? Shower skipping?"

"I'm not babbling," Sam said. "I'm just . . ." He shut his eyes, trying to think. He could see the showers in the Bunk House. He could hear the air conditioner humming, he remembered its cool breath on his neck while he read a book and the boys played Ping-Pong. Too vivid for a dream.

But he could also remember his house in West Virginia.

Tall and white. With fences. And horses. No water pipes. No lights. Lanterns with little flames. A well he had to pump till his hands blistered. Baths in the kitchen. Baby lambs. Chopping kindling and nicking his knuckle. Millie cooking when the sickness came. Cooking till there wasn't anything more to boil in water than month-old chicken bones. He remembered the men nailing the lid onto the box that held his mother. He remembered her living face smiling at him. Her rough hands. Her soft kiss on his forehead. He could see them sliding the box up onto the wagon beside the bigger one that held his father. It all felt so long ago.

But now he knew what a telephone was. And a television. And a stereo. And a refrigerator. He couldn't have made those up. He wasn't that smart.

The steam engine gasped, jerking the train forward. It gasped again and iron wheels squealed on the rails. And again. The train was moving a little more each time.

Sam opened his eyes and looked at his sister. He leaned forward, beautifully bent elbows on his knees. "Millie, I need you to listen and not be worried even if this doesn't make sense. I don't remember much from West Virginia, and I'm sorry I said that about Dad. But for me it was a very long time ago. I was hurt and then someone hid me in the future to keep me safe." He leaned back, and his heel scraped over a piece of paper on the floor. "I don't remember why, but I know there was a reason."

Millie's brows were as low as they could go. She touched Sam's forehead with the back of her hand, and grabbed his wrist to feel his pulse.

Sam was looking at the paper on the floor between his boots. It was a note.

WHEN THE COWBOYS STAND, RACE FORWARD TWO CARS.

FT

"FT?" Sam said it out loud. His memory was roaring now. Centuries were sorting themselves out. "Father Tiempo."

"What about him?" The voice was hard and deep like a canyon in the air. Two long-limbed cowboys blocked the aisle. One was more cowboy than the other, the one with the voice. He had a droopy black mustache, spurs, a sweat-soaked bandanna, and a two-gun holster. The other had a similar holster, but he wore it with a suit. His trousers were tucked into high black boots with silver buckles, and a bowler hat sat on the back of his head. His face was smooth and freshly shaven. His smiling eyes were arctic blue. Sam knew them.

"Can we help you, gentlemen?" Millie asked.

Sam's whole body had tightened. He'd seen the note

too late. And now there was nowhere to go. He could dive through the glass and out of the train, but he'd be leaving his sister behind. He could dive over the bench, but that would leave her exposed, and they would just shoot him in the back. His fingers clenched the edge of his bench. At least his elbows were bendy now. He could throw a punch before he died.

The real cowboy touched his hat. "Kind of you to ask, miss. Folks call me Rattles on account of how many I kill. My friend here is known as the Tinman on account of how he likes to collect the badges of fallen sheriffs, deputies, marshals, and assorted lawdogs."

"That I do," the Tinman said. He touched his hat and grinned. His voice was crisp and proper. "You'll excuse us not sharing our Christian names."

"No," Millie said. "I don't think I will. What do you want with us?" Her voice was nearly sharp enough to draw blood.

"Tiny," said Sam. He kept his voice low and cold. "People will call you *Tiny*, on account of how stretched out you get moving between times. Also, you won't like what I do to your face."

Rattles drew a long bowie knife from his belt and stroked his mustache. "Miss, would you mind holding your brother down while we cut out his heart? We've had just about enough of that Navajo priest dancing him away through time after we kill him fair and square."

"To be honest," Tiny said, sniffing, "it's shameful the way some types don't know when they've lost. But we can't all be winners." He tossed a wink and a tongue click at Millie.

Sam's hands were fast. Faster than Tiny's wink. As Tiny's eyelid began to close, Sam lunged. As Tiny's tongue clicked against his teeth, Sam's hand closed on the butt of his holstered revolver. As Tiny's eyelid opened, Sam was trying to draw the weapon backward.

And failing.

Rattles was quick, too. His fist cracked into Sam's cheek, slamming his head against the back of the bench. Sam's hand slipped from Tiny's gun, but he'd partially cocked the revolver's hammer.

The hammer snapped forward.

The gunshot shook the windows. Millie screamed. Tiny yelped and fell, grabbing his knee. Rattles snarled, clamping Sam's throat tight with one hand, pressing the knife against Sam's ribs with the other.

Millie rocked back, pulled up her skirt, and stomped him in the ear. Rattles dropped Sam's throat and grabbed her ankle.

The sleeping Indian had thrown off his blanket and was running down the aisle. His hair was pure white and his face was scarred with deep creases.

He raised both arms high, then wind and hissing sand roared through the train car.

Tiny shot him from the floor. Father Tiempo staggered forward and fell. As he did, he pointed, and sand devoured his two enemies. They were gone. The priest sprawled facedown in the aisle, his blood creeping through the sand.

Millie was frozen on her bench in shock. But for the clatter and rock of the rails, the train car was silent. The other passengers were stunned and staring. Sam crawled out beside the priest and felt for his neck. No pulse. The old man was dead. But he'd written something in the sand with his finger.

NO

Sam looked back at his sister. Millie's eyes were wide, wondering.

"Dead." Sam coughed on the word. His throat was practically crushed. His jaw was throbbing. He had a shallow knife prick between his ribs just above his heart.

Which meant his mind was perfectly clear. And he wanted to cry.

"I'm sorry." He touched the priest's bony back. "It's always my fault, isn't it? Every time."

GLORY SHIVERED AND RUBBED HER LEGS. THE DENIM warmed up her palms, but it was her sun-torched skin that was now chilled by the night air. She wouldn't have expected to end the day cold, but she also wouldn't have expected to end the day by sitting cross-legged beside a dead railroad with a sleeping priest. Whenever she had wanted to move around, he had barked at her.

The sun was down, the burros were snoring on their feet, and the moon had yet to come up. Warmth was still rising out of the canyon beside her, but cooler air was crawling across the plateau. And over the last hour, that breeze had been growing.

She hadn't thought to wear warm clothes—or pack any—but shorts would have been worse than her old jeans. Her bare arms were the problem. To distract herself, she pulled the old copy of *The Legend of Poncho* out of her pack and dug around for the little flashlight she had thought to throw in. Switching it on, she pointed it over at the priest. The light was dull and orange. Tired batteries. But not as tired as he looked.

Father Tiempo had his legs crossed and he was slumped forward with his chin on his chest. He had set an empty hourglass on a rock in front of him a long while back and had barely moved since. While Glory watched, his shoulders rose slowly with an incredibly long breath. Fully inflated, all motion paused, and then the breath poured out of him in a ghostly rush and the process began again.

"So . . . ," Glory said.

The priest said nothing.

"Any thoughts on timing?" she asked. "I'm starting to wish I'd brought a sleeping bag."

Glory shivered, rubbed her bare arms and then opened the book, flipping through the yellowing pages all the way to the end.

"Okay, Sam Miracle," she whispered. "How much did you tear out?"

But the final pages were completely intact. There was a little ad for two other novels by J. P. Hawke, and before that, a page that said only "The End." Across from that there was about half a page of prose, the last lines of the last chapter of *The Legend of Poncho*.

At first, Glory thought Sam must have lied about tearing out pages. Or maybe there had been two different copies back at SADDYR. But then she actually read the final lines.

Gloria sat in her wheelchair and wept beside the loose soil of Sam Miracle's grave. The loss of her own legs caused not a single tear. But the loss of her hero did more than break her heart . . . it broke her very soul.

The western sun set slowly on her sorrow. And when it

was gone, a final darkness swallowed Gloria Spalding. It swallowed her dreams. It swallowed her story. Only the darkness knows where she may be, and how her life ended.

"That's awful!" Glory slammed the book shut and pointed her flashlight at the priest. "That's seriously the worst ending to any book that I've ever read."

The priest said nothing.

"That can't be real, can it? First off, it made me seem like a total sap, like I was in love with Sam. Second, I lose my legs? I'm weeping in a wheelchair? And Sam is still dead." She held the paperback up. "How am I even in the book? I've never been in the book before. Why would Jude do that?"

The priest remained silent.

"Hey!" Glory lobbed her flashlight at the priest, orange light looping in the night. It bounced off his back and skittered across the rocks, breaking the glass. The light died.

"What was the point of that?" Father Tiempo asked. Glory blinked, her eyes trying to adjust to the first hints of moon dawn.

"It doesn't matter," Glory said. "Batteries were dying, anyway, and I didn't bring any backups. Do I really lose my legs? Because I am seriously reconsidering this whole thing!"

The priest's shape straightened in the low light.

"Such courage," he said quietly. "What happened to the bold girl?"

"It's not about courage," Glory said. "I'm just being practical. If Sam still dies, why lose my legs, too?"

"Will you give your legs if it means saving his life?"

Glory was silent. It was hard to tell, but she was pretty sure the priest was staring at her.

"Courage before a battle is a simple thing," the priest said quietly. "Sacrifices are easily promised."

"How did the book change?" Glory asked. "How did I get into the story at all?"

"You chose to enter the real story. Jude will have made changes in his telling of it. And will make more, depending."

"But hold on." Glory leaned forward until she could see the priest a little better. "We have to stop right now. If that's how this all ends, you have to get Sam back and try something else right away."

"You have only just begun to affect this story," Father Tiempo said. "Many more choices still wait for you."

Suddenly, the priest gasped, inhaling sharply. He was holding his breath.

Glory gave him a moment. But only a moment.

"So . . . ," she said. "What was that?"

The priest exhaled and picked up the empty hourglass

in front of him. "I was waiting for something clear. What I have is not good."

"Why not?" Glory asked. "What's bad about it?"

"I have been killed," the priest said. "Shot. My final years given up for a confused boy. And the sacrifice may not even save his life. I do not understand my final message."

Glory bit her lower lip. "Killed?"

"Yes," the priest said. "And my only note to myself was 'NO.' If Sam was killed as well, then perhaps the *no* was in reference to our now inevitable defeat. Or simply to prevent me from sending you to join him. But more likely it was in reference to the previous written message, which instructed Sam to move forward two cars. No, he didn't move. That is the most likely. In that case it is an instruction to modify where in the train I attempt to place you. If Sam stays where he is, then he will never survive the crash. You must be sent there to save him, and soon."

The priest faced Glory. "The boy's unreliability is infuriating. He understood and acted on the note perfectly well in his last attempt. But this time . . ." He shrugged. "No. I can't have died that quickly. Pitiful effort. Surely, I could have been more specific."

"I'm sorry you died," Glory said.

"As am I." Father Tiempo rose to his feet. "But at least someone has died. It means that there is room for your soul to join the moment. I have made my decision. I will send you into Sam's original train car. If he is still there, take him forward two cars immediately. Sam must survive the crash. I'm sure another older me will join you as soon as possible, but don't wait for me. Act. How many cars forward?"

"Two," Glory said.

"Good. And *quickly*." The priest took the nearest burro by the reins and led it back along the track, counting his paces. Glory followed.

"Right here," he said, stopping the burro. Then he turned and faced Glory, holding out the small empty hourglass. "Take this and you will know when time is being disrupted around you. Keep it close and it will keep you rooted."

The glass was cold and heavy in her hand. Both ends were open and uncapped.

Father Tiempo stepped back from the burro. "Now stand on the saddle."

"Stand?" Glory looked from the fat-backed animal to the priest and then back again. "What do I do if it moves?"

"You fall," Father Tiempo said. "And we try again quickly."

Glory tucked the hourglass into a water bottle pouch on her backpack. Then she swung herself up onto the saddle. Father Tiempo crossed the tracks and turned to face her from the other side.

Glory wobbled on her knees, bracing herself on the hard leather of the saddle. One foot, one knee, and both hands. More wobbling. And then . . . two feet and one hand. She let go and stood up tall, both arms extended for balance like a tightrope walker.

The moon edged one lip above the horizon, trickling silver across the desert. With arms out, backpack on, breathing slowly, Glory watched the silver trickle become a flood. She watched the light paint the priest, and she saw that his eyes were closed.

"The time is now," the priest said. His arms rose, but his eyes were still closed. "Leap out above the tracks. You will not land."

Glory didn't jump. She didn't leap. She stood on the burro and tried to inhale. But her breath fluttered and escaped like a startled bird. Pain sprouted in her chest, like her heart was beating against needles.

"Now!" the priest said.

Father Tiempo opened his eyes. Glory shut hers.

And she jumped.

With arms flailing and legs kicking, she looked down at the old rails beneath her. And then moonlit sand erased her with a stinging wind.

While dazed passengers watched, Sam dragged his sister across the priest's body, pulling her toward the front of the car. Millie was pulling back against him.

"Samuel! Our trunk!"

"It doesn't matter," he said. "The note said we have to move forward!"

He pointed across a family out their window. Men on horses were galloping alongside the train. Sam slammed into the door at the end of the car and dragged his sister onto the little platform. Rock and rails rattled past beneath the huge iron coupling that bound the cars together. Sam jumped over it, grabbed onto a swaying handrail, and leaned back for his sister.

Millie grabbed his hand and jumped.

The men on the galloping horses were whooping and laughing and pointing.

Sam didn't need them to point to know what was coming. He could remember falling. He could remember the bridge blowing. He could remember being shot from above when his legs were broken. Being crushed. Being burned. Being sliced. He could remember the cold breath that meant death had come for him again.

The front of the train had to be faster to get across the canyon in time. But everyone in the back of the train was going to die. Unless . . .

He dropped to his knees and walked his hands

carefully out onto the shaking iron hinge between the cars. There was a heavy pin—a rod—with a ring in the top. If he pulled it . . .

A bullet skipped off the iron in front of him, throwing sparks up into his face. Squinting, he grabbed the ring and pulled.

Hopeless. He might as well have been trying to lift a mountain.

"Samuel!" Millie's scream cut through the roar of the rails.

A heavy hand grabbed Sam's shirt between the shoulder blades, and jerked him up.

GLORY TUMBLED TO THE FLOOR INSIDE A ROCKING TRAIN car. The knee of her jeans tore open on a loose floorboard as sand rained down around her. People lined the windows, looking out. Gunshots outside. There was blood mixed with sand in the aisle. And Father Tiempo was lying facedown in the middle of it.

She pulled herself up onto her feet and looked around. No Sam. He was already gone. Glory raced forward, jumping over the priest's body and banging through the little door at the front of the car.

Another old Father Tiempo was shoving Sam and Millie into the next car as bullets splintered the wall around them. Then he leaned down over the iron hinge between the cars. She looked back at the body in the car behind her. How could the priest still be alive? Bullets were punching into his shoulder, his ribs, his arm.

Father Tiempo touched the fat iron pin in the hinge, and it dissolved into sand. Glory's car slowed slightly. The priest's car jerked forward. He looked up at her, and surprise flashed in his eyes as he tumbled out onto the tracks. She bit back a scream and looked away. Now the old man had died twice.

The horses and the gunfire followed the front of the train. Glory watched it accelerating away toward the edge of the canyon. A big man pushed out of the car behind her.

"Go, Sam," Glory said. "Go!"

"They gonna blow the bridge?" The man had to yell to be heard.

Glory nodded. "At least it looks that way in like a hundred and fifty years!"

The man wheeled back into the train car, bellowing as he went.

"Everybody get to the back of the train!"

Glory stayed, balancing on the front edge of the rattling platform, watching the approaching bridge. The outlaws on their horses veered away from the canyon. The steaming engine and five cars made it out onto the bridge. The engine and the first two cars made it across.

And then the explosion. Timbers sprayed up into the sky, riding on flame. The train's back heaved and rolled. The engine twisted and fell, sliding, spinning across boulders and over cacti. Four cars tumbled after it. The fifth slammed against the canyon wall, hanging. The rest dropped into the oblivion of smoke and flame, sending up a shrieking crunch as they hit the hidden bottom.

The outlaws whooped and screamed and fired into the air.

Glory's half of the train clattered toward the shattered bridge. It had slowed, but not enough. She stared through the smoke at the broken train on the far side, its carcass fiery and steaming and heaped up like an imagined monster.

She hoped Sam and his sister had made it across the canyon. But how could she hope that for anyone? The wreckage on the other side was horrifying.

As her half of the train reached the canyon, Glory stepped to the side of the platform and jumped. She landed hard and rolled clear of the following train. Car after car nosed down and dove into the smoke-filled canyon beside her, filling the desert with the crash and scream of iron thunder until the entire train had vanished.

The hooting outlaws didn't care about one strange girl in strange clothes, breathing hard with her backpack on and blood on her knees. They circled their horses around and galloped back toward the crowd of passengers who had jumped from the rear of the train and were huddling together on the tracks.

Glory knew that Sam might be dead. And if another version of Father Tiempo didn't come for her, she knew that she had just leapt into a time that she would never escape. Fear, cold and heavy, was filling her limbs and pooling in her gut. Glory swallowed hard and inhaled slowly.

Somehow, she had to cross the canyon.

SAM MIRACLE HAD BLOOD IN HIS EYES. HE WAS DANGLING from a net full of cheese, kicking and twisting against the ceiling of a suspended cargo car. When the bridge had blown, he had pushed Millie down between two bales of cotton. Then the train had rolled, slamming him into the ceiling. Every bale and barrel and box in the cargo car had hit the ceiling after him. For a moment, they had teetered on the lip of the canyon, and then metal had screamed. The car had tipped and fallen, slamming against the rock wall, hanging from the cars that had reached the other side.

The side of the cargo car had been crushed. The big doors had been torn from their hinges. Thick sour smoke rolled around Sam, singeing his lungs and mixing tears with the blood in his eyes.

Memory roared through him along with the burning taste of smoke. Millie holding him tight in a lightless crawl space. Thugs yelling downstairs, searching for someone . . . for him. Millie rocking him to sleep in the dark, singing their mother's quiet songs when the thugs had gone, when their mother would never sing them again. The taste of the smoke while the barn had burned.

Sam spat and blinked and looked around.

"Millie?" No answer. The blood was coming from his scalp. Small cut, much blood. He hoped. There wasn't any pain. No pain anywhere. Only fear. Had his sister fallen? Had the cotton bales crushed her? Was she burning with the bridge rubble at the bottom of the canyon? He would burn with her. He would find her. He would never let himself forget her again.

Sam scrambled against the ceiling, and then gave up, gasping. His body was warm, but he was shivering. And he smelled like he'd been dipped in whisky. Most likely thanks to the bottle that had cut his head.

"Millie!" Sam couldn't yell any louder. He kicked and twisted, still dangling from the net full of cheese, scanning the remaining contents of the car through red stickiness and smoke. No cotton. Almost all the cargo was gone. Along with his sister.

Sam shut his eyes. His arms were shaking harder than the rest of him, but his fingers were curled through the net. He wouldn't fall. Not by accident.

Sam's father had been sick for months before he'd finally stopped talking. Sam was with him on the front porch, staring out at the fields that should have been planted, at the pen that would have been holding the sheep if they hadn't all been stolen away by the mountain people. At the charred ruins of the barn. His father had always been as sure as sunlight, as full of laughter as the great gold maples in fall. But no more.

Before that moment on the porch, Sam was sure he had already heard his father's last message. He'd felt the rough hand on the back of his neck, and a weakened arm had pulled him close enough for a leather-scented whisper.

Proud of you, boy.

So, sitting beside the leafless branches of his father in his old rocker, tucked under the three heavy quilts Millie had given him, Sam was expecting nothing more than his father's slow painful breathing. But then . . .

"You left your sister?"

Sam jumped to his feet. His father's thin unshaven face was hard and angry. But his eyes were closed. His voice had been as firm and clear as it had ever been.

"No, sir. I didn't," Sam said. "Millie's upstairs. She's here."

"Better you died," his father said. "Leaving my girl like that."

Sam's father didn't survive the afternoon. And it didn't matter that he'd been delirious and ill and dying, those were the last words he'd spoken on this earth. And he had meant them.

It was time to let go. Sam took a breath and prepared to drop.

Sam.

It might have been Millie's voice, but whoever it was wasn't anywhere below him. Sam looked up.

"Sam!"

Sam held his breath. The metal in the train car was groaning. Fire was popping and gnawing on the timbers from the bridge.

"Sam!"

A gun fired.

Sam climbed without a plan. He scurried up the ceiling, grabbing at beams and chains as he went. He hooked his leg out the gaping door in the side of the car, and swung out into the hot smoke. Powered by panic, he clawed his way up the outside of the train car like a rat, too desperate to fail.

Rolling up onto the very top of the dangling car, he scrambled to his feet, ran at the canyon wall, and leapt for a jutting boulder at the lip.

The rock tore his palms, but he didn't feel it. His father's dying dream had been wrong. Sam would never leave his sister. He would never lose. He jerked his chin up above the boulder and then pulled and pressed himself forward until his chest and ribs were resting on stone. Then he rolled forward and stood, panting.

Steam and coal smoke from the crumpled train engine had swallowed the plain. Through the vapor, the sun was as small and dull as a white dime. Cargo was strewn around the edge of the canyon. Bales of cotton. Shattered cases of whisky. Fire.

"Millie?"

Sam threw his arm up over his mouth and nose and moved slowly into the wreckage with eyes streaming. Why had the outlaws done this? What did they want? Robbing a train made some kind of sense, but destroying it? Blowing the bridge? Ruining the cargo?

He rolled a bale of cotton over, revealing a shattered barrel of coffee beans. Coughing, he flipped over a wooden bench. A cowboy, badly broken and clearly dead, lay facedown on an obliterated cactus.

"Samuel Miracle!" The roar carved through the smoke and bounced back up from the canyon in a rolling echo. It was a man's voice, rough and wild and full of violent thrill—like an animal sensing a kill.

Sam's throat clenched at the sound of his name. He knew the voice. He hated the voice. But how could he? He'd never been in Arizona. He'd never been anywhere outside West Virginia until one week ago.

"Samuel Miracle, I grow bored of this game! I have won, you have lost, and once again that fool of a priest will dance you through time so that we might begin again."

Sam dropped into a crouch beside the dead cowboy's boots. His arms stopped shaking. His heart was pumping frozen blood, sharp with ice, cutting him with fear. The gash on his scalp thumped with the beat. The open tears on his palms began to scream.

Pain. Sam shut his eyes. SADDYR. Glory. West Virginia. His father on the porch. Train wreck after train wreck. His arms shattered and fused tight. Father Tiempo telling him to hide. To survive. Not to fight. No matter what.

"If you run," the voice continued, "your sister will suffer again. Every time you have escaped, she has lived on through agonies you couldn't even imagine. And every time you return, you set her back to the start—fresh, unbroken, ready for new torture, new pain, and another slow death. Have you heard of Prometheus, Sam Miracle? The titan chained to a rock, cursed to have an eagle tear out and eat his liver every morning, cursed to have his liver grow back every night?" Laughter rolled through the smoke, tumbling over its own echo from the canyon, and then dying slowly into a growl. "Your sweet sister is Prometheus, Sam. You and your priest have chained her to a rock. You regrow her liver every time I have eaten it. But I am no eagle, Sam Miracle. I am the Vulture. And I would rather eat you."

Sam lowered himself to his belly, peering beneath the smoke for any sign of movement.

"Sam? Am I talking to myself, Sam?" The voice was closer. Boots crunched on stone. Whispers. And then: "We can end this. Millie can remain unchained, uneaten, unharmed. I can release her to whatever future she may find. Your life for hers, Sam?"

Sam looked back at the dead cowboy. He was wearing a two-gun holster. Sam slid his arm underneath him, reaching for the buckle. His hand crumpled paper. A note.

DON'T! STAY HIDDEN AND UNDAMAGED!
FT

So Father Tiempo was still alive. Somehow. Maybe. But the priest didn't matter to Sam. Not right now. He threw the note away, slowly pulled the holster free, and rose to his knees. When he'd buckled it on, he cupped his hands to throw his voice off the still-groaning train wreckage.

"Fight me!"

Catcalls and hooting bounced off the rocks. Sam

clenched his fists and tried to slow his breathing. Anger, hotter than the sun and the smoke, burned in his chest.

"Let her go and I'll fight you!" Sam yelled. "If I die, I die, but let my sister go! Millie? Can you hear me?"

"No, she can't," El Buitre said. "But I can."

Sam spun around. The man was barely more than thirty feet behind him. Tall. Slim hips and wide shoulders, shining black vest and no fewer than seven golden watch chains, heavy with pearls. His eyes were both hungry and happy—the eyes of an animal about to feed. Nose like a knife. Narrow black beard oiled into a spike. Black hair rolling back in waves down his neck. Teeth like piano keys. A holster with even more pearl than his watch chains. Two silver guns shining like the moon on black water.

Men flanked him on either side with revolvers drawn. There was Tiny with his motorcycle boots and bowler hat, now elongated and slender, with the facial scar he had been missing on the train. Rattles was there, but the mustache he'd had on the train had grown even larger and was now white. More shapes were lost in the smoke behind them.

Sam was alone.

"Where's my sister?" Sam asked. "I'll fight you for my sister."

The outlaws fanned out around Sam.

"I will fight you," El Buitre said. He rocked his head slowly from side to side and then bobbed it, like a bird. "But once I have cut your heart from your still-living body and ended this charade forever, I am still keeping your sister." He grinned. "Someone has to look after her."

Sam flexed his fingers. Fear and anger and smoke blurred his still blood-sticky eyes. His father had taught him to shoot, how to calm himself and aim. But that had been a little rifle and they had been hunting for food; this was quick-draw, he was facing a human, and his heart was kicking in his chest like a trapped dog.

"I'm supposed to kill you," Sam said. He tried to drain his body's tension out of his feet, the way his father had described. But it all got stuck in his lungs.

"Then do it." El Buitre's lip curled into a snarl. "Kill me. Put the world to rights and end my rule before it even truly begins."

The Vulture drew out a gold watch and wound it slowly with long fingers. As he did, his six remaining watches slipped free of his vest on their own and floated in the air around him, gently rattling their gold-and-pearl chains.

Sam blinked and squinted, unsure of what he was seeing.

Three watches rose over El Buitre's left shoulder and three rose over his right until the drooping chains had spread above the outlaw like golden wings. No longer winding the seventh watch, the Vulture grinned and let it float above his palm. A tiny spinning tornado of sand sprouted up from the watch's face.

Sam ignored it all and focused on the chest of the tall man in front of him. He imagined his hands jerking the revolvers up faster than sight, faster than thought, faster than time. He envisioned two shots throwing the outlaw back into the smoke as his golden watch chains rattled down around him.

A slow breath. And then Sam Miracle's hands snapped toward his holsters. And El Buitre slapped his little tornado watch straight up.

Sam's hands weren't faster than sight. Or thought. He suddenly felt like he was trying to move through water. Through invisible tar. And El Buitre was a blur. Sam's fingers didn't even close before the outlaw's twin silver barrels were spitting fire. Bullets shattered Sam's wrists. They punched through his forearms. They splintered his elbows. While El Buitre's guns blazed, Sam's arms snapped and swung like a rag doll's. Five rounds in each arm. And one more for each shoulder. Sam slipped, staggered backward, hung in the air for an impossibly slow moment, and then slammed into the ground.

The world was a place of smoke and silence.

Seven watches floated back to their master and were pocketed.

Rattles stepped over Sam, pushing back his hat and drawing his long bowie knife as he did. The outlaw was grinning under his huge white mustache, and when he spoke, Sam heard nothing.

Cold wind ripped away the smoke and a column of swirling sand poured down from the sky above Sam. White-haired Father Tiempo arrived spinning in the storm, hurling wind and sand in every direction.

A dozen guns began to fire. Sam felt cold. And he couldn't move. He wished the dime sun above him would shine harder. He wondered if death would bring a blanket, or if he could just borrow his father's quilts.

Sam Miracle swallowed. His throat felt like torn paper and ash.

But he hadn't left his sister. No, sir. Never. Not him.

He shut his eyes and waited for the blankets, but the words that came in his father's voice were even warmer.

Proud of you, boy.

Sam Miracle smiled.

6

Arms

HOURS HAD PASSED, AND MOST OF THE SMOKE HAD CLEARED by the time Glory had crossed the canyon. Her water was long gone and her eyes felt like shattered glass. Climbing through the wreckage at the bottom of the canyon had left her with peeled shins and singed hands. Climbing back up the other side of the canyon had moved new pain to her knees.

She had tried not to think about what she would find. She'd heard the guns and the shouting in the smoke. Even worse, she'd heard hours of silence after, broken only by the groan and crash of a shifting train car or by the squalling of an unseen vulture. She knew it wouldn't be good.

But she had never expected this.

Squinting in the sunlight, Glory moved through the mounded ring of bodies. Sand had drifted over them, between them, and around them—hiding legs, arms, and even full torsos. There were more than she could count, and every last one of them was Father Tiempo.

Dozens of him. All shot dead.

At the outside of the ring, the priest's hair was white and his face creased and hard. But as she moved carefully through the ring, he grew younger. His hair darkened. His face softened. The very youngest version of the man had fallen near the center of the priestly ring, beside the body of Sam Miracle.

A startled sob jumped out of Glory when she saw Sam. His shattered arms were black with cracking blood and pointing in a different direction at every bullet break. His eyes were shut, but his cracked lips were parted. His ribs rose slightly. And then fell.

He was still alive.

She dropped to her knees beside him, trying not to cry.

"Sam, I'm here," she said. "It's Glory. I'm here." She wasn't sure if she should touch him. Or where. Definitely not his hands or his shoulders or his arms. Oh, his poor, poor arms.

She touched his chest and felt his slow breathing. He couldn't last very long. Not after losing that much blood. Not in the sun.

"Stay alive, Sam. I'll think of something. Just stay alive." She looked around at the piled-up priests. The story the bodies told was a strange one, but she thought she understood it. Father Tiempo had died defending Sam. And he had known that he would. He had sent his oldest self to die. And then a slightly younger self. He had died younger each time, giving more and more of the end of his life until . . . what? He had given too much?

She looked back at Sam's face. A living version of the priest wasn't here now. Was Tiempo dead for good or had he run out of life that he could spend? Or maybe he had just left Sam to die and had gone back to an earlier time to steer Sam into avoiding this next time.

No. He'd tried that already. He had said that he was risking everything on this one throw. She looked around at the priest's bodies. That's what he had meant. Father Tiempo had spent himself to save Sam. This moment and this attempt had cost him how much? She couldn't say.

Sam's eyes cracked open. They met Glory's, and then fluttered. She leaned over him, holding their attention. And then his voice hatched out of his throat.

"Millie? Father said not to. I didn't. I didn't leave you."

"Shhhh," Glory said. She didn't need to correct him. "You don't have to talk."

"Alive?"

Glory nodded. "You are. Yes. You're alive, Sam. Be strong, okay? I don't know what to do, but I'll think of something."

"Hurts," Sam said. "Been here. Before."

Hurts didn't even begin to describe how bad he looked. Glory wiped her cheeks quickly. "Why didn't you hide?" she asked. "Father Tiempo said to hide. To survive. But you tried to fight."

Sam shut his eyes. Glory watched his throat spasm a swallow.

"The book," he said. "I'm. Not. Poncho. Couldn't leave you. Won't."

Tears darted down Glory's cheeks, and another sob broke loose like a laugh. She'd told him Poncho deserved to die for leaving his sister. That she had wanted him to die at the end of the book. How could she be so stupid?

"I know you're not Poncho. You're Sam Miracle. The book can change. It already did. It will change more."

Sam had fought. But Millie was gone, anyway, and the priest was pretty thoroughly dead, and Sam was dying in the sun. And even if he didn't die, he would never use his arms the same way again. If he had arms at all.

"I'm so sorry," Glory said. "I'm such an idiot, but I didn't know we'd be living it. I didn't know it could be real."

Sam's eyes opened again. They turned away from the train wreck.

"Water," he said. "Please. That way. Been here."

"Yes!" Glory scrambled to her feet and adjusted her backpack. She pointed. "That way?"

But Sam was unconscious. Hooking her backpack straps tight, Glory began to run.

THE CREEK WAS AT LEAST A MILE AWAY, OVER BOULDERS AND through dense tangles of sage, and it was more pale mud than water, but Glory couldn't have been any happier to see it. She dropped onto her stomach in the mud and sipped off a trickle at the top. Then she filled her water bottle and ran back to Sam.

She trickled water onto his lips and into his mouth, but his eyes didn't open. She thought about dumping water on his wounds, but that might cause more harm than good. If more harm could possibly be done to him. She settled for pouring the rest of the water on his forehead and neck and chest. He needed to be out of the sun, but there was no way she could move him—his arms might come all the way off. She stripped the black outer robes from two of the Father Tiempos, and then pitched them in a tent over Sam's body, using dead cactus arms for poles. Then she ran back to the stream.

Back and forth, as the sun dropped into the west, Glory shuttled water. She bathed Sam's forehead. She squeezed out cloths into his mouth and on his throat. She listened to him breathe. Finally, parched and blistered herself, Glory widened the tent, and wriggled inside. She didn't watch the darkness fall. She slept.

Hours passed. Cold crept in under the coats and all the way into her bones.

Coyotes woke her.

Snarling in the darkness.

Glory snapped back into consciousness, her heart pounding blood and adrenaline through cold veins. She reached out and felt for Sam. He wasn't breathing. She slid her hand under his shirt. His chest was still warm against her icy hand. And there was a breath, faint and ghostly beneath his ribs. Sam moaned slightly and Glory jerked her hand away. The snarling outside the tent stopped. But only briefly.

Holding her breath, Glory lifted the corner of her makeshift tent. A quick shape darted away. Two other shadows leapt and rolled and circled each other, growling. There were shadows all around, nosing through the bodies.

And one of them was creeping toward her. A big one.

Head low and steady, shoulders rolling. Moonlight dying in the animal's eyes. Glory didn't move. She didn't breathe. The coyote stopped, eight feet away, staring. Quick sniffs sampling the air. One leap and it would be on her. Glory wanted to scream, but a scream would draw all of them. This one might still leave. Dear God, make it leave.

The coyote raised a paw. But behind it, a swaying lantern was coming slowly down the tracks. As it approached, the other coyotes stopped their nosing and their snarling, and they turned. Finally, the animal closest to Glory stood up tall and turned with them.

A sharp whistle raced down the tracks and every coyote tensed. One more sent them racing away.

Glory gasped for air and shivered relief, but she wasn't about to call for help. For all she knew, she could be watching Rattles or Tiny coming back for Sam's body. She slowly lowered the tent flap and slid a little closer to Sam.

The lantern was on a small cart, pulled by a mule, led by a man. The man was humming something that swayed like a lullaby, mixing in a few verses of song here and there—some in English and some most definitely not.

The solemn bells are ringing
And though my grave is singing
I've yet to reap my corn

My sons are all unborn
So give Death a poison cake
Beside a quiet lake
And I shall steal his pony

The humming man was wearing high boots, a loose vest over bare skin, and a tall top hat. He led his mule and cart straight to the ring of fallen priests. There, he paused for a long moment, his face sorrowful in shadow. Then he removed his hat, made the sign of the cross, took the lantern off the cart, and wove his way through the bodies to the tent of cloaks.

Glory held perfectly still. The man was bigger than he had looked. And old to be so straight and strong. His long white hair was bound back tight with a strip of black cloth. His mostly bare chest was crowded with necklaces, and his wide belt was hidden behind knives and bottles. With one hand, he lifted the tent and threw it to the side. Glory yelped and slid away. Without even looking at her, the man held out the lantern for her to hold. When she took it, he began to chant and hum quietly, bending over Sam, assessing his damaged arms with thick gentle fingers. Slowly, and with a very somber face, he folded Sam's arms tidily onto his chest. Then, scooping him up easily, he carried him toward the cart.

Without needing to be told, Glory followed, holding the lantern high. The big man slid Sam carefully onto a bed of furs in the back of the cart, and then he turned to Glory.

"Daughter of tomorrow," he said. "Do you choose to come with me or to die here?"

"What? I'm coming!" Glory said. "No way I'm letting you take him—"

The big man touched her head and her tongue wobbled to a stop. Thick rippling cold poured through her, relaxing every muscle, soothing her sunburnt skin, but somehow warming her insides. Her eyes shut. Her legs gave out. She didn't even feel the large hands catch her and lift her into the back of the cart.

WHILE THE NIGHT ANIMALS WATCHED, THE GREAT MAN stood before the dark ring of dead priests. He drew a small paper card from his vest. Then, breathing a quiet blessing of farewell, he flicked the paper out into the ring, and returned to his cart. With his top hat back on, and the lantern swinging on the cart, he clicked his mule away.

The card whispered across the sand.

BROTHER, I WILL BE FALLEN BEYOND MY STRENGTH.
CARRY MY BURDEN.
ATSA

✧ ✧ ✧

THE TOP FLOOR OF THE ROYAL SHARON PALACE HOTEL WAS seven stories above the cobbled San Francisco street. But the rooftop tower rose another seven stories above that. It rose high above the shouting and the fighting and the chatter and the clatter of iron horseshoes on stone.

It even rose above the fog.

On the very top floor, in a circular room, carefully bent window panes shivered in their wrought iron frames as the morning breeze blew in off the sea. The sun had risen above the fog, and the world outside was a chain of hilltop islands, peering up through the flat blanket of cloud. The city was mostly hidden. The bay was invisible. But the sunlight roamed free.

Inside, sprawling on black silk sheets with seven gold-and-pearl watch chains in a tangle around him, William Sharon stared at the ceiling and wished that he had the energy to yell. He was that tired. And that disappointed. And now the sun was in his eyes.

He threw his arm over his face and groaned.

The bed was carved ebony, darker even than the black marble floors. At the head, two large feathered wings stretched up, almost reaching the gold vaulted ceiling. At the foot, two enormous talons gripped black globes—carefully mapped with the world. But the globes had been pierced by the talons and were collapsing into skulls.

In addition to the bed, the room held a hulking desk, a hulking fireplace, a hulking chair, and a tall slender bookshelf overloaded with books, files, journals, logs, and parchments rolled up like scrolls.

An iron spiral staircase rose up through the ceiling to the tower rooftop and receded down through the marble floor.

It had taken William fourteen years lived in one tower to accumulate all that he had. He had repeated days over and over until he'd gotten them just right—until all the right people had been killed, the right secrets stolen, the right properties burned—until he had maximized his gain. And then he had moved on to the next day. Some months had taken years. But the longer he had been at it, the more efficient he had become. Now, he could repeat a week once and know that he had squeezed as much blood and gold and power out of it as he could possibly squeeze.

William Sharon, aka Bill Rose, aka Bill the Vulture, aka Bill Buitre, aka Boss Buitre, aka El Buitre, had married and unmarried, murdered and unmurdered, invested and destroyed. He had shot judges and bought judges. He'd looked for the best gold mines in the future and had taken violent possession of them in the past. And he'd made even more money on failing mines. He had made friends incredibly rich, only to pluck their lives when the time was right.

And he always knew when the time was right.

He'd been a senator. And a bank robber. When his best friend and the founder of the Bank of California had finished building his mansion and had nearly finished The Palace Hotel, Bill the Vulture had crashed his most valuable asset (the Commodore Mine), created a run on the bank, and then pushed his friend into the San Francisco Bay with a hammer tap to the head.

The Vulture had taken everything—the bank and all its holdings, the mansion, the hotel, and a hundred other properties. He didn't need anything more from this time.

El Buitre was ready to move on.

But he couldn't.

He wasn't repeating weeks now in order to gain. He was repeating weeks because he was still living in the month of his death. And the boy had escaped him again.

At first, it had been infuriating. And then boring. Now it had become insufferable.

What had the priest been thinking, dying like that? As Father Tiempo had scattered the outlaws through the years, they had cut him down easily. But he hadn't stopped coming. He hadn't stopped dying until the last remaining outlaws had fired their very last rounds and had been tossed through the centuries.

Tiempo was a fool. He could never get those years of his life back, and he'd laid them down for a boy already hopelessly broken. As good as dead.

William Sharon sat up on his vast bed. Seven pearly watch chains rattled behind him. He still hadn't changed his clothes since returning from Arizona, and his sheets were full of sand.

A wide woman with gray-streaked hair pulled back into a tight bun stood beside the stairwell in the floor. One lightly tapping toe was just visible beneath her black floor-length skirt, and a bulging gray metallic blouse was buttoned all the way up into a lacy cuff beneath her fat chin. Her pale face was pillow smooth and pillow shaped, and she gripped a leather-bound book with short, thick fingers, tipped with silver nails. She had no eyebrows, and her eyes were deadly and burrowed well back in her face like twin vipers in twin dens, ready to strike any fool who might pass by.

She wore a large golden two-headed vulture brooch above her left breast. A clock was set in its feathered belly; two pearls were gripped in its talons.

William Sharon looked at her, and then looked out of his tower window, across the clouds. He wasn't in the mood for Mrs. Dervish.

The tapping of her foot filled the room.

"What?" he said. "Speak, woman, and stop that tapping before I cut your foot off."

Her tapping grew louder. When she spoke, it was like her shrill voice was dragging nails across the stone floor. "I told you this would fail, William. Unnecessary risks were taken. Do you even care what I think?"

"No."

"May I remind you where you would be without me?"

El Buitre's nostrils flared as he looked at her. "No, Dervish, you may not."

Mrs. Dervish held up the big leather book. "The story had changed already before your attempt, and the boy was still doomed. Poncho would have come to you, William, if he dared. I could have protected you. We could have taken his heart at our leisure, but now . . . the priest will have hidden him again."

William Sharon rolled his shoulders, his frustration simmering into fury.

"I do not require your protection, Dervish. I am in no danger." He stared into the visible black tips of her eyes, licking his teeth beneath his thin lips. "But you are. Do not forget to whom you speak."

Mrs. Dervish snorted. Holding up the leather book, she opened it, pages facing the Vulture. Raising her bald brows, she flipped through the pages slowly, without glancing down.

El Buitre blinked in surprise. His lip curled, and he

jerked his beard into a tighter point.

"Blank," Mrs. Dervish said. "The priest has outsmarted you."

"The priest is finished," El Buitre snarled. "Pages have been blank before."

"Never this many." Mrs. Dervish took a step forward. "Not since the very first change. Anything could happen, William. *Anything.*"

Faster than sight, the Vulture slipped a knife out of his sleeve, flinging it at the woman. The blade flashed, and then Mrs. Dervish slammed the book shut like she was catching a fly. The long thin blade stuck out of the spine toward her face, but the handle was firmly trapped in the pages. Small dust tendrils spooled slowly away from the book.

"Madam, begone," the Vulture said quietly. "You'll have his heart. We will end this thing."

"No," said Mrs. Dervish primly. "We will finally begin." She looked at the knife in the book, and then back at William Sharon, slumping over the side of his bed.

An elongated man in a tight suit and bowler hat was creeping up the stairs through the floor behind Mrs. Dervish. She stepped aside, retreating down the stairs on clicking shoes once the tall man in the motorcycle boots cleared the stairwell.

"Boss?"

"Don't call me that," William growled. "You know my name, Tiny. Get your bones all the way in here and tell me what you've learned. Where's he hiding the boy?"

"I couldn't say, Mr. Buitre," Tiny said. His long fingers adjusted his eye patch and then picked nervously at the deep scar on his cheek.

The Vulture filled his chest. "I've given you a month in these last three days. A month." He pushed back his long black curls and then scratched his thick mustache. "Tiny, you are useless. Shall I kill you? You were the Tinman once. You were a terror. Now you are a ghost, a gas, nothing more terrible to me than an unpleasant odor."

"Sir, Boss," Tiny stammered and pulled off his bowler hat. "Mr. Buitre, I've done my level best for you."

El Buitre rose to his feet. He flexed his fingers and looked around the room. "Shall I strap on my guns and let you draw, Tinman? Should I be frightened?" He looked back into Tiny's one eye. "Could you beat me? Are you fast enough to kill the Vulture? If you are, I'll leave you everything. Perhaps Mrs. Dervish will chain these watches to your black heart and build you an empire across time. After all, there's no point in my living"—he moved toward the lanky outlaw, raising his voice with each step—"*if I can't find the boy!*"

"Sir," Tiny said. "Mr. Buitre. We've checked every moment at that bridge that matched the exact position of the moon one hundred years in both directions. Rattles and a few others went forward while I went backward. We checked more than two thousand nights, sir. Then we moved further in increments of seven like the priest always favors. All the way up to seven hundred years each way, sir. And . . . well . . . I think he tricked us."

Mr. William Sharon Vulture Buitre raised his eyebrows. "I beg your pardon?"

Tiny straightened to his full height and blinked his one eye. "We assumed that the priest was fighting us off in order to ghost the boy away the way he always has. He lost much of his life doing it, so it mattered to him dearly."

El Buitre waited.

"But he didn't," Tiny said. "Ghost him away through time, I mean. He didn't take him anywhere. Once he scattered us all through the years we were just trying to find our way back to you. But the priest . . . did nothing. He tricked us. We assumed he would hide the boy the way he always has, and we went searching, but the boy never left that time. He was just lying there in the desert right where you shot him."

The Vulture stiffened his long fingers and then curled them each slowly into fists, cracking one knuckle at a time.

"You're sure of this?" he asked.

"We are." Tiny nodded. He licked his lips, nervously.

"When we realized what had happened, we returned to the moment right after we had first been scattered. We saw the boy's body."

"And?" El Buitre asked. "Was he still living?"

"He was. But the priest was with him. We killed him. And killed him. Even more than when you were there, and he flung us away through time. Younger and angrier versions of him fell in a ring all the way around the boy. And as the last priest died, he threw up an enormous sandstorm that spun like a tornado above all of his bodies. It swept us clean out of that time and wouldn't let us back. Disappeared whole train cars. The next closest time we could reach was fourteen hours later. No one there but dozens of the dead priest. But there were wagon tracks in the sand. Someone took the boy."

"Someone?" El Buitre asked. "But how does that help the boy? If he isn't dead, his arms are at least destroyed. They must come off if he's to survive. Even the priest isn't fool enough to think he could face me with stumps on his shoulders."

The arch-outlaw walked to his bent glass windows and looked out over the fog. His mind, trained to track time through seven layers at once, capable of fiery patience and an intense and bloodthirsty pursuit of perfection for every day that he lived, capable of beating even lesser demons and their fortune-tellers at the poker table, could not understand what Father Tiempo could possibly be planning.

"Ridiculous," he said out loud. "If he wants to offer up a single prayer against me, he must move the boy back and try again to overcome my strike at the train. But then why die? Why give up so much of his own life when he could have vanished with the boy at the outset?"

"Maybe he died a little too much," Tiny said behind him. "Maybe he had a plan, but we just beat him."

El Buitre thought about this. Maybe. Maybe the priest was finally done. Maybe the boy was dead in the desert and his soul had departed from the earth, never to relocate again, never to come searching for the Vulture with the blessing of Providence upon him and a weapon in his hand.

Maybe El Buitre could finally live forward, braving the week he had long ago seen to be his last.

"I think he's dead," Tiny said. "I do. I think it's over, Boss."

El Buitre wanted to believe it. Badly. But believing was a fool's game.

"When his heart is ash in my hand, I will believe. Get me the boy's heart." He pocketed his watches, picked up his gun belt, and turned around, strapping it on as he did. Then he looked up at Tiny with a grin, his fingers tickling the butts of the twin silver-and-pearl revolvers. "Try me, Tinman?"

The lanky man took a step back toward the stairs, shaking his head. "Not with all those timepieces on, Boss. I know how they favors you."

Turning, he raced for the stairs, long legs tumbling like the legs of an awkward insect. When he had gone, El Buitre pulled both of his guns sloth-slowly, thumb-cocking them as he did.

"Boom, boom, little boy." He smiled and holstered his guns.

Snakes

Sᴀᴍ Mɪʀᴀᴄʟᴇ ʜᴀᴅ ᴀ ᴅʀᴇᴀᴍ. Hᴇ ᴡᴀs sɪᴛᴛɪɴɢ ᴏɴ ᴀ sᴛᴏᴏʟ in a cave lined with mirrors. He was wearing a barber's apron tight around his neck, and he was waiting for a haircut. The floor was crawling with fat-bellied snakes, so he kept his legs tucked up beneath him. A tall Indian wearing a top hat and no shirt was seated in a red-velvet easy chair, reading a newspaper. The snakes didn't bother the Indian. He had his legs extended straight out onto the slithering rug, boots crossed at the ankle. Every time he turned a page, he winked at Sam.

Underneath the apron, Sam had no arms.

"Who are you?" Sam asked.

"My father named me Pistol Bullet," the Indian said. His voice was distracted, his eyes roaming the newspaper. "Because he wanted me to be frightening to our enemies. A priest named me Emmanuel, because he wanted me to be a savior to my people. But men called me Manuelito, because I am large and *ito* means 'little,' and there is often joy in calling a thing what it is not." He smiled at the pages in front of him. "But Manuelito fits me well, because my body may be large, but I was only a little savior."

Manuelito looked up. "My brother wanders time on the path set before him by God's angels. But I am at rest. Men think I am dead. But I am here when he needs me. He brings me broken things in need of healing."

"And you fix them?" Sam asked.

Manuelito shook his head. "I heal them. Sometimes that means breaking them differently. If a boy's arms are so damaged and mutilated that he cannot live, a healer may remove the arms to save the life. He makes things worse to make them better."

Hot fear flooded through Sam. He wriggled his torso under the barber's apron.

"You took my arms?" he asked. His eyes were burning. He blinked quickly. "They were bad before, but I liked having them."

Manuelito set his newspaper down on his knee. He

removed his top hat and set it on the newspaper. His dark eyes had grown quite serious.

"I did not take them. Not in the way you mean. My brother wanted me to heal them," the Indian said. "But that I could not do. He wanted your arms strong and fast, so that your enemies would fear you, and so that you could be a savior to all who have come under the shadow of the Vulture who flies against time. And that I could do. Is this what you want, even if I must break them differently? Terribly. Fearfully. You could live more simply with them gone. I can still remove them."

"Arms," Sam said. He nodded and hot tears darted over his freckles and down his neck into the apron. "Yes, please help me. If you can."

Manuelito set his hat back on his head and winked. "I can." He picked up his newspaper and opened it. "I *may*. And, I already have. Your left arm is a matter of justice. Your right is a young and foolish volunteer. You are strong enough to wake now, but there's no hurry if you'd rather not. I have also given your memory some calming. It has been through much." He snapped the paper up in front of his face. "When you do wake . . . try not to be frightened."

THE DREAM FADED. FOR HOURS. FIRST INTO DARKNESS, AND then into nothingness, and finally it faded into light as warm and golden as the dawn.

Sam opened his eyes. The ceiling above him was stone. The wall beside him was stone. He was lying on a low wooden cot and he wasn't wearing a shirt. Instead, his hands and arms were bundled in bandages from his knuckles to his shoulders. He sat up and tried to rub his eyes. Needle-sharp pricks danced along his arms as they moved. And they didn't really move like arms at all. They were strong, but . . . floppy. His left hand missed his face completely and floated in the air behind his ear.

Sam swallowed hard, suddenly nervous. And then two snakes began to rattle behind him.

After a week of sleep, Sam exploded off the cot and spun around. His feet were bare, and the stone floor was dotted with sand and loose rocks.

The snakes were still behind him.

Yelling, Sam jumped back up onto the cot and turned in a tight circle. The whole cave was echoing with the rattling, but Sam couldn't see a single snake.

"Sam!" Glory was running toward him from somewhere. "It's okay, it's okay! Calm down!"

Sam stopped spinning and looked at her. His chest was heaving. Panic sweat was running down his face. First one rattle stopped, and then the other.

"What's going on?" Sam asked. "I dreamed a big Indian. I think."

A boy Sam's size ran into the room behind Glory. His

143

hair was thick, perfectly black, and cut in jagged clumps around his protruding ears and the worn-penny earrings that dangled from them. He wore a coarse wool poncho that hid his arms, a tangle of long braided-leather necklaces, and a red cloth strip tight around his head—just like Peter had done back at SADDYR. Sam's mind was so sharp with memory, it surprised him. The recent past was crystal clear . . . all the way up to guns firing at the train wreck.

"The big Indian is real," Glory said. "This is his cave." She looked back at the boy behind her. "And this is his son, Baptisto. He doesn't speak much English, but he's smart."

The boy stepped forward and stuck his hand out from beneath his poncho, ready to shake.

"I am Tisto," he said and nodded.

"Sam," Sam said, but his right hand didn't go anywhere near Tisto's. Instead, it slid slowly up his chest and then hooked itself around the back of his neck. Sam blinked and jerked it back down by his side.

"Did you hear the rattlesnakes?" Sam asked. Cold dizziness washed across the backs of his eyes. His voice didn't feel like his own. "Am I crazy?"

"I heard them," Glory said, nodding. He could tell she was working hard to hold his eyes, to reassure him. "And you are crazy. And Father Tiempo is crazy and his brother is crazy and the whole world is crazy. Now how about you sit down?"

"I don't want to sit down!" The cold in Sam's skull exploded into heat, and his voice was rising. "Why would I sit?"

"Because your arms are the craziest of all and I don't want you freaking out again." Glory's words were slow and smooth. She touched his chest, gently pushing him backward.

Sam sat down on the cot and stared at his bandaged arms, breathing heavily. When he relaxed, he could feel them trying to bend and twist. So he didn't relax. At all.

"Okay," Glory said. "For the record, I need you to know that I didn't want him to do this. I didn't want him to amputate your arms either. I wanted him to make them perfectly normal, like they had never been shot. But apparently that wasn't an option. He said he could fuse them up solid and put them in painful braces forever, cut them totally off, or . . . this."

Sam wasn't looking at her. He was gripping his knees and staring at the backs of his bandaged hands. The skin was tickling. Wriggling a little. Like his veins were moving by themselves.

Glory leaned forward and took Sam's left hand, untucking the end of the white bandage as she did. Tisto stepped back and crossed his arms. He didn't seem interested in what was beneath the bandages. His eyes were locked on Sam's face, and they weren't impressed.

"Are you ready?" Glory asked.

Finally, Sam looked up at her. His heart was rabbit-kicking against his ribs. "Does it matter?"

"Not really," Glory said, and she began to unwind the bandage. "Don't look yet." She paused. Sam was staring straight down at his hand.

"I'm serious," said Glory. "Let me unwrap it first."

Sam knocked Glory's hand away and tore at the bandages. He stood up, shaking white cloth coils down to the floor of the cave. As he did, the rattles started up behind him. But Sam didn't spin around. He was looking at golden scales patterned with black and white. They covered a mounded muscle that ran down the center of his wrist onto his arm. The scaled muscle flexed, and Sam felt it tense inside his arm just like it was his.

He clawed the bandage loose up to his elbow and then shook it off.

The rattling grew louder, and his forearm bent into a tight quivering U. Two vicious golden eyes with hard slanted pupils stared at him from the back of his hand. A sharp scale horn rose up above each eye, but there was no mouth. The skull of the rattlesnake, minus its lower jaw, had been grown onto the back of his hand. His own skin stretched up like the edges of a tent, and then merged with the scales.

"This one is Cindy," Glory said. "Manuelito just calls her Cin. She's a big old Mojave Sidewinder."

"She hates people," Tisto added. "All people."

Sam was having trouble processing. There was a snake in his arm, steering his arm, bending his arm into curves that didn't belong on anything human. There were eyes and horns on the back of his hand. And they looked angry.

"Cindy," Sam said, and his voice was flat—stunned. "It's stuck to me."

"*She*," Glory said. "Not *it*. The rattles are on your shoulder blades. If you get nervous or mad, you rattle."

Sam relaxed, just to see what Cindy would do with his arm without him.

Faster than fingers snapping, his hand slammed into his face. He tumbled backward and onto the cot. Forcing his hand away, he made his fingers hook onto the edge of the bed. Cindy tried to jerk the hand loose again, but Sam clenched tight. Blood was trickling out of his nose and his lips felt instantly swollen against his throbbing teeth. His eyes were watering. In his entire life, Sam had never been punched as hard as he had just punched himself.

Tisto shook his head and pointed at Sam's offending hand. His tongue buzzed quickly like a rattle and then he spat out a sharp hiss. Cindy stopped fighting Sam immediately, but she remained tense.

"She just needs to get used to you," Glory said. "You'll have to practice controlling her. But the other one isn't so bad. Just a little goofy. And a boy."

Sam sniffed and wiped his nose against his shoulder. The rattling hadn't stopped and he was panting hard. All he wanted to do was shut his eyes and not think about anything that had just happened.

Which wasn't easy when he could feel his arms flexing without him, when he could feel them trying to twist and slide free of his shoulders.

It was a nightmare. He would wake up in bed sweating with a fever, and his SADDYR brothers would jump out of their bunks and make sure he was all right. His arms would be stiff again. Stiff and safe and useless.

But he wasn't waking up. And his mind was clean and uncluttered, unlike any dream he'd had in years. The wriggling in his arms was real, as real as anything he had ever felt in all of his confused living.

Rolling over quickly, Sam threw up on the floor. There was nothing strange at all about the mess. It was exactly the same kind of mess that he'd made hundreds of times eating at SADDYR. Which was strangely reassuring. And vomiting had somehow stopped his nosebleed. For a moment, he ignored the tickling slither of his arms.

When he finally looked back up at Glory, she had her arms crossed, and her cheeks shone with quickly smudged tears. Her lip was shaking. Baptisto was watching her, curious. The pennies below his ears bounced when he looked back at Sam.

"She cries often," Baptisto said. "While you sleep. While my father cuts you. While you heal."

"I did not!" Glory said. "And why shouldn't I? It's been awful!"

"Please don't cry," Sam said. "Please."

"I'm not." She quickly slapped a tear off her cheek, sniffed, and then recrossed her arms. Her jaw was jutted out angrily.

"You already did," Sam said. "Just don't cry anymore. Not for me." He sat up slowly, keeping his arms tense. Then he began unwinding the bandages on his right arm. "The way El Buitre shot me, I shouldn't have arms at all right now."

"Why didn't you hide?" Glory asked. "Father Tiempo told you to stay hidden. He told you to save your arms. Did you forget?"

Sam shook his head. "No. For once, I remembered. I still remember. Father Tiempo was wrong. You hated Poncho because he left his sister. So did I." Sam stopped and stared at the heart-shaped rosy-peach head on the back of his right hand. No horns. Smoother color. Blue granite eyes—rounder, but still hooded and vicious. Sam's hand looked around and then arched its back and rubbed its scales on the side of his knee. Baptisto nodded, pleased by the rosy snake's behavior.

"It will be better with this one. I will tell my father." Then, tucking his arms back underneath his poncho, the boy left the room.

"Speck," Glory said. "Short for Speckle."

"I couldn't hide," Sam said. "I couldn't leave my sister. I had to try, even if I got my arms shot off." Sam looked up into Glory's eyes. "I'd rather have snakes in my arms." He forced a smile. "At least these arms bend. And they must be pretty quick."

"I think that was the point," Glory said. "And your bloody nose already found out how quick they are."

Sam was unwinding the rest of his bandages, all the way up to his bare shoulders, tracing the scale-wrapped strip of muscled snake to where the rattles stuck out from the backs of his shoulders, just below his neck. Cindy's rattle was huge, and she buzzed it quickly as Sam traced her long flexing back with the fingers on his other hand. Speck's rattle was almost as thick, but shorter by a few segments, and much calmer.

"Will this be in the book now?" He looked up. "Do you think the ending will change?" The shock of what he was seeing and feeling was growing into amazement. "They could help, right?"

"You know," Glory said, watching. "There's a difference

between real life and books. Don't act like they're the same."

"Sure," Sam said. "Getting life right is a lot harder. If I was just a book, Father Tiempo could have given up a long time ago. Come on, I'm curious."

"Most of the book is blank now," Glory said. "Right before the train wreck the ending was still there but . . . different. Now it's just gone."

Sam wasn't listening. He held up both of his hands, fingers splayed. The horned snake head on the back of his left hand—Cindy—tugged slightly at his skin, trying to arch herself free of Sam's arm. But she had been grafted in too deep. She could only ripple her scales, tickling Sam's skin along the seams.

Manuelito appeared in the mouth of the cave. He wasn't wearing his top hat, but everything else about him echoed Sam's dream—his size, his thick white hair, the high boots, the heavy bundle of necklaces on his bare chest. Baptisto stood in his father's shadow.

"Samuel Miracle, it is a pleasure to meet your conscious self." Manuelito held up a belt with two holstered revolvers. "If you're feeling strong enough, training with your serpent-assisted arms should commence. There is not much time, and more cannot be bought."

"Training?" Sam asked. "For what?"

"For survival," Manuelito said. "For victory, if our

prayers are heard. You must face the Vulture. And when you do, you will die for the last time. Or you will live."

Sam received the heavy holsters with strangely swaying hands. The big man crossed thick arms across his bare chest.

"I hope that you are not repulsed by your situation," Manuelito said.

"No," Sam said, looking at his arms. "I mean . . . yeah. A little. I did throw up. It really doesn't feel real."

"You must become accustomed to your new limbs. If you are ready, Baptisto will assist you."

"I'm not sure I'll ever be ready," Sam said. "Am I supposed to thank you?"

Manuelito smiled. "My young friend, if you are still living in a year, you may thank me then."

Manuelito slapped his son on the shoulder and spoke a string of words that sounded like water slipping across stone. Tisto nodded, and his father left.

Glory looked at the young Navajo. "Can I stay?"

Tisto looked at Sam. His eyebrows were up, waiting for Sam to answer the question.

Anger flooded through Sam and he shut his eyes tight against it. "I don't care," he snarled. "Just . . . don't ask me anything right now." He swallowed hard, exhaled, and looked up at Glory. She was worried, chewing her lip, but obviously not leaving.

Tisto took the gun belt from Sam's hands and set it on the cot. As he did, Cindy struck, jerking Sam's left hand and fingers into Tisto's side.

The boy spun around, snatching Sam's wrist and squeezing hard.

"Sorry," Sam said. "I wasn't trying to—"

Tisto jerked Sam's hand up to his own face. He bent Sam's fingers down and leaned his nose forward to within an inch of Sam's knuckles. He was staring directly into Cindy's vicious, unblinking eyes.

Cindy's head tugged against the skin on the back of Sam's hand while her fat rattle buzzed on his shoulder. She knotted Sam's arm up harder than a cramp, but Tisto pressed his face even closer.

"Shut your eyes," the boy said. "And try to think of nothing."

"Excuse me?" Sam asked.

Glory stepped closer to Sam, eyeing the Navajo boy. "What are you doing?"

"Hush," Tisto said. "Shut your eyes, please, and clear your mind."

Sam shut his eyes. He was used to letting his mind wander, rambling through layers of foggy memory, but he was not used to clearing it. He was picturing SADDYR, with Jude writing in the corner and the pinball machine going, and the music on, and . . .

153

"I can't do it," Sam said.

"Look at the night sky." Baptisto's voice was smooth. "There are no stars. The moon has gone. There is only nothing. Can you see it?"

Sam nodded. Darkness swallowed him.

And then something warm trickled up his left arm and into his shoulder beneath the buzzing rattle. The ghostly warmth oozed up inside his neck, left bitterness on the back of his tongue, and spread out like a word made of steam inside his skull.

Kill.

He didn't hear it. He *felt* it. And he could feel the warmth of Baptisto's face an inch away from his hand. His knuckles couldn't feel it. His skin couldn't feel it. The sensation came from the tickling head of Cindy and flowed into the back of his hand.

"What can you feel?"

"Your face in front of my face," Sam said. The warmth shifted side to side and then rose higher. "You're moving."

"Good. What else do you sense?" the boy asked.

"Hate," said Sam. "Cindy wants to kill you."

"Open."

Sam opened his eyes as the boy dropped his hand and took a step back.

"Good," Baptisto said. The pennies swung below his ears as he nodded.

Kill.

The rattling had slowed, but the level of furious rage pulsing through Sam's hand had not.

"She still hates you," Sam said. "She wants you dead."

"Of course," Tisto said. "But I am not offended. Cindy wants all things dead."

"I'm confused." Glory looked back and forth between the boys. "What just happened?"

Baptisto ignored her, focusing on Sam. "When you calm the noise inside, you will know how your vipers feel. Cindy is old and her hate great, so her voice will always be louder. But Speckle can be heard as well. Also, these two can see the heat of bodies in the darkness. When there is no light, trust your hands to guide you."

"Okay," Sam said. "How do you know this?"

"My father taught me when I was young," Baptisto said. "But I do not need the animal grown into me. I need only a touch of the skin and the oldest words of my people to learn what a beast might teach me."

"Wait," Glory said. "You can understand animals? Could you show me?"

"Yes," Baptisto said. "And no. There's not time. Eyes shut again," he said to Sam. "Now arms straight out from your sides if you can. You must practice sensing them, and you must teach them to sense you."

Over and over again, the boy gave Sam simple

commands, and over and over again, Sam failed to accomplish them. He couldn't gently touch his own ear with his left hand. Cindy struck him in the face every time he tried. He couldn't even clap his hands. Cindy would recoil and Speck would float up or down or out—anywhere but where Sam wanted his hand to be. It was easier with his eyes open, because he could see what the snake was doing and fight it. But that wasn't good enough for Tisto. Sam had to control his arms by instinct, and without sight.

Frustrated, sweating, and a little bruised, Sam stretched, twisted his torso, and tried to relax. With his eyes closed, he imagined the night sky without stars and tried to feel the new sensations, impulses, and desires that flowed up his arms from the reptilian brains on the backs of his hands. But all he got was anger and warmth on the left and confusion on the right. He could begin a motion easily, but the snakes always decided how to finish . . . if they finished what he had started at all.

"What now?" Sam asked with eyes clenched tight. "Punch myself in the face? I can do that. Or maybe I should lose my right hand behind my back."

"Do not think of failing," Tisto said. "Think of knowing. Glory now moves silently around the room. Know what your hands know. Point to her."

Sam breathed evenly, trying to lose his mind in

156

darkness and feel any rumors of warmth the snakes might send him.

Kill.

"Oh, shut up," Sam said aloud. He had no idea where Glory was, but his left hand was moving in front of him by itself.

"Good," Tisto said.

"That isn't me," said Sam. "It's moving by itself."

Tisto sighed. "The right hand then. What does Speck know?"

Sam focused on his floating right hand. Cindy was still tracking Glory, but Speck seemed to be tracking everything. Sam's arm slid forward, twisted and slid backward, looped around and slid forward again. After a moment, he recognized the pattern. His right hand was tracing a slow figure eight over and over again. And at different points in the motion, different impressions ghosted into his brain. And they were the same every time.

Rat. Boy. Girl. Snakes. Snake. Fear. Rat. Boy. Girl. Snakes. Snake. Fear. Rat. Boy. Girl. Snakes. Snake. Fear.

Sam tried to focus on identifying one thing at a time, matching the impressions he received with Speck's motion.

"There's a rat somewhere behind me," Sam said. "Tisto is on my right. Glory is in front to my right. Then he thinks there are a lot of snakes straight ahead. One snake on my left—Cindy, I guess—then he tugs away from my arm a little bit, gets scared, and starts over."

A new sensation flooded into the room. Speck relaxed instantly. Cindy tensed and slid in tight against Sam's hip. Her rattle twitched just enough to tickle Sam's skin.

Sam opened his eyes and looked around. Tisto had his arms crossed over his poncho. The boy nodded slightly.

"The rat is in a box. Snakes are in a den behind the wall in front of you. You listened."

Glory was staring at Sam, chewing a nail, looking even more nervous about the new situation than Sam felt.

Manuelito had reentered the room, and both snakes had responded. The big man looked from Sam to Tisto and asked his son a question in their mysterious liquid language.

Tisto shrugged at Sam. Not disappointed. Not impressed.

"I'm sorry," Sam said. "I can get better."

Glory forced an encouraging smile at him. "Practice makes perfect."

"Cindy is too strong," Tisto said in English. "But the other may function in time."

"Too strong may not be strong enough." Manuelito grimaced and scratched his broad chest beneath his necklaces. Then he stepped forward and picked up the gun belt off the cot. "The time to learn is now. Come."

While Baptisto and Glory trailed behind, Sam

followed the big man out of the room and down stairs cut into the stone. The ceiling rose higher and higher, arching into a red-and-yellow dome, bright with sunlight. Where the cave was larger, square buildings of mud and stone were clustered in rows. Manuelito led Sam through the narrow streets and walkways of the tiny ghost city until they finally stood in the vast gaping mouth of the cave, overlooking the rolling red rock and green sage hills of nowhere.

"There," Manuelito said. He pointed at a long gravel shelf below the cave mouth. Sagebrush dotted it. A huge saguaro cactus huddled at one end, bent by the weight of at least a dozen ancient arms.

A few rusty cans were scattered on the gravel shelf. Manuelito handed Sam the gun belt and watched the tense curves of Sam's scaled arms as he buckled it on.

"Walk on down," Manuelito said.

Glory moved forward with Sam, but the big man dropped a hand onto her shoulder.

"He will struggle to control his arms. We will remain here, well out of view."

Glory scrunched her face in disappointment, but she forced a quick smile at Sam. He inflated his cheeks in response. He was still more confused than nervous.

"Good luck," she said. "You'll be fine."

Sam tried walking down the steep slope, but the loose

159

gravel on the smooth rock made walking impossible. He arrived at the gravel shelf in a small avalanche. Dust climbed slowly up into the sky around him. A few small stones skittered all the way across the shelf and dropped off the other side.

But the world was silent.

Sam stood and looked back up at the cave. No one was watching. His legs were coated with dust and his arms swayed heavily, like socks full of sand, as he slapped it off. His hands mostly went where he wanted them, but his arms bent wherever they felt like bending to get there.

Cindy didn't like it at all. Her rattle buzzed on Sam's left shoulder and she fought his motion, stiffening his arm up into an S.

The desire to kill him washed up his arm.

"Oh, stop," Sam said. "This is already weird, don't make it harder."

He forced his left hand up until he was looking into the snake's horned yellow eyes between his knuckles. The rattle quickened and Sam tensed every muscle in his arm that his brain could reach. She was trying to strike him again, trying to smash his hand into his face.

And then Sam's other arm jerked him suddenly backward and down. He spun, staggering sideways, barely keeping his feet. Cindy swam Sam's left arm through the air toward his other fist.

Cactus spines dotted the knuckles on Sam's right hand. His fingers were closed tight around a squirming lizard. On the back of his hand, the muscles in Speck's rosy-scaled cheeks had mounded them up into a strange little smile.

"Oh, come on!" Sam said. "Really?" He forced his fingers open and the lizard dropped onto his foot before darting under the nearest stone. Speck's smile vanished. The snake's stony blue eyes stared into Sam's.

Sam felt the ticklish urge to swallow something whole.

"No! You can't eat it through my palm," said Sam. "And I'm not eating it for you."

Manuelito's voice rolled down from the cave above.

"If it was unclear, I intended for you to attempt to shoot those cans!"

"Right!" Sam shouted back. His rattling had stopped, but both of his hands were floating by his sides, scanning the ground and trying to tug him down to get closer.

He grabbed the butt of the revolver on his right hip and looked for the nearest tin can. Speck didn't fight him, so he drew the heavy weapon, cocked the hammer with his thumb, and aimed. Speck tensed, sending a rigid prickling shiver up Sam's arm. The snake was staring sideways down the barrel.

Even with his old fused arms, he never could have held such a heavy gun at arm's length without a wobble.

But with the snake's strength there wasn't even a quiver in Sam's arm, and no hint of muscle burn. Nothing more than a quiet throb in his old bones.

Sam pulled the trigger and the old can leapt into the air. The whining ricochet echoed across the desert.

Cindy snapped around, nosing Sam's left hand through the air to get a closer look at the power in Speck's grip. Sam shoved Cindy straight down at his side while he aimed at the can again.

He missed, but Cindy still snapped his hand up to see. This time, he forced her down and grabbed his belt with his left hand, holding on tight while he took aim with his right.

Speck forced his right hand slightly up. Sam pushed it back down to where he wanted it. Speck rippled ticklishly from his wrist to his shoulder, forcing the barrel back up again.

"Fine," Sam said, and he pulled the trigger. The can skipped and tumbled through the sagebrush. Cindy jerked, but Sam held on to his belt just tight enough to keep her down.

"Three in a row now," Sam whispered. "Got that?"

He cocked the revolver, pointed at a more distant can, and fired. While it hopped into the air, he cocked the gun again and let Speck drive his arm. The can split in half while it was still in the air. Sam cocked the revolver again and shoved the barrel toward one of the halves. Speck took over, tracking it down. Another bullet hit it just before it bounced.

Sam holstered his gun and stood still, breathing hard. The gunshots rolled back to him from across the hills.

"Wow." He looked at the pink snake in his hand. "Speck . . . I like you." The snake was happy, too. An electric thrill shivered up Sam's arm.

Letting go of his belt, he used his Cindy hand to rub Speck's head, and then ran his thumb down the length of the snake's rippling body.

Lowering Speck, he lifted his left hand and looked Cindy in the eyes.

"You have horns, and you already smacked me in the face, but I can like you too, if you behave." The gnarly old snake gave him no reaction at all. So Sam focused on a can and reached for his other gun.

As soon as his fingers closed around the butt of the revolver, Sam's left arm cracked like a whip. The barrel pointed almost straight up, and Sam's thumb jerked back the hammer. With that first shot, a crow dropped, trailing feathers, and the gun barrel was already swinging down. A beetle exploded in the dirt fifteen feet away. A lizard vanished off a rock. A spider splattered into a cactus.

"Stop it!" Sam yelled, ducking away from his swinging arm. "Stop it, stop it!"

The revolver fired twice more, and two more small creatures perished. Sam dropped into a crouch, with his right arm sheltering his face.

Kill.

Click. Click. Click.

Cindy was still trying to fire. Sam lowered his right arm and looked up and straight into his own smoking gun barrel, and into the two golden horn-hooded eyes beside it.

His own thumb cocked the hammer. His own finger pulled the trigger.

Click.

Sam jumped to his feet, throwing the revolver into the sage. Anger surged through him, pounding through his ringing ears, roaring in his lungs.

"You're insane!" He grabbed his left wrist with his right hand, squeezing harder than he thought possible, squeezing until his fingers twitched and the pain was screaming louder than both of the buzzing rattles on his shoulders. There was a sharp stone between Sam's feet. He wanted to crush the snake with it. Or gouge it out of his skin.

"Samuel!" Manuelito shouted down from the cave mouth. He was visible now. "Come. Eat. And I will help with the anger."

Sam threw his left hand away. It swung down and hit his thigh and then crept up behind his back.

"No!" Sam forced his hand back around and grabbed his belt. "You stay where I can see you . . . *you* . . . sick little snake."

He picked up his thrown revolver with his right hand and muttered insults at Cindy as he scrambled back up the slope to the cave.

MANUELITO AND GLORY AND TISTO STOOD IN FRONT OF THE little ghost town, waiting for him.

"I hate this one!" Sam shouted. He kicked a rock, spat, and held his left hand up in the air away from his body. "What happens to my arm if I get rid of it?"

Glory looked up at the tall Indian. "Can he still switch? I think it would be good."

She was wearing her backpack again, and *The Legend of Poncho* was in her hands.

Sam glanced at the book and then up at Glory. She quickly brushed a loose strand of hair back out of her face.

"What is it?" Sam asked. "How does it end?"

"I told you it was blank," Glory said. Her voice was flat. Too flat.

"Still?" Sam asked.

Glory bit both of her lips.

"Tell me," Sam said. "There's no point in not telling me." He peered down at Cindy. "This is bad enough already."

165

"Parts are still blank," Glory said. "But the ending isn't good."

"The book," Manuelito sighed and turned away. "I do not care about this thing. Maybe you are reading it, but it is not yet written, because you have unfinished living. Come, eat, and discuss your real troubles."

A tiny table, gray and weathered like driftwood, was set up just outside the nearest square house in the cave mouth. Three stools had been set beside it for Sam, Glory, and Tisto. The large red easy chair from Sam's dream waited for Manuelito's big frame.

On the table there was a heavy clay pot full of water with three matching clay cups. Fleshy yellow slices of what could only be cactus were piled up on a wooden tray beside small skewers of flat flame-darkened meat. A short tower of dark-brown flatbread sat on an old blue handkerchief.

Sam was hungry. He didn't ask what kind of meat he was eating, because he didn't care. He gnawed on the bread even though it tasted like a woodpile, and the warm water was sweeter in his throat than anything he had ever tasted.

While Sam kept his hands moving, he had no trouble controlling them. It was when he let them rest that Speck got distracted and slid his right arm down off the table to look under his chair, and Cindy tensed his left arm in a partial coil and rattled at Glory.

"Speckle was a pet snake at a miner's camp from a

166

very young age," Manuelito said. "Many believe that a rattlesnake cannot be trained, and for the common man, that is truth. But Speck came close. The camp cook loved him, cared for him, and let him loose at nights to hunt rats in his kitchen. But when the mines dried up and the men left, Speck was set free for the first time in his life. When I found him, he seemed quite insane, slithering after me in the open without any hate. So I kept him. When you had need, he was willing."

Sam set his right hand flat on the table and watched the rosy snake ripple his scales in the sun.

"How did you know he was willing?" Sam asked.

"As my brother Atsa is given mastery of time, I am given mastery of beasts." Manuelito tore a piece of flatbread in half. "I have the words to teach them and the touch to hear them." He popped the bread in his mouth and began to chew. "But Cindy was a different choice. She is a killer. A nightmare."

Sam's left hand was frozen six inches above the table. Cindy's horn-hooded eyes were still locked on Glory. Glory chewed slowly, glancing up and down between Sam's hand and his face.

Manuelito continued. "The most vicious of her kind retreat into deep isolation, but not Cindy. Railway camps. Stables. Schoolyards. She sought people out. And where she went, people died."

Sam shivered. "Why on earth would you use her?" he asked. "It might have been better if you'd just cut my left arm off."

"Maybe," Manuelito said. "But every hero needs to be part nightmare. Moses turned a river to blood and called down the Angel of Death. Samson tore a lion open with his bare hands and killed hundreds with a donkey bone. When the world was young, my father Naayéé' Neizghání bound lightning to an arrow and crawled deep into the dark caves below our feet to kill the Horned Monster alone. He was the greater nightmare. If your will is stronger than the snake's, if you master her, then she will no longer be wicked. But she will still be deadly. And the wicked will learn fear. If you are fire, you need not fear the dark." Manuelito laughed. "If you had not needed so dangerous an arm, she would have become a belt. I'd given her fair warning, and she still tried to kill me in my sleep."

"But what if Sam can't control her?" Glory asked. "What do we do then? I can't let him face El Buitre like that."

"*You* can't let him?" Manuelito looked at her, smiling slightly. "Are you the queen of permissions?"

Glory sniffed. "I'm here to keep him from making the same mistakes over again. To make sure he wins. And if he doesn't learn to control Cindy . . . we have to start over or something. Try something else. Another life maybe."

"My brother," Manuelito said quietly, "has bet too much of his life on this one already. I was not even able to honor his bodies. There will be no more starting over."

Glory reached for the pot of water and Sam's left hand struck, slamming into her wrist, snapping Sam's fingers tight around it. Cindy's horned head flexed and tugged, trying to tear free of Sam's skin. He forced his fingers open, blushing while Glory stared at him.

"Sorry," he said. And then he tucked his hand under his leg and sat on Cindy.

A brown-and-white-speckled bird with a needle-sharp bill and white stripes on its head swooped down onto the table, chirruping like a tree frog. Manuelito handed it a crust of bread, and when it darted away he stood, shading his eyes and peering out over the hills.

He pointed. "It is good that you are healthy and fed. Men have finally come. And there is murder in their hearts. Your next lesson will increase in difficulty."

Down in the red rock and sage, a mile or more from the high mouth of the cave, six riders were pushing their horses hard.

Manuelito looked back down at Sam, where he was still hunched forward, sitting on his left hand. The big man spoke, first in his own windy tongue, and then in English.

"To the monsters, be monstrous. Be danger, and in all the world, there can be no place called Dangerous by the ones you love."

Baptisto rose from his stool and clenched his right fist.

"You must be a new legend," the boy said, thumping his chest. "With your heart first and then with your hands." He looked out over the valley. "And both must be now."

Millie rocked slowly in her seat. Dizziness was overpowering and closing her eyes didn't help. Every time she blinked she practically tumbled forward into the chessboard on the little table in front of her.

The room had a marble floor, but it didn't feel solid at all. It swayed. It rose and fell. One moment, she felt too light for her body—and the contents of her stomach felt even lighter—and the next moment she felt heavy enough to crush the chair beneath her into splinters and punch through the floor.

She had hit her head when she'd been thrown from the train wreck, but the gash on her scalp was almost completely healed. She had been fed, though nothing nice. And she'd been given cold metallic water. So she wasn't dehydrated or starving. Her wrists were sore where they were tied together on her lap, and her ankles chafed where they were chained to the floor, but neither of those things explained how sickeningly disoriented she felt.

The problem was the darkness.

The room she was in held only her chair, a little table with the small wooden chessboard set in the middle of the game, and an oil lantern hanging from a gold chain above her head. Thousands of splintered and broken chess pieces were strewn across the floor as far as she could see. Which was not very far.

The room had no walls and no ceiling. It was enclosed only with darkness—darkness so thick and swollen that it looked like the heaving belly of some living liquid.

While Millie watched, it crept toward her, pushing the light back, swinging the lantern above her. And then it receded and she felt suddenly heavy. Chess pieces swirled and skittered across the floor around her, but the pieces on the board were undisturbed, as if they had grown roots into their squares.

Millie didn't know how long she had been sitting there. Not long. But maybe forever.

She was waiting.

For the man with the floating watches.

For the game on the board to end.

For the lamp to go out.

For the darkness to swallow her.

Again.

She knew that it had before. The sorrow inside her

was old and familiar. The fear that filled her was like a childhood memory.

Hope was unfamiliar. She could hope for her brother to come. She could hope for them both to survive and find sunlight again. But that wasn't what she remembered. Not ever. But still . . . it was there inside her. Like the lantern, with darkness all around, but never burning out.

Reaching up with her bound hands, Millie leaned over the chessboard. She reached across the white pieces and put her fingertip on the black king's crown. Breathing hard, she flipped him over.

The piece snapped into thirds and spun off the table onto the floor.

Waiting, Millie wiped her damp forehead with the back of her hand. A moment later, every piece on the board snapped and splintered. The lantern swung. The darkness seethed.

Millie heard footsteps rising on metal stairs somewhere behind her. The woman was coming, just like she always did. Coming to reset the board.

Coil and Strike

Manuelito was as still as the cliffs as he watched the dust rise around the distant horses. Finally, he lifted his face to the sun and shut his eyes, breathing slowly. From that pose, he spoke, and Tisto moved closer. The words of father and the words of son rippled quickly over and around one another.

Tisto finally nodded, squinting down at the threat.

"What now?" Glory asked. "What do we do?"

"Come," Manuelito said, and turning back into the cave, he began to run.

Sam and Glory raced through the open cave city, but

Manuelito's strides were too long and too many for them to keep pace. Baptisto ran just behind his father, poncho flapping, occasionally glancing back to make sure Sam and Glory were still there.

"All the way back!" Manuelito shouted over his shoulder. "Tisto will lead you. After the opening volleys, I will come to you there." The big man veered away down a tiny side street between collapsing stone houses.

Sam immediately slowed. Baptisto didn't.

"C'mon!" Glory tugged on his arm and then quickly let go when her fingers touched scales.

"Pretty gross, huh?" Sam said.

"Don't be stupid," said Glory. "We have to hurry."

Sam jogged. "Is any of this in the book? How does the story end now?"

"I guess it is. At least, outlaws find us hiding in a cave, and we have to escape. But there isn't anything about your snakes." Glory moved along beside him, suddenly silent. Well ahead of them, Tisto slowed.

"But what about the ending? Let me guess," Sam said. "Happily ever after for the bad guys but not for my sister and not for me."

"Millie lives," Glory said.

"Seriously?" Sam stared at Glory, trying to find the catch. "That's a lot better than it was."

"But you're still dead," Glory said. "And so am I. And you're the one who does it."

"What? I kill you?" Sam shook his head. "No way! That's just stupid."

"With your left hand, Sam." Glory watched Cindy swinging at Sam's side as they jogged. "Don't think about it now. We'll figure it out later. We'll change it."

The cave floor rose steeply as they left most of the buildings behind. A stair had been cut into the uneven rock and they climbed it quickly. Above them, the roof of the cave sloped down steeply. The sides banked in. At the top of the stair, a large jagged crack like a lightning bolt veered up from the floor. Water trickled down its edges.

Baptisto had already gone in.

Glory ducked through as soon as they reached the top of the stairs, but Sam hesitated, looking back over the small ancient city behind him. A gunshot rang through the cave, but he saw nothing. He could feel Cindy's rattle beginning to quiver slightly on his shoulder.

"Sam!"

Sam ducked through the crack. The little cot he had woken on was right where he had danced on it. The white of his bandages decorated the floor. But now he noticed more. There were shelves. Countless bottles of what had to be medicines. A stone bowl on the floor with water trickling in and overflowing out. A stack of newspapers. A pile of animal hides. Two other cots, pushed against the wall. And a bench covered with knives—huge cleavers and small saws and tiny bladed needles. He didn't want to know which of those had been used to seam the snakes into his arms.

Sam saw no exits beyond the large crack. But Tisto was dragging a large battered wooden box out from under a shelf. He looked at Sam and pointed at it. It was labeled with white stenciled letters.

1,000 Metallic
Center-Primed
Cartridges
Solid Ball—.45 Caliber

Glory stood in the center of the room, gnawing her thumbnail. Sam jerked open the bullet box. He had no idea if they would fit the revolvers in his gun belt, but it was worth a try. He pulled his right revolver and stared at it.

"How do I empty these?" Sam asked, but Tisto wasn't looking. He had pulled off his poncho and was strapping on a gun belt of his own.

Glory took the gun out of Sam's hands, thumbed a small lever, flipped the cylinder out the side, and pushed in a rod that sent six dirty brass shells pinging across the stone floor.

Cindy rattled at her.

"Oh, shut up," Glory said. She handed the open revolver to Sam, slapped his left hand down, and pulled the other gun out of the holster.

"I hate guns," Glory said. "I mean, I didn't mind them in books and movies, but when my dad took me shooting for real, it totally freaked me out. Maybe that was the whole point. But he said it was all about self-defense. Probably because he always kept you punks around." She pinged six more shells onto the floor, and then dug some of the bullets out of the box and began loading. "Mom spent the whole morning telling me horrific story after horrific story, mostly of terrible accidents, or people getting killed with their own guns. And then Dad was like, 'Here, make this crazy steel thing explode in your hands,' all big smiles, flinging a piece of metal at that piece of paper on the fence post. I almost threw up before I even pulled the trigger, I was so scared something would go wrong."

"But did you hit the paper?" Sam asked.

"Moron." Glory snapped the loaded cylinder shut and shoved the revolver into Sam's holster. "Of course I did."

Sam holstered the other gun and turned around.

Baptisto was standing at the crack, his face far more

serious than the stone. Now that he'd shed the poncho, he was wearing a loose, badly stained sleeveless and collarless shirt. Sam could see the veins pulsating in his dark neck. The snakes in both of Sam's hands could sense the boy's stress.

Tisto flattened his palm toward the floor. "Stay here. I'll be right back."

"What are you talking about?" Glory shook her head. "No! We're waiting here like your dad told us to."

"I cannot leave him," Tisto said. "He is the stone beneath me."

"I'll come," Sam said.

"No way!" Glory said. "You're not thinking, Sam. Do you remember me? What's my name? I'm going to slap you in a second if you don't answer."

"Gloria Spalding. I remember you." Sam stepped toward the crack as Tisto disappeared through it. "More clearly than anything. More clearly than the pain in my elbows at SADDYR. More clearly than the Vulture's bullets ripping through my arms. If you hadn't risked everything to come with me . . . I'd be dead."

Glory blinked. "You can't, Sam. In the book you don't fight. We escape."

"You told me how that ended," Sam said. "So I'm going to change something right now." He smiled. "See if I can't erase a few more pages."

He didn't wait for an answer. And as he ducked back through the crack, another shot echoed through the cave.

Tiny, in his tight suit, bowler hat, and buckled boots, was halfway up the stairs with a gun already drawn and pointing at Tisto. Tiny froze when he saw Sam. He smiled, and his one icy eye sparkled.

Sam tensed. Cindy and Speck filled the cave with buzzing. Tiny glanced around his feet to be sure he was clear of any snakes, and then he looked back up.

Tiny laughed. "Samuel Miracle! There seems to be a Navajo boy between us. Shall I shoot you through him?"

Tisto flexed his fingers above his pistol grips.

"Don't," Tiny said. "I only need to kill one child today, and him slowly." Tiny cocked his gun. "I take your heart from you while you still breathe, Samuel. That's all the Vulture needs."

Sam walked down the stairs behind the Navajo boy, and then stepped around in front of him.

Tisto sniffed, clearly irritated, but Sam didn't care.

"So, Tiny," Sam said. "If I kill you, then you'll stay dead?"

Tiny's lip curled.

"You ever read *The Legend of Poncho*?" Sam asked. "In the book, you were called the Tinman because you killed sheriffs and kept their badges."

"The Boss just might have a copy lying around," Tiny

said, grinning. "And that's the truth about the Tinman. Sheriffs. Deputies. Marshals. And a New York copper or four when I was just getting started."

"And you shot me," said Sam. "And Glory. If the priest hadn't saved us, we would have died."

"Ooh," said Tiny. "Someone is remembering things. Did the priest mix you a memory potion? But you don't remember nearly as much as I do. That wasn't the only time I've shot you. I've killed you more times than the Vulture himself. Like me to tell you how many times we hurt your sister?"

Sam's rattling grew, echoing through the cave. He flexed his fingers. His mind floated back to SADDYR, to his first time reading *Poncho*, to the Tinman's final scene in a burning saloon and the gruff line spoken by the book's hero.

"No need for me to be cruel," Sam growled. "I'll put this one through your eye patch and let your good eye be."

"Oh, that version of the story was nipped in the bud, kid." Tiny smiled, taking another step forward. Sam's eyes were on the man's gun. "And you're nowhere near fast enough to touch *me* with lead. Pull, girlie. See if you can even get one of those pieces clear of leather before I drop your skinny carcass just like the Vulture at the train."

The tension in Sam's arms was incredible. Both snakes were coiled and ready to strike. Both were sending clouds of fear and fury up into Sam's head. They were both cocked and ready to explode, and Sam knew the trigger was inside of him.

Sam's mind was slower than his hand. He focused on Tiny's chest. The biggest target. He envisioned hitting it. And then he twitched his right arm—the one he was more likely to control. The rest happened all at once.

Sam felt like he was still reaching when the revolver went off, like he had just shot himself in the leg. But his arm was already up and smoke was rising from the barrel. Tiny's gun clattered down the stairs, and Tiny was grabbing his hand.

Sam blinked. He'd missed. But he'd gotten lucky. He aimed again at Tiny's chest, and cocked the hammer. But as he fired, Speck moved his hand.

The butt exploded off Tiny's second revolver, still in its holster.

Tiny turned and ran.

Cindy was twitching, but Sam curled his fingers tight around his belt, holding her back. He walked down the stairs after the outlaw.

A man stepped out from behind a stone building, rifle raised. Sam swung his arm toward him and Speck fired. The weapon flipped out of his hands.

"Tisto! What are you doing?" Manuelito quickly descended the stairs behind Sam. He was draped with bandoleers full of bullets, wearing three holsters and his top hat, and carrying two rifles. He aimed both from the waist, and fired down into the shadows.

"I thought . . ." Tisto looked from his father back to Sam. "I wanted to fight."

"Into the back! Now!" His hands were full, but he kicked at his son and then Sam, steering them back up the stairs.

Sam retreated slowly. "Can we catch one? I need to know where they're keeping my sister."

"Catch one?" the Indian snorted. "You won't catch any of these fools. Go!"

Sam skipped steps back up to the crack, and slipped through it after Tisto as a bullet slapped into the limestone wall beside him. Inside, two of the shelves that had been loaded with medicines had been rolled clear of opposite walls. Two dark doorways faced each other across the room. Glory stood in one doorway, bouncing nervously, and gnawing on her lip. She had *The Legend of Poncho* wide open in her hands and she was reading as fast as she could. Rattlesnakes were pouring into the room out of the doorway across from her, but she didn't seem to notice. A dozen fat snakes were already on the floor around Sam's cot. Dozens more were following.

Rattles exploded everywhere.

"Sam!" Glory shouted. "Quick!"

Sam jumped over one snake and then two more as they spun into coils. His own rattles were buzzing again, and they grew louder with his fear.

He hit the cool stone wall and then slid into the dark doorway beside Glory.

"Nothing," Glory whispered. "A few pages disappeared and then came right back. I tried to read fast, but I couldn't tell if anything had changed."

Manuelito squeezed back into the room.

"Come on, then! Come!" He picked up Tisto's poncho and then buzzed his tongue against the roof of his mouth. "Come!"

The snakes accelerated, slithering into the room until they had woven a loose carpet of serpent bodies across the entire floor. The interwoven snakes parted around Manuelito's boots as he walked straight to Sam and Glory with Baptisto trailing behind him. The big man pushed all three kids deep into the darkness, handed Glory one of his rifles and his son's poncho, backed his bulk into the tight space after them, and then pulled the rolling shelf closed, shutting them all inside.

Sam's rattles were still buzzing.

Manuelito hissed sharply and both snakes went silent. The big man grabbed his son by the shoulder and squeezed the two of them between Sam and Glory to take the lead. Sam's left hand slammed into the Indian's chest as he passed.

"Cin!" Manuelito slapped Sam's arm down. "Keep your focus, Samuel. Clear your mind. It is no different than what you have practiced already. Trust your hands, especially when they can see and you cannot."

Sam held his hands up, and felt them both drifting away, but they were nearly invisible to him.

"Stay close to me if you can. I will talk as we go so you know where I am."

Manuelito's boots scuffed away.

"You first," Glory said, shoving Sam. "I don't want one of your hands grabbing me in the dark."

Both of Sam's arms veered to the right just before he thumped into a wall. Glory thumped into his back. Manuelito's steps had quickened, and were rising in the darkness to their right. He could hear him whispering something stern to Tisto in their own language.

"Stairs!" Manuelito shouted. "Several flights. Quickly!"

"Glory, grab on to my shoulder," Sam said.

Her hand stumbled down the back of his head and settled on Cindy's rattle. With a squeak, she jerked her hand away.

"You're still not wearing a shirt," she said. "I don't

184

want to touch . . . those."

"Well, get over it," Sam said. "Because they can steer. Grab on."

"Wait," Glory said. "I have a rifle and this book and a poncho." Sam heard her shrug off her backpack followed by quick zipping and the whistle and rustle as she slipped back into the straps. "Okay," she said. "Now I can do this."

Glory set her hand between his shoulder blades, away from the snakes, and Sam began to feel his way blindly up the stairwell. He didn't extend his arms. He kept them bent at what had once been his elbows, with his hands palm down.

The snakes seemed more relaxed in the cool darkness. *Peace*, Cindy felt.

Safe, felt Speck.

Hidden flowed up both of Sam's arms.

Speck and Cindy moved at the same time as the tunnel changed—curving gently left and then banking hard right, turning left and finally doubling back and up to the right. But the snakes didn't move in the same way. Speck was direct, but Cindy sidled. Even when Sam was moving straight, she would fight to wriggle a coil of Sam's arm out beside her head. In the dark, the sensation was heightened. Her muscles flexing inside Sam's arm. Her scales tickling his skin. Ripples and curves in his arm where

185

there should have been solid bone.

On the final turn, she threw Sam's elbow forward like a hose.

"Cindy! Stop it!" He slapped his hand against his thigh and shivered. "It tickles, okay? And it grosses me out. Just move my wrist, not my whole arm!"

"She doesn't know English," Glory said. "I don't think words will help her."

"They help me," Sam said. "She flops all sideways and it makes my arm feel like a garden hose, or a jump rope, or something that isn't at all like an arm."

Gross, Sam thought. He tried to shove thoughts of *grossness* down his left arm into the horned head on his left hand. Not that Cindy would care even if she understood.

Sam started moving again. High up ahead, daylight spilled onto visible stairs.

Glory dropped her hand off his back. "She is a sidewinder, so it makes sense."

"No," said Sam. "It doesn't. It doesn't make sense at all. Why does my arm wriggle sideways? Because my bones and joints were wrecked and a Navajo healer grew a sidewinder into it. Oh. Right. That makes sense."

Sam slowed slightly, catching his breath. "I probably wouldn't mind if it didn't tickle."

"Do you remember SADDYR?" Glory asked. "Do

you remember not being able to bend your arms?"

Sam didn't answer.

"Because I'm supposed to keep you remembering everything," Glory said. "And I think remembering how awful that was could help you cope with this."

"Cope?" said Sam. "Why would I want to cope?" His voice grew louder and the words burst out of him between heavy breaths. "I got my sister back and then lost her again. I got my arms back and then lost them again. The man who saved me more times than anyone will ever know just died because of me. Died *for* me. I don't think he'd want me to cope. Manuelito didn't graft vipers into my arms so that I would cope."

"That's not what I meant," Glory said.

"I'm not coping!" Sam said, climbing stairs. "I want to save my sister and smash every little thing the Vulture has planned. Let him cope with me."

The temperature rose steeply as Sam and Glory approached the day-lit exit. The two of them climbed up out of the tunnel and onto the sloping shoulders of the enormous rock that enclosed the cave below. Sam shut his eyes against the light and Glory moved past him, still holding Manuelito's rifle.

"What is he doing?"

Sam opened his eyes and squinted. Glory was pointing at the big form of Manuelito, stretched out on his belly fifty yards away, peering down over the edge of the rock. Baptisto was bellied down beside him. While they watched, the big man slid back from the edge, stood up, and then jogged back toward them. Tisto stayed down with a rifle at his shoulder.

"One guard for all six horses," Manuelito said. "And the heavy saddlebags mean supplies. We steal two and you head north until you hit the railroad. Follow the rail to Tombstone. From there, trains are the quickest route to California. If your sister is alive, she will be with the Vulture in San Francisco. He will not kill her until you have been killed. Simple prudence. She is useful bait."

"We're going right now?" Sam spread his arms, and felt the ripples of pleasure both snakes took from the sun. But he didn't feel the same. In the light, his ribs were like pale tiger stripes across his chest. "I don't even have a shirt."

"A shirt will come more easily than a strong horse. Come."

"Wait!" Glory jumped forward. "Shouldn't I check the book first? I don't even know what changed this last time. Won't leaving this quickly change it all again?"

Manuelito stared at her. "Gloria Spalding, there is no time to play oracle with the book. If you want to know the weather, look at the sky. If you want to live well, be courageous in the most terrible of all the moments you are given. Do that, and in many years, Sam's friend will write his book, and it will match your living."

Manuelito hopped back into a jog, winding through scruffy sage until the rock pitched forward down a steep slide. Sam and Glory followed him down, hopping sideways, dragging one hand at a time on the slope behind them when they slid.

When they reached the bottom, dust spun in a cloud around them, and Manuelito held a thick finger up to his lips. They were hidden between a city of boulders and the huge stone hill that enclosed the cave, and judging from how far down they had come, Sam thought they had to be about level with the shelf below the cave mouth where he had done his practice shooting.

Manuelito inched forward, leaning out around the boulders to get a look.

Dust continued to rise.

"Count thirty," he whispered, "then fire into the air." Without explaining, he disappeared around the corner.

Glory looked at Sam and coughed quietly into her arm. Leaning back against the slope, she rested the rifle on her knee. Sam began to count.

"So," she said quietly. "Tombstone?"

A gun fired above them and a rock shattered between her feet. Glory yelped and scurried forward. Sam spun around and flopped onto the slope as another bullet punched rock. On the top of a big rock, a man had his left arm hooked tight around a choking Tisto's neck. With his right, the man was taking careful aim with a long-barreled revolver.

Sam didn't aim at all. He snatched his right gun, pointed the barrel at the sky, and let Speck do the rest.

The gunshot thundered in his right ear, he heard the man above him curse, Tisto scrambled free, and a moment later, the long-barreled revolver slid to a stop in front of Sam's face. There was blood on the handle where the butt had splintered around a bullet crater.

The man on the rock was gone.

"Glory?" Sam pushed off the slope and raced out into the open.

Six horses, all tied together, tossed their heads and stamped, whickering nervousness. A man with a huge white mustache stood in front of them with two guns drawn. One gun was pointing at Manuelito, the other was pointing at Glory. Manuelito was on his knees, bleeding from his shoulder. The outlaw moved his gun off Manuelito and onto Sam.

Rattles. From the train. Sam felt a pain prick of memory over his heart, where the man's knife tip had been.

"Why, Samuel Miracle," the man said. "Two old friends meet again. You know, my hair was black when I first started killing you."

Glory suddenly laughed out loud. "You're Rattles!"

The man looked at her, running his eyes over her modern shorts and shirt. "Girlie, I don't know where you think we've met, or what this savage here has been doing to you to addle your sense, but we've never had the pleasure."

"You say that in the book," Glory said. "At least in the first version I remember reading. Not exactly, but close enough that you have to be Rattles. Poncho was out of bullets, and you knocked him down, kicked him in the face, and then rolled your spur slowly up his ribs and said"—Glory lowered her voice to growl—"'My hair will be white by the time I've finished killing you.'" She pointed at him. "You're Rattles. You are. You're crazy scared of snakes and that's how Poncho killed you. There was a den in the cave and Poncho had nothing to lose so he grabbed a rattler and whipped you with it. You died in the desert."

Rattles looked from Glory to Sam. "Never happened. Never. Nothing but a bad dream. The Vulture took care of me. I'm standing right here, ain't I? And I don't go into caves." He squinted at Sam. "What you got on your arms, boy? Crazy savage give you tattoos?"

Rattles whistled sharply, fluttering his mustache.

"Shoot him," Manuelito said. "Now, Sam. Before the others come."

Sam took a step forward and Rattles swung his other gun onto him. Sam was staring down two barrels. He swallowed hard and cold fear washed down into his arms. Immediately, both of his snakes began buzzing their tails on his shoulders and Rattles jumped in surprise, sweeping his eyes over the rock around him.

Speck whipped up his revolver, and Sam extended his tense, scaled arm. "Drop your guns and I won't shoot you. This time."

"Yes, you will," Manuelito said. "Do it. Now."

Rattles snarled at Manuelito and cocked both his guns.

Sam aimed at the man's mustache. And he pulled the trigger. Rattles screamed as the bullet hit his fist. Both of the outlaw's guns fired and a hot whistle licked Sam's left ear. Glory and Manuelito ducked, and Glory's rifle fired, kicking her backward into a sitting position on the ground.

Rattles slipped and fell. Glory had grazed his leg. His right hand was empty and bleeding, but his left still held a revolver. He raised his gun again and Sam fired once more. Rattles's second gun bounced away into the sage. The outlaw scrambled up onto his feet and ran and slid and tumbled down the slope, taking cover behind boulders and cacti while Sam and Glory watched.

"Miracle," Manuelito said, breathing hard. "Such

rabid dogs must be ended, not toyed with. He could have killed two of us even after you fired. When he aims for hearts, do not aim for fingers." He slowly rose to his feet, wincing in pain.

"I know," Sam said.

"Never take a life without need . . . not even of an insect." Manuelito led the jumpy horses forward, untangling the reins of two of them. His right arm was hanging limp beneath his bloody shoulder. "Grieve when that need comes, but do not hesitate when defending the lives of others."

"It was Speck," Sam said. "He doesn't want to hurt people."

"Then use Cindy."

"Cindy would have shot him and then you and Glory and three of the horses." Sam looked down into the yellow horned eyes on his left hand.

"You must gain control of the nightmare. Practice commanding her until your command is certain." Manuelito crouched and grabbed the back of Sam's belt with his left hand and then heaved him easily up onto the saddle of a big, gray Appaloosa stallion with a white speckled rump. He turned to help Glory, but she had already picked her horse: a pretty golden palomino mare with an empty rifle scabbard hanging from the saddle. Glory slid Manuelito's rifle into the scabbard, hopped into the high stirrup, and swung quickly up onto the horse.

Gunfire echoed across the valley. Shots fired from above the cave. Rocks clattered and bounced down the shoulder, and then Tisto emerged, bloody and painted with dust. Keeping his rifle pointed up, he retreated toward the horses.

The Appaloosa stamped and danced sideways. The palomino under Glory posed calmly, ears forward, listening, blond tail swishing softly.

Manuelito stood up straight and removed his hat. His eyes were as cool and calm as cave shadows. "Samuel Miracle, I pray that I have not woven too heavy a curse into your flesh. Bear it. And bless the world when you pluck El Buitre from the sky."

"But I don't have a shirt," Sam said.

"And Glory doesn't have a dress," said Manuelito. "Not your biggest problems."

"Sam Miracle," Tisto said over his shoulder. "I wish that I could have been the one chosen for your struggle. But I will not be a child with envy." His eyes drifted toward Glory and then back to Sam. "Please wear my poncho when you have become the famous one."

Sam wasn't sure he would survive, let alone become famous. But he didn't want to argue. So he nodded. Baptisto seemed satisfied.

Manuelito tapped his tall black hat back onto his

head. "If you ever see my brother again, greet him for me. Now go. My son and I stand here against your hunters. You will have a strong start. North," he said, but he wasn't talking to Sam and Glory. All six horses looked at him. Manuelito clicked his tongue and spoke again, and this time, his words sounded like a wind combed by cactus thorns.

All six horses leapt away. Manuelito picked up his rifle with his good hand. After a moment, he whispered a quiet blessing after Sam and Glory, and then turned to face the cave.

At the bottom of the slope between the hills, piercing through the clatter of iron-shod hooves on stone and rising above the snorting of the spotted stallion beneath him, Sam heard the high rolling echo of gunfire behind him.

Strangers in Town

SAM LEANED HIS BRUISED BARE BACK AGAINST A ROCK AND shut his eyes. The sun was down and even the dusky afterglow had almost faded. If Glory wanted a camp-fire, she could build one. He was sore from riding, but he was much sorer from being thrown off his stupid spot-ted horse and crashing down through the spiky tufts and branches of a Joshua tree.

And it was all Cindy's fault. Speck had been fine the whole time, but after a couple of hours of boredom, Cindy had started to rattle and had slammed Sam's left hand into the back of the horse's neck and the horse had

196

spooked and spun and bucked and Sam had gone flying.

The stallion had taken off.

The other four horses had been trailing not too far behind, and an old ragged pinto had let Sam up on her back. At least until Cindy had started rattling again. The mare had reared and Sam had somersaulted backward over her rump. The other horses had scattered.

The day had ended with Sam perched behind Glory on the palomino, riding slowly beside an empty and arrow-straight railway through the desert.

Sam dozed until the smell of smoke woke him. When he opened his eyes, his left hand was perched in the air in front of his face and yellow-eyed Cindy was staring at him from above his dangling fingers.

"Oh, stop," Sam said. He didn't even have the energy to be angry at the snake. He shoved his hand under his thigh and looked at Glory. She had started a small fire and was on her knees, rooting through the saddlebags. She was holding what looked like a striped wool blanket as she pulled out three apples, a flask, and a stack of jerky wrapped in a handkerchief.

"I really need a shirt," Sam said. The air was getting cool fast. "Are there any shirts?"

Glory took aim and threw the blanket at him. "Guess what that is."

Sam moaned. "I'm not guessing anything."

"Oh, come on. It's Tisto's. You might not be famous yet, but there's a hole for your head in the middle." She grinned at Sam. "Put it on. It's a poncho for Poncho." She turned back to the saddlebags. "I really wish we hadn't let the other horses go. There's no money here and we'll need some if we're going to get food and clothes and train tickets in Tombstone."

Sam examined the poncho and then exhaled hard. "I wish Father Tiempo was here. Is it weird to miss someone you barely knew?" He kicked a rock away with his heel. "This all feels . . . *hopeless* . . . without him."

Glory shook her head. "Don't say that. Please." She wished the same thing. She felt the same way. But hopelessness was poison. They had to hope. She slipped the priest's hourglass out of her pack. The thick blown glass had a gently rippling surface like water barely thinking about a breeze. It was cold against her fingertips, and she could just feel the bumps where tiny bubbles had been trapped inside and stretched into daggers.

"So Tisto gives me his poncho and says he wishes he was me. Why?" Sam asked. Glory didn't look at him. "It can't be the snake arms. My sister is being held by outlaws somewhere in San Francisco and rescuing her means I have to find someone who has killed me more times than I'll ever remember. What do I have that anyone would want?"

Glory didn't say anything. She set the hourglass on a flat stone like the priest had done beside the railroad, and she stared at it. There were so many incomprehensible things about the last few days—and the last couple of years that Sam had been at SADDYR—that what Tisto may or may not envy about Sam simply wasn't interesting to her. Even though she knew the answer.

The Navajo boy was strong and well trained. Obviously he'd be attracted to adventure. Sam had arrived weak and broken but with a great destiny—more attractive to Tisto because it was likely tragic. But worst of all, Sam had Glory. And Tisto knew that better than Sam did. She had tended him every day he'd been asleep and healing in the cave. She'd been the one wringing out rags in his dry mouth, keeping him hydrated. Manuelito had given her balm to apply to the seams between the snake skin and Sam's arms, and she had done it twice a day, while Tisto had held Sam's hands down. And, of course, she was risking her whole life to help a boy she barely knew rescue his sister and stop a legendary villain.

Only, she didn't feel like she barely knew Sam. She had loved his Poncho character with the kind of loyalty that went well beyond a normal readerly commitment. Which was why she'd wanted him to die at the end of the book. Because Poncho had not just betrayed his sister, he had betrayed Glory. He had failed to be the character he was so clearly supposed to be. He had lost his way and forgotten his purpose.

Millie had practically raised him! She had kept him safe. She had been the strong and perfect sister as the two orphans had been tossed through their wild western adventures. The kind of sister that Glory would want to be. And Poncho had loved his sister back. Millie had meant more to him than anything else in the world.

And he'd let her die. Just like that. Revenge wasn't good enough. He should have rescued her.

Siblings should never abandon each other. Glory knew this, because she had been abandoned. She couldn't change what had happened to her, but she could help change the end of a book that had made her just as angry. She and Sam would find Millie. El Buitre would die and Millie would live. Sam would be the brother and hero he ought to be. Just with snake arms . . .

Glory could finally stop hating Poncho. Maybe. Then again, maybe Millie would die and Sam would die horribly, and she would die last of all, knowing that she'd made the whole story worse.

"Water?" Sam asked. He leaned forward and pulled the poncho over his head. Itchy wool tumbled down his sweat-sticky back.

"No water," Glory said. Her voice was cold, but she tried to correct it quickly. She sniffed at the flask. "Just whisky or paint thinner or something worse."

Behind Glory, a young cactus, tall and armless, striped the darkening blue sky. From the low spot where she and Sam were sitting, the level line of the railway carved a hard black horizon. The silhouette of the cactus was as straight as a ship's mast, but the rail was much straighter than any deck.

Sam leaned his head back and looked straight up. Glory followed his look with her own. There were stars. There were always stars. But tonight, out in the desert, in the past, with a boy with snake scales shifting and rippling on his arms, with hands that could see in the dark, the stars seemed more dangerous, like a vast army invading the sky.

"What was it like?" Sam asked. "When he put the snakes in?"

Glory set the saddlebags down and moved closer to the fire, staring at the small flames.

"You were a mess," she said. "A total nightmare. He got your arms all straightened out and cleaned. I had to help him." Glory looked at Sam, feeling her stomach roll a little as she remembered the gore, the shattered bone. There was no point in describing it all for him. "Manuelito sang and he whispered and the bleeding stopped. His fingers and his voice change things. The real problem was the bones. The joints. He said that he could have healed it all with enough time—a year or more—but that you would have hands slower than a ninety-year-old."

Sam rolled his shoulders under the wool poncho and extended his arms straight out from his sides. Glory shivered. The cool night air tingled on her human skin, and she wondered how it felt on scales. Sam rolled both serpentine arms over and looked at the marks where the bullets had torn through him. The scars could have been years old, and even in the low light, they were crisscrossed with a cobweb weave. Glory had traced all of it with a fingernail while Sam and the snakes had still been unconscious.

Glory watched Sam study the memorials of his wounds.

"Manuelito sealed up the holes with his fingertips," Glory said. "Like stitches without string, he traced the pattern slower than a snail, breathed on it, and the skin grew back together. He did the same thing once the snakes were in—between your skin and theirs."

Sam lowered both his hands to the ground and looked back up at the stars. Both of his hands shifted slightly, twisting in place, but he didn't seem to notice. At first, Glory thought he was forgetting, that his mind was wandering again, that she would need to remember for him. She slid closer in the darkness, close enough to see that his eyes weren't empty and unfocused. They were full of pain and weariness.

"Do your arms hurt?" Glory asked. "I mean, I'm sure they must."

Sam nodded. "Bones ache a lot where I was shot. And my skin tickles all along the scales. Always. Trying not to think about it."

"So what are you thinking about?"

Sam sniffed and blinked slowly. His eyes were wet.

"My sister," he said. "Millie. Just remembering things. It hurts worse than the bone."

"The pain helps you remember," Glory said. She nudged a burning stick further into the fire with her toe.

"Remembering hurts worse than any pain," Sam said. "If Millie is hurt . . . if she dies . . ."

"Don't," Glory said. "We'll get there. You'll save her. It's different this time."

"How?" Sam asked, and he shut his eyes.

Glory watched him drift away, his lips parting, his jaw going slowly slack, his hands and arms freely crawling over and around him.

"You have me," Glory said quietly. "And those things."

As Sam began to snore, Glory unzipped the backpack and pulled out her beat-up copy of *Poncho*. Leaning closer to the fire, she flipped to the end.

THE VULTURE DABBED BROTH FROM HIS FRESHLY OILED mustache. The large dining room was alive with laughter and the assault of silver on china. The ceiling was thirty feet high, intricately carved and painted with gold. A garden of floral iron rails lined the walkways high above the room. Palm trees stood guard in every corner, growing in stolen Greek urns, thousands of years old. At one end of the room, on a dais of polished Egyptian granite taken from the grave of a pharaoh, in front of a row of carved lion-headed gods, El Buitre was alone at a table big enough for eight, sipping clear soup from a gold spoon.

Long before he had earned his outlaw name, when plain-old William Sharon had stopped gunslinging in Nevada and begun his real work in San Francisco, the wealthy diners in the city's lavish restaurants had still owned their own successes. Now . . . those who were still living at all worked for one man. And it was an honor to do so and keep breathing. William Sharon was a prophet, a mogul, a devil, a god of certain knowledge and deadly strength. More than a vulture. *The* Vulture. The one and only.

Before the Gold Rush, William Sharon had walked the California hills and had somehow staked all of the most profitable gold claims simply by the smell of the air. William Sharon had started every boom business on the bay. His fishing boats knew where the fish would be. His pearl divers returned with chests from Spanish shipwrecks. He sold shares in businesses before unexpected fires. He took out insurance on ships one day before they sank, and on his business partners hours before their suicides. His newspaper announced national and international truths before telegrams could even carry across the continent.

Not one person in the city would bet against William Sharon no matter the contest—boxing, dogs, horses, or even turtle races. William Sharon knew things. He knew what men planned to do before they had bothered to think about it themselves. And he was never wrong. At least, that's what people thought. The truth was both simpler and more complicated. In the early years, William Sharon had been wrong quite often. But with assistance and instruction from Mrs. Dervish, he had always doubled back and gotten things right. Now, the only opportunities that slipped through his fingers were too small to even bother with.

Only one thing remained for him to get finally, permanently, and emphatically right. And if he did, if Sam Miracle was stopped, if the boy's heart was taken and his soul was prevented from yet another retreat through time, William Sharon's alter ego, El Buitre, could spread his wings over the next century, and truly put his abilities to the test. There would be world wars, he knew that already. And he was eager to taste them. To tame them.

Where men find death and decay, a vulture finds wealth.

But he did have a weak stomach, especially in the evenings. Clear soup was all he could manage.

William Sharon set down his napkin and drew out the largest of his gold pocket watches. He set it on the table, faceup, although it floated centimeters above the tablecloth. Then he drew out a second, slightly larger watch and placed it beside the first. They clinked quietly against each other as they drifted. Both watch chains stretched back into his vest above his heart. He continued until all seven watches were arranged in a triangle. He admired each one with a twist or two, and then waited. All seven ticked differently. But they weren't just out of sync. It was like each one was counting something different, something longer, something shorter, something slower, something faster. The sevenfold ticking was chaos—like seven very different dogs barking.

And then it wasn't.

Mr. Sharon shut his eyes. The ticks became one long swirl—like the arcing blade of a windmill, slow in the center, but falcon-fast at the tip. He heard the diners scream and plates crash, but it was all faraway and muffled, something happening inside a building across the street. And then he opened his eyes, and looked up at the man pointing the gun.

Time hadn't slowed down. The Vulture had sped up.

The man with the gun was named Lloyd Batchcraft.

He had a massive mustache, a large belly, and his fat cheeks and throat were covered with shaving cream. He had knocked into a table as he rushed into the restaurant and he was already pointing his gun straight at William Sharon's heart.

To El Buitre's eyes, Lloyd Batchcraft was barely faster than a statue. A dollop of shaving cream was wobbling in the air beside his face, only just beginning to think about falling. Instead of flipping over, the table Lloyd had collided with perched up on a single leg. Instead of shattering against the floor, plates slowly grew cracks and crumbled no faster than stones in the desert.

William Sharon smiled. If he hadn't moved to San Francisco, Lloyd Batchcraft would have been a mining tycoon worth many millions of dollars and the owner of an entire fleet of steamboats. Instead, he was a barber. At least he had been until thirty minutes previously. And then Mr. Sharon's bank had seized his barbershop, thanks to a contract that poor Lloyd Batchcraft had absolutely no memory of signing.

Lloyd's finger finished pulling the trigger on his gun. The hammer swung down like a tree branch swaying in the breeze. Flame grew out of the barrel's mouth as slowly as a summer sunrise. The bullet nosed out of the flame like a mushroom in autumn leaves.

El Buitre drew his gun, checked the chamber, took

casual aim, stifled a yawn, and then fired six times. While his own swarm of slugs inched through the air toward Lloyd, he reloaded his gun and holstered it. Then, leaning sharply to one side, he rearranged his watches.

The ticking tangled differently. Time flew. Plates shattered. A table tumbled. Gunshots bellowed. Lloyd Batchcraft's bullet smacked into a statue above William Sharon's shoulder. All six of El Buitre's bullets smacked into poor Lloyd Batchcraft, tumbling him onto his back.

The clatter and the echoes and Lloyd Batchcraft all died. William Sharon snapped his fingers and began pocketing his watches. While diners stared, amazed at how fast, how practically invisible the great William Sharon's movements had been, two waiters hurried to clean up the mess while a third waiter jumped forward to see what the great Vulture needed.

"Take the body to the kitchen and put him in the crab tank. Then tell Mrs. Dervish to bring me the Miracle girl." The Vulture tucked away his final watch and smoothed his vest. "It's time we had words."

GLORY WAS SITTING UP, HUDDLING BENEATH A SCRATCHY blanket. The hourglass was perched on a stone beside her, *The Legend of Poncho* was on her lap, and the fire was sleeping in quiet coals at her feet. The horse was tethered to a cactus behind her. She had found men's long johns in the saddlebags along with the blanket, and both had disgusted her. But she was wearing the long johns now—over her denim and shirt—and she had the blanket tucked tight around her. It made her feel like a flea farm.

Glory was trying hard not to think. She didn't want to think about the choice she had made, about what came next, about whether or not Father Tiempo was completely and totally dead, about Sam's arms shattered and sticky, and now scaly, bendy, and alert.

But not thinking was harder than having a mouthful of gum and not chewing.

Reading the end of the book hadn't helped. Why had she signed up for this, really? It wasn't just to have an adventure, although that had sounded fun. At least until everything got so very real. She had come because people should never leave other people to do hard things alone. She believed that. She had been let down in her life, and she never, ever, ever wanted to let down anyone around her. Especially not the hero of her favorite book.

And now, the last few days of her life had been wilder than anything that had come before. But she had been able to simply move through the moments, making crazy decisions as easily as if she had been in a dream. Yet seeing her name in *The Legend of Poncho* changed things. Strangely, it made her danger seem more real. She might die. If the latest version of the book was the final version, she would die—wounded in a gunfight and then trampled by horses. Poncho had carried her body to a graveyard and had stood above her in wordless sorrow. A nice scene, so long as it was imaginary.

Glory refused to accept her fictional end, but it still made her feel like throwing up her apple and jerky. She didn't know how dead the priest might be. But if he was all the way dead . . . even if she survived, she might never see her own century again, let alone the Spaldings, or flush toilets, or television, or an ice-cold Coke. And if she did die like the book described, Sam wouldn't even say a thing! Not a word! It was a ridiculous thing to worry about, but she still did.

She'd known that living a story would be so much harder than just reading one. But she hadn't really known how much longer and lonelier and . . . *scarier* it could be.

She did now.

While Sam snored in the dirt with just a poncho over his bare torso, Glory shivered. And she stared at the sky. Earlier, before the moon had come and gone, the stars had crowded the dark heavens, a mayhem of pale fire and heat too far away to be felt. Glory had slept and then marveled, and slept some more. It was like sitting beneath a weed patch of worlds. Exactly like that. Because that's what it was. Too many to count in countless lifetimes of counting.

Glory yawned.

The stars were mostly gone now, and dawn was erasing the darkness. Only the planets were left, shining in the blue.

And in the light, Glory could see Sam's snakes watching her. Speck was on Sam's hip. Cindy held Sam's left hand up in the air with his limp fingers dangling beneath her head. She was listening. Glory listened, too. Faintly, she heard slow hooves on rock.

A jackrabbit hopped past Sam's sleeping body, and Speck darted out, snatching it by the foot. While the rabbit kicked and jumped, dragging Sam's arm around the rocks, Sam snored on. Glory shrugged off the blanket and stood. Hitching up the baggy legs of her long johns, she moved toward the railroad, trying to listen.

SAM WAS DREAMING. HE WAS STRETCHED OUT ON A TABLE on the front porch of his house in West Virginia, but the whole house was inside the huge cave in Arizona and the boys from SADDYR had gathered around to watch Mr. Spalding help Manuelito graft rattlesnakes into Sam's arms. Trains were chugging around the ceiling and crashing out the cave mouth into the sky.

Sam's dying father was in his rocking chair, tucked in tight under his blanket.

El Buitre was peering down at Sam over Manuelito's

shoulder. Manuelito was sharpening a knife. Baptisto was glaring at Sam with his arms crossed.

"My arms are fine," Sam said. "Really. They are." He tried to sit up on the table, but Mr. Spalding pushed him back down.

"Don't fight," Sam's father whispered from his rocking chair. "You need the snakes."

El Buitre scratched his oiled mustache and smiled. "Lead will break those pretty bones right up. But you do realize the snakes won't help him one bit. They'll kill him before I even get a chance."

Manuelito shrugged. "I must try."

Sam tried to roll off the table.

"Boys!" Mr. Spalding shouted, and Sam's Bunk House brothers from SADDYR jumped up onto the porch, and an army of hands pinned him down.

Sam kicked and writhed. Mr. Spalding clamped his hand over Sam's throat and began to squeeze.

"There you go," El Buitre said. "What did I tell you?"

Sam choked. He kicked. He fought for air. His head felt like it was going to explode with blood. He was dying. And dying didn't feel like a dream.

"Where is Glory?" The voice was Father Tiempo's, young and sharp. "You can't leave her here. Where is she?"

The priest's face was right in front of Sam's. His breath smelled like dirt.

"Open your eyes," Father Tiempo said. "Right now Samuel Miracle. Open them."

Sam's eyes opened. He was on his side, kicking loose sand and rock, his cheek and open mouth and dry tongue grinding across dirt.

His left hand was clamped tight over his own throat.

His right hand was bouncing all over, clinging to an angry jackrabbit's foot.

The sky was rosy with dawn's fingers. Glory's silhouette stood beside the railroad looking up at six men on six horses.

Sam let the rabbit go and then jerked his left hand off his throat. Gasping, sputtering, pulling in rib-splitting lungfuls of life, he rose to his knees. The poncho draped around him.

Glory and the men all stared at him.

"The spastic kid stays," a heavy cowboy said. "But, missy, you and that horse are coming with us. You're too pretty to leave out here." He drew his gun and pointed it down at Glory. "Saddle up, sister."

"Hey," Sam rasped. Adrenaline and anger were boiling inside him. Panic. Terror. Frustration. Every emotion that comes from having your own hand try to murder you in your sleep. "No way!" He panted for enough breath to snarl. "Drop your gun and ride off."

213

Six cowboys grinned.

"You a short little toad." The heavy one laughed. "This don't concern you, Poncho. Get back to kicking in the dirt."

Sam wasn't in the mood. Speck jerked his right revolver from under his poncho and fired.

The big cowboy squealed as the shot smacked the gun from his hand. And Sam didn't stop. As five more guns rose up in five more hands, five more shots slapped, sparked, punched, stung, and struck.

Revolvers clattered in the rocks. The cowboys whooped and spurred their horses away like the thunderous echoes of the gunshots, trailing a pillar of dust behind them.

Sam was still breathing hard, and the gunpowder in the air burned his throat.

Kill.

The desire washed up Sam's left arm just as Cindy tried to draw his other weapon.

"No!" Sam shouted, locking his left arm in place and splaying his fingers. "What's your problem? Don't even touch it. You tried to kill me!"

Glory looked at Sam. "He called you Poncho."

"I don't care what he called me." Sam shrugged. "Who were those guys?"

"I don't know." Glory looked at the dust trail

dissipating over the railroad. "But we should go before they come back." She stooped, rolled up the legs of her long johns, and tucked them into her shoes. "We need to be on the first possible train to San Francisco. And I'm starving. And I don't feel like chewing jerky for breakfast."

Glory rode in front. The farther away the snakes were from the horse's head, the better.

Sam rode on the back, leaning forward on her backpack, trying to sleep without Glory noticing. But every time he dozed off, Speck dragged his right hand around Glory's waist while Cindy slid up and perched his left hand on her shoulder.

"Sam!" Glory tried to shrug Cindy off.

"What? I'm here." Sam mumbled the words straight down into her backpack.

"Wake up! Seriously." Glory thumped her elbow back against Sam's head. He jerked upright and his hands released.

Glory twisted in the saddle, glancing back at him. "I get that this is totally crazy and you're still not strong from being shot and you're hungry and tired, but you can't forget why we're here. Stay focused. And don't sleep on me, all right?"

Sam blinked. Dirt had grown his freckles together into one big smudge.

"Why *are* we here?" he asked. "And remind me again why you're wearing dirty long johns?"

"You're here to kill the Vulture," Glory said. "Because your sister needs you."

"But why are you wearing long johns?"

Sam could see a town on the horizon over Glory's shoulder, and the railroad they were following bent in a slow curve toward it.

"That Tombstone?" Sam asked.

"Must be," Glory said. She heeled the horse forward.

"Wake me up when we're there." Sam leaned his head back down onto the backpack. Glory elbowed him in the stomach.

"We're there," Glory said. She elbowed him three more times. "We're there, we're there, we're there."

Sand spilled out of Glory's backpack into Sam's face.

Sam sat up and slid back onto the horse's rump. Glory bent backward in front of him. Her pack was expanding quickly, spilling sand, busting zippers.

"Sam!" Glory yelped. "Stop it. You're pulling me off."

"I'm not even touching you," Sam said. "Something's in your pack."

Glory tried to slip out of the pack, but the straps were digging deep into her shoulders. Cindy began to rattle. The horse reared and Sam slid over the rump and hit the ground. It bucked and Glory spun through the air, landing on her back in a tangle of sagebrush.

As the horse galloped away, Sam began to laugh.

"Not funny!" Glory shouted. She writhed free of her pack, stood up, and then dragged it out of the brush.

The pack was still spilling sand out of every seam. Pale sand—almost white—was growing quickly into a mound. While Sam watched, Glory dropped onto her knees and dug into the pack.

Glory stood up, breathing hard, puffing her hair back out of her face. She held the hourglass out at arm's length, and a pillar of sand was streaming out of it.

Sam was stunned. "What on earth? Where did you get that?"

Glory didn't answer. She moved quickly over to Sam, spilling sand across his legs. But she wasn't even looking at the hourglass. She turned in a slow circle, scanning the landscape. Her worry erased Sam's amusement.

"The priest gave it to me," Glory said. "Someone is messing with time. But he said the hourglass would keep us rooted."

Sam stood up quickly and the sand trickled off his legs. "What does that mean?"

"I think we'll know soon," Glory said.

Sam's rattles quivered. He felt . . . blurry. Like he did whenever his dreams changed. Whenever his mind started seeing something different than his eyes. "Foggy,"

Sam said. He didn't know why.

Glory slapped his face, and Sam jerked in surprise. His cheek burned.

"Focus," Glory said, shaking out her hand. "This isn't a game. If that didn't hurt enough to keep your brain clear, then I'll keep trying until something works."

Sam blinked. He wasn't sure where he'd been going a minute ago, but his sister and the man with all the watch chains were in the front of his mind now.

The sand spilling from the hourglass had slowed, but it was still flowing.

"Well, we're not waiting here for whatever is coming." Glory looked at Sam. "Stay really close. Let's walk on the white sand if we can."

Glory shook out her backpack and then put it back on. Then she turned and began to walk toward Tombstone. The crotch of her long johns hung almost to her knees. She had the top rolled down and the sleeves tied around her waist.

Sam hopped up and jogged after her, poncho flapping against his bare skin.

"Glory!" His rattles both buzzed. He tried to focus on his arms for just a moment. "Stop it!" he snarled. Glory glanced back at him. "Not you!" he said quickly. "That was for the snakes. Sorry! And thank you. That's for you." Glory turned away and kept moving. Sam caught up to her quickly. She held the hourglass out in front of her, and the two of them walked silently side by side, keeping their steps on the pale scattering sand, following the long, slowly bending railroad.

Memories arranged themselves awkwardly in Sam's head.

"Did you check the book at all?" Sam finally asked. "How does it end?"

Glory's face was slick with sweat, and she was squinting against the sun, but her voice was flat and cold. "You don't want to know."

"Yeah," Sam said. "I do."

"Nope." She shook her head. And that was that. The way her jaw was set, Sam knew asking again would get him nowhere.

AFTER A FEW HUNDRED YARDS, GLORY FINALLY LOOKED AT Sam. She looked at his face, at his hands, at his guns, at his feet scuffing and scrambling across the loose, freshly fallen white sand. Then she looked up into his clear but distracted eyes. This was the hero that she had loved and then hated, that she had wanted to help and even save. She didn't have much, but she had risked all of it to change a boy named Sam Miracle into the legend she had always wanted him to be.

She wasn't sure it was working.

Glory looked ahead to the ramshackle town on the horizon.

"I'm not telling you what the book says right now, Sam, because we're going to tear out all of those pages anyway. All of them. And then some extras just in case."

She would have smiled, but the hourglass jerked her forward. Glory tripped, staggered, and slid down onto her knees.

SAM WATCHED GLORY FALL. HE WATCHED THE HOURGLASS turn over in her hands and all the sand that had poured out began streaming back in. Then he felt the ground shake beneath him, and not because a girl had fallen.

Glory blinked and spat as sand attacked her in a cloud. She left the hourglass on a rock and slid away backward as a white, stinging tornado formed above it, funneling down inside.

"How is this helpful?" Glory scrambled up onto her feet, covering her face with her hands.

Sam didn't answer. He didn't hear her. The entire sand path they had walked was roiling toward them, and even that didn't hold his attention. He was watching the landscape change all around them.

"Glory . . ."

Sam reached for her without looking, and Cindy clamped his fingers tight onto her arm.

Glory didn't even try to pull away.

"Am I dreaming?" Sam asked.

"Maybe," said Glory. "But I'm in the same dream."

All around them, brick walls with soaring black iron peaks and glistening glass domes were erupting out of the ground. Boulders and rocks shattered into gravel and became smooth. A huge iron obelisk crowned with a vulture hatched up out of a single massive boulder. Gold clocks dangled from its wings.

There were workers doing all of it—humans, Sam assumed—but they were barely visible, gusts of wind and streaks of vapor, forms spread so thin by their speed that eyes could not possibly track them. Sam stepped away from the sand toward the obelisk.

"Sam!" Glory grabbed his poncho and pulled him back. "Stay here. Father Tiempo said the hourglass would keep us rooted."

Sam and Glory stood side by side, blinking and squinting out of their hissing cloud of sand as the walls climbed and the world changed around them.

"Oh no," Glory said. She spun in a circle. "We're in trouble."

"Is it a prison?" Sam asked. He looked back over his shoulder. Walls were rising on every side. Walls without doors. They were completely penned in.

Glory snatched the hourglass off the rock and raised

the tornado of sand up above her head like a torch.

She grabbed Sam's right hand, and Speck gripped her fingers tight.

"C'mon!" she yelled. "Run!"

A tall black wall now stood between Sam and Glory and Tombstone. Together, they raced straight toward it, trailing their hissing funnel cloud behind them like a steam engine's plume.

"Is it real?" Sam asked. "Can we run through it?"

Glory didn't answer, but the wall did. Sam's left hand hit cold black stone and Cindy immediately flinched, pulling his hand back.

"There has to be a door." Glory spun around. "Do you see one?"

Sam wasn't looking for a door. The sandstorm was twisting in the air directly above them, swinging its hips like a kid with a Hula-Hoop. On each twist, it grazed the wall, and when it did, the funnel went suddenly dark with black sand.

"Glory!" Sam grabbed her shoulder and pointed straight up. "Whip it! Let it eat the wall."

"Samuel Miracle!" The voice was El Buitre's, but it sounded like it belonged to a multitude, like echoes stacked on echoes.

Sam spun around. A small door had opened in the bottom of the towering obelisk one hundred feet behind them. While Sam watched, the Vulture eased himself out of the doorway into the sunlight. He flickered where he stood, sprouting streaks like a smudged painting. His seven chained watches weren't just floating; they were snapping and lashing at the air all around him.

"You should not have taken such a direct route. You should not have taken such a direct time. Now put down your glass," El Buitre said. "That trinket will not keep you from me. The darkness I walk is outside of every *where* and every *when*."

Glory swung the hourglass above her head, and cracked her enormous sand whip across the gravel courtyard. As she did, the writhing funnel cloud grew, disintegrating the surface of every wall it touched and slurping up the fresh gravel on the ground. Glory's storm blackened again, and the hissing sand began to rattle and crack as it collected larger stones.

Sam stepped closer to Glory as her devastation grew. The faint wisps and gusts that had been building the walls were being swallowed up all around them. Sam was sure he heard a scream.

The Vulture retreated back into his doorway and began to laugh.

"That was unkind! One hundred men have been working for three years on these walls."

Sam moved forward, rattles buzzing, snake arms

taut, fingers flexing. Sand and gravel whipped through his hair.

El Buitre stepped to one side of the doorway and beckoned for Sam to enter.

"Set down the trinket and I will take you to your sister. There is only one outer darkness. Through all of my doors, she is. But when she dies of madness, I promise to bury her under the earthly sun."

Sam took another step toward the outlaw, his quivering arms ready to explode into action. As he moved away from Glory, the Vulture sharpened and solidified. As did the walls all around him.

"Sam, no!" Glory hurried forward, bringing her swirling storm whip around and lashing it straight down at the Vulture and his tower.

The Vulture drew both of his pearl-gripped guns and emptied them at Glory.

But he and his bullets vanished beneath the vicious funnel cloud. With a hiss louder than the ocean eating islands of lava, the tower collapsed into a massive seeping black dune. Glory spun, immediately attacking the wall with her hourglass storm, lashing a huge breach in the wall. Then she grabbed Sam's wrist and dragged him through cold shin-deep sand, and out into the hot Arizona desert.

Once clear of the sand, Sam and Glory ran. They ran

until the sweat was burning their eyes more than the sun, until their insides had stitched into knots and their lungs were splitting with hot desert air. They ran until the last of the rippling changes in the landscape had vanished behind them and their vast sandstorm tail had died down to a few whispering grains. And then, finally, gasping, when they had reached the outer edge of old Tombstone, they slowed to a cautious walk.

Sam cleared his throat and spat with every other breath. His arms, writhing unpleasantly from his body heat, both slid under his poncho to get out of the sun.

Glory stuck the hourglass back in her pack.

"Will he try that again?" Sam asked. "Changing everything around us?"

"Didn't work that time," Glory said. "But he'll try something."

TOMBSTONE WAS SPRAWLING. THERE WERE BARNS AND warehouses and mills and hundreds of tiny miners' shanties and tents and a huge water tower painted with an enormous and confusing advertisement: "Go to Bangley and Schlagensteins. They Are the Bosses, You Bet!"

Sam in his poncho and Glory in her baggy long johns drew smiles from men shaving or spit-bathing over horse troughs. Long teams of steers or mules—sixteen to a wagon—lumbered past with rough ore piled high.

There were so many loud saloons and so many tired women in absurd dresses with feathers in their hair that Sam lost count. And the mines were right in town. Beside a brick hotel, massive timbers bridged a hole. And there was another beside a tall mansion painted with three different shades of pink.

Sam stopped in the center of a wide dusty street, instinctively keeping his arms tucked under his poncho.

"Have I ever been here before?" Sam asked, turning in place.

"Don't know," Glory said. "Not in the book."

"I think I'd remember."

They moved on slowly, cautiously. Sam followed Glory's lead.

A fat man with a donkey laughed loudly at Glory, drawing more smiles from anyone who bothered to pay mind to the two kids on the dirt road.

"Man," Sam whispered. "We need to get you some clothes."

"We need to find the train station." Glory wiped off her sweat-damp forehead and pushed back her hair. "I'm fine."

On one side of the street, a barber with the longest white beard Sam had ever seen—the tangled ends were tucked into the man's belt—was leaning against a wooden horse rail. On the other side of the street, the charred remains of a torched saloon slumped together.

"Excuse me." Glory gave the barber a smile. "Where is the train station?"

The barber grinned, skinny arms crossed over a sagging beard-upholstered belly.

"What she means," Sam said, "is where do we get her some clothes? And where do we get food? Are we allowed in saloons? They all look like bars."

"Money?" the barber asked. "You two have any?"

"What's that to you?" Glory stepped closer to Sam, not for protection, but to offer *him* protection. Millie had always done the same thing. Sam pushed around her.

"We have enough," Sam said. The man didn't need to know the truth. "Food, clothes, and the train station. That's all we need. If you'd point us along our way, it would be appreciated."

Sam smiled, but the barber's grin vanished. The man slipped quickly away from the horse rail, retreating back to his shop door.

A rifle cocked loudly behind Sam. He spun around as three men in long coats and flat-brimmed hats walked toward him. All of them had spectacular mustaches. The shortest of the men held the rifle at his waist, pointing at Sam. Glory backed away.

Behind the men, Sam recognized the heavy cowboy who had tried to take Glory at the railroad. His right hand was mittened with bandages.

"That's the Poncho Kid," the cowboy said. "Couldn't even see his hands till he'd already pulled on me."

"We're going to need your guns," the man with the rifle said. "Get your hands out from under that poncho. And they'd better come up empty."

~10~

The Legend Begins

"HE DIDN'T DO ANYTHING WRONG," GLORY SAID. "THAT idiot was trying to kidnap me. And he drew first."

"Here's the problem," Sam said. "I need my guns."

"No," the short man with the rifle said. "You don't." His face was almost perfectly rectangular and his mustache drooped down over his mouth like a straggly curtain. It puffed when he talked.

"Could you tell us the best train for San Francisco?" Sam asked. "We'll move right along."

The two taller men simply stared. And spat. One of them was thin and gaunt and sickly, with moist mushroom-clammy skin. His mustache was tidy and waxed tight. A single tuft of hair on his chin punctuated his lower lip. The other man was easily twice as thick. He had a round face, and heavy unshaven cheeks to match his rough gray mustache. He picked at his teeth and then flicked something away.

"Listen," he said. His voice was like tree bark. "Poncho, you may be a kid, but I'm the sheriff here, and when a man's been shot and he points the finger, a judge has to be called, and that means I'm going to need you to give me whatever guns you've got strapped on and then wait behind bars till a trial can be arranged. Shouldn't be more than a week. I'll even buy some clothes for the girl here and find her a place to stay while she waits."

Sam shook his head. "I'm sorry. I can't. An outlaw took my sister to San Francisco, and I don't have much time to get there. Maybe no time at all." He looked back at Glory for confirmation. She nodded.

Sam faced the men and flexed the fingers on his right hand. Speck could easily take out the short rifleman with the hair curtain on his lip, and then deal with whatever guns were pulled next. The sickly guy looked like he could faint before anything even happened. And that just left the guy with the fat face. Sam wasn't even nervous.

And then he remembered. The revolver on his right hip—Speck's revolver—was completely empty. He'd never reloaded after the cowboys at the railroad.

Fear chilled him. If he fought, he would have to use Cindy, and if he used Cindy . . . six things were going to die. Not things. People. Maybe Glory. Maybe him.

Sam coughed and cleared his throat. His forehead was suddenly damp, and he could see that all three men noticed.

"This is bad," Sam said. He raised his right hand up out of the poncho, fingers splayed and palm facing the sheriff. "This hand, I can control. Well . . . a little bit. But it doesn't like to hurt people even when I want it to. If I draw with this hand, you might get a little hurt, but it wouldn't kill anybody. But that gun is empty." He swallowed. "My left hand doesn't care what it shoots so long as something dies. Even me. I really don't want to use my left hand. Please don't make me."

Kill.

Sam pushed the desire back down, trying to force his own message into the vicious brain attached to his left hand.

No. No. No.

KILL.

It wasn't working. He could feel Cindy's excitement. Even the horns above her eyes were trembling. She wasn't frightened. She wasn't even rattling. She was hunting. Sam took a step back. Paper crumpled in the dirt beneath his feet. He looked down.

231

DON'T HURT THE EARP BROTHERS.

FT

Relief poured through Sam. Somewhere, the priest was still alive. He hadn't been completely destroyed protecting Sam. Sam felt like he'd just shrugged a bag of rocks off his shoulders. He'd been so busy surviving, he hadn't realized how much the priest's death had been weighing on him. But why couldn't he have said something more? Sam would have really appreciated some direct and perfectly clear instructions. And some encouragement. He would have preferred something like:

GOOD JOB, SAM. YOU'RE HANDLING EVERYTHING
PERFECTLY. MILLIE IS FINE AND WAITING FOR YOU.
I'M INCLUDING SOME MONEY, TRAIN TICKETS, A MAP,
SOME COLD BOTTLES OF COKE AND A BAG OF CHIPS,
A SHIRT FOR YOU THAT DOESN'T ITCH, AND SOME
NORMAL CLOTHES FOR GLORY SO SHE CAN GET RID OF
THOSE RIDICULOUS LONG JOHNS.

"Sam?"

Sam blinked. His mind had left Tombstone completely. Now it came flying back. Glory was looking worried.

"I'm fine," Sam said. "Look."

He nudged Glory and tapped the paper with his toe.

Glory snatched it off the ground and laughed out loud.

"Father Tiempo's alive!" she said. "Man, that's a relief!" She grinned at the lawdogs. "Have you heard of him? Father Tiempo? Maybe we won't be stuck here forever. We aren't from here, you probably guessed that, and he's pretty much our only way back."

The three men stared at Glory like her brain had been sunbaked.

"You're the Earp brothers?" Sam asked. "All three of you? I know you're probably famous, but I've only heard of Wyatt Earp. And you aren't in the *Poncho* book. Well . . . maybe you are now, but you weren't when I last read it. Aren't you good guys? I'm not supposed to hurt you."

The men exchanged slow glances and then all of them spat. The sickly one tugged at the hair tuft on his chin.

"We're the law," said the man with the rifle, and his mustache puffed. "That the same thing?"

"No, Morgan," the sheriff said. He scratched his fat scruffy cheek and then hitched his thumbs in his gun belt. "It ain't the same. I'm Virgil." He nodded at the gaunt man next to him. "This is Doc Holliday, an honorary Earp and the man to see if your teeth are paining you. Wyatt is out hunting down some dog of a cowboy or other."

Doc Holliday nosed the tip of his boot in the dirt and then stepped forward. He looked even thinner when he moved and his cheeks were practically caved in. His hair might have been blond once, but now it was on its way to ash. When he spoke, his voice was quiet, climbing out of phlegmy lungs.

"What I'd like to know, is how a boy your age could possibly think that he could hurt us?" The man cleared his throat, locking eyes with Sam. They were cold eyes, blue that had died and gone to gray, like Sam's father's before the end. Only these eyes had a hardness to them, a knife's point, a desire to kill. Sam felt like he was looking into Cindy's eyes.

"And I'd like to know," Doc continued, "who the outlaw is who took your sister, and who you're planning to gun down in 'Frisco. Not many outlaws working on their own in that town. Point of fact, I only know of one running things out that way, and if it's him you're after, I'd be a kind man just to put you in the ground right now and spare you the travel. You have no kind of chance, and that's coming from a born gambler."

"Sam." Glory pulled on the back of his poncho. "Come on. The Earps aren't going to shoot a couple kids in the street."

"Oh, but darling, Doc Holliday will." Doc grinned, swallowed a cough, and slid away toward the center of the street, tucking his long coat behind him, leaving his pale, bony right hand free. "Only one man currently in this world faster than Doc, and he spreads his vulture wings over San Francisco. Here's a practice bout for you, Poncho. If you can't get past me, well . . ." He pursed his lips and shrugged.

Sam shook his head. "I'm not supposed to hurt you."

"Sweet of you, child," Doc said. "But you won't. Go ahead. Draw. Friendly right hand or killer left, I don't particularly care which you use in pursuit of my demise." He sniffed and then coughed lightly behind a tight smile.

"He'll kill you," Glory said, stepping back. "He really will."

"I'm not fighting you," Sam said.

Glory chimed in, pointing at Virgil. "That one said you're an honorary Earp and we have instructions not to hurt the Earp brothers."

"Your poor stolen sister," Doc said. "Her brother not even willing to fight a dentist to get to her. If you draw on me, kid, I swear on the tears of three dozen angels that I won't kill or maim you. You can hold out hope of dying in San Francisco."

Kill.

Sam blinked. His left arm felt as taut as a violin string, humming like it was freshly plucked. Sweat rolled down the center of his back, tickling him all the way to his gun belt. He was going to do it. The man was practically begging for it, and grinning while he did.

"I know two men faster than you, Holliday! Not one."

Sam spun around. Three men on horses were riding slowly down the center of the street. Tiny, in his tight suit and tall motorcycle boots, led the way. He was wearing sunglasses and his bowler hat. Rattles, with his huge white mustache, rode next to him. The third man had a bushy red beard, caked with blood. He was wearing Manuelito's top hat.

Sam's heart jumped in his chest when he saw it. He didn't want it to mean anything. It could have just fallen off. Sam tried to envision Manuelito and Tisto safely hidden in the caves.

"His hat," Glory whispered. Sam could hear the fear in her voice. "Sam . . ."

Tiny slid off his horse, smiling. "Doc."

"Tinman," Holliday said. He pinched his tuft of chin hair and smiled. "Why, I thought you were dead and feeding the daffodils."

"How would I be dead? No, just been occupied. Mostly with this kid here." Tiny sniffed at the air. "You haven't forgotten Wyoming, have you? Two of you drew on me and I left you both bleeding. Would have finished you off then, but I always like saving some for later." He glanced at Morgan and Virgil. "Would love to add some badges to my tin collection, but where's the Earp that matters? No offense."

Glory and Sam were exactly between the two gun-fighters. Glory slowly pulled Sam backward out of the street.

Morgan Earp looked at Sam, but he kept his rifle on Rattles. "Don't you go anywhere."

Up and down the road, people were steering clear. Wagons crawled away out of sight. One hundred yards in both directions, pedestrians retreated, until the whole town seemed silent.

"We need the boy alive, Doc," Tiny said. "And I've been hunting through all sorts of lifetimes, and I'm tired, so I'll be taking him now." Tiny glanced at Sam.

Glory and Sam backed up onto a wooden sidewalk in front of a window painted "General Store."

"I saw him first," Doc said. He cleared his throat and then spat. "When I've finished with you, I'll finish with him."

Tiny flexed his right hand. "I'm afraid that doesn't fit with my plans."

Sam's heart was thumping. His arms could feel the blood flow, the adrenaline, the fear.

Cindy began to rattle. Sam didn't even notice. He was focused on the growing tension, wondering if he would make it all worse if he drew his gun. He wasn't even sure if he could make Cindy shoot Tiny first, but he was pretty sure he wouldn't be able to stop her from shooting anybody else.

Doc Holliday was the first to look around his feet, checking for the snake.

Tiny did the same. Rattles wheeled his horse around, scanning the ground.

Glory put her hand up on Sam's shoulder, pinning Cindy's buzzing rattle flat beneath the poncho. Speck started up immediately and Glory pinned his flat, too.

Doc and Tiny both looked at Sam.

Sam smiled. "Don't worry about me," he said. "You two get on with your thing." Then he grabbed Glory's hand, and they ran straight into the general store.

Expecting bullets, Sam and Glory both stayed low as they scrambled between shelves. There were shouts behind them, but no gunfire.

Sam careened into a pyramid made of bags of flour, knocked a small crate of whisky bottles off a shelf, and then smacked into a high wooden counter. Glory went around it. Sam rolled over the top as the front door banged open and Rattles stepped in.

A fat clerk in suspenders was already sitting on the floor behind the counter, reading a newspaper called *The Epitaph.*

"No, you can't hide in here!" he said. "Absolutely not! Leave immediately."

Sam carefully drew his left gun, keeping his barrel up and his finger off the trigger. Cindy buzzed crazily with excitement, and her yellow eyes gleamed beneath her horned brows as Sam flipped open the revolver and tapped all but one bullet out. And still he kept his finger off the trigger and his thumb off the hammer. Cindy's muscles were rippling inside his arm, but he held her back.

Calm, Sam thought. *Careful. Only the one I have to hurt.*

KILL.

The clerk stared at the backs of Sam's hands. His eyes went wide, but not as wide as his mouth.

"He's called Poncho," Glory hissed at the clerk. "And no one is faster than he is. No one! And he never hurts anyone unless he absolutely has to. And his hands can see in the dark, and he's walked through time hunting evil, and even snakes obey him."

"No I haven't and no they don't," Sam said. "I wish they would." He bobbed his head up over the counter to take a look and immediately backed down. A gun fired and a jar of pickles behind the counter shattered. Vinegar and glass rained down.

"Here's the deal, Rattles!" Sam yelled. "Leave now, or I guess you're going to be the first villain I actually kill. At least this time around. Do you want me to count to three?"

Gunshots began popping like fireworks in the street outside.

Rattles laughed. Sam could hear his boots move forward across the wood floor.

"No way out, boy. Red is at the back door. Tiny will have the Earps mopped up shortly."

A window exploded.

"I can count down from three or up to three," Sam said. "Either way is fine."

Glory slapped Sam in the shoulder. Both of his rattles roared to life beneath his poncho. "Just do it already." Then she yelled over the counter. "You know how you hate snakes? Well, this kid is your worst nightmare."

More gunfire outside. Cans tumbled off a shelf.

"One!" Sam yelled.

"I'm ready, boy," Rattles growled. "Just you rise on up."

"Two!" Sam yelled. He slid his hand down onto the butt of the gun. Cindy was as rigid as steel inside his arm. He slid his finger onto the trigger.

"Two and a half!"

For a moment, Cindy was perfectly still. Quiet. No rage flowing up into Sam's mind. For a moment, Sam felt like he might be in control.

And then his left arm exploded forward, dragging Sam into a cupboard under the counter, snapping shelves under his weight. Sam's thumb jumped up, cocking the hammer. Footsteps raced from right to left through the store and then twin guns roared. Bullets punched through the wood just above Sam's head, spitting splinters against his neck and into his hair.

Rattle buzzing, Cindy bent Sam's arm, tracking her target through the wood. Sam shut his eyes and he could see the moving outline of a man made only of body heat.

Cindy fired right at it.

Sam yelped. The shot was so loud it was like the round had gone off inside his skull. Shrieking needles burrowed deep into his ears, followed by wool. Gunpowder burned inside his nostrils and in the back of his throat.

His body began to shake, and he wanted to cry.

He didn't hear Rattles tumble to the floor. He didn't hear the clicking as Cindy continued to cock and fire, but he could feel his thumb and finger moving. He didn't look to see what she was trying to fire at.

Sam hurt. And the hurt was somewhere much deeper than his body. It shook inside him. It wanted to peel him open and crawl out. Hot tears streamed down his cheeks and his ribs quaked.

One hundred versions of Sam's life lined up in his memory, sharper and tidier than they had ever been. Perfectly preserved versions of him, of his living, of his story. A record of El Buitre's vandalism, of Father Tiempo's doomed interventions.

Killing hurt Sam more than being killed ever had. And that hurt brought everything back.

It was like watching a game of chess where every single possible move has been made and countered, unmade and made and countered again. A priest playing against a vulture. A flurry of moves and failures and defeats, one hundred years of game swirling through Sam's mind in a cyclone of seconds. The pieces moved and reset and moved and reset, until every option was painfully exhausted. Pieces were lost—sacrificed. And those pieces were people.

He'd remembered flashes before, but never all at once, and with such razor brutality.

In Baltimore, his grandfather had died fighting burglars. Died fighting kidnappers on the docks. Died fighting trained dogs, but always he had kept men from taking small Sam. His mother had taken a hunter's stray bullet. A knife. Been trampled by horses. His father had eaten poisoned bread, drunk from a poisoned well, been run off a cliff by outlaws, been scorched carrying Sam from a burning barn. They had died because they loved him, plain and simple, not because they wanted him to go fight some vulture. They had died over and over and over again, because they had loved him over and over and over again.

And priests had died, too. Dozens of them.

And Millie. Too many times. And Glory.

Glory, too? Sam remembered lying in the Spaldings' living room with her, both of them bleeding, both of them dying. The priest had moved their souls. Those bodies had died.

Not this time. Not Millie. Not Glory. He couldn't let it happen.

GLORY HELD HER BREATH. HER EARDRUMS WERE THROB-bing and her heart was jumping. The fighting outside was a lot more than a gunfight. It sounded like a war. She had no idea how they would get out. Nobody out there had been friendly. Inside the store, Rattles hadn't stirred since he'd crashed to the floor, and Sam was still flopped on his face inside the counter.

"Sam? Are you hit?" His back was shaking. Was he laughing? Crying?

The clerk folded his newspaper and set it down, now undisturbed.

"Girlie," he said. "You know I sell clothes. And gloves. If Poncho there should ever want to hide those hands."

Glory crawled forward, leaning over Sam. His left arm was twisted around; Cindy cocked the pistol, pointing it at her face.

"Stop!" She slammed Cindy down with both hands and then jerked the gun away. Then she tossed it to the clerk. "Load this." Then she grabbed Sam by the belt and dragged him out of the counter cupboard.

Men were shouting in the street outside.

Sam sat up and handed Glory his empty gun. The clerk slid a box of ammunition out of a cupboard.

"What now?" Glory asked.

Sam stared at her. "I killed him."

"You don't know that." She loaded one gun as quickly as she could while the clerk loaded the other. "Maybe a stray bullet got him from outside."

Sam looked down at Cindy, splaying the fingers on his left hand.

"I know," Sam said. "I . . . *saw.*"

Cindy's sharp eyes sparkled beneath her scale horns. She had stopped rattling but she was still explosive with excitement, tickling him with smooth shivering pulses from shoulder blade to knuckle. On his right hand, Speck just seemed nervous. Twitchy.

Sam grabbed on to the edge of the high counter and pulled himself up. Twenty feet away, Rattles lay on his back with both of his guns drawn.

"I killed him." Sam clenched his fists and tensed his arms until every muscle fiber shook beneath skin and scales. The bullet breaks in his bones ached like new. He wanted to yell, but his voice came out cold. "I hate this. Hate, hate, hate."

"Sam . . ." Glory stood up beside him.

"I want it to end." Sam took back his revolver from Glory, tucking it into his right holster. "They keep killing everyone and Father Tiempo just lets them. He lets them all die just so that I won't. Like they're all worth sacrificing just to give me a chance at killing the Vulture. My mother, my father, my grandfather, my sister. You."

"Me? No. Not yet, at least. And the priest says you died a lot, too," Glory said. "And he died more than anybody." She took the loaded gun from the clerk on the floor, along with the open box of bullets. Then she shoved the gun into Sam's left holster. "That Red guy probably really is out back, but we'll have a better chance there than out front." She looked back down at the clerk. "Fastest way to the train station?"

Before the clerk could answer, Sam vaulted the counter and began walking for the front door.

"Sam!" Glory yelled. "Stop! Don't be stupid."

Sam stepped over Rattles. The man Cindy—no, *he*—had killed lay faceup with his legs twisted beneath him. A single bloody bullet hole marked his heart. Sam looked straight into the dead man's eyes. He felt like he should say

245

something. Instead, he bent over and took both of Rattles's guns, quickly checking the chambers. Two rounds in the left gun, three in the right.

Cindy immediately tried to cock and fire, but Sam slammed the back of his hand against a shelf.

KILL.

"No!" Sam snarled the command like a wolf. Cindy twitched his finger toward the trigger, but Sam forced it back. Focusing his anger, he shot threats down his arm like talons, but hot and smoking.

Obey! I will cut you out of me with broken glass. I will burn my whole arm off if I have to but you will obey me you stupid Cindy snake do you understand me or I will do it right now!

Cindy was as still and silent as a possum playing dead.

Good, Sam thought. *Obey.*

"Sam?" Glory asked. She sounded scared. "I know you're upset, but please let's try the back. Please?"

Sam shrugged his poncho up onto his shoulders, and then, with both of Rattles's guns pointed straight up, he moved to the front door. His brain itched with strange knowledge. Layered-up lives. Archived failures.

He was done. No more people dying for him. No more people killing to get to him. He was right here, and he was ready. If he died now, then he wasn't good enough to beat El Buitre anyway, and no one else would ever have to die protecting him. But if he died now, at least bad men would die with him.

His heartbeat was slow, but each thrum was an earthquake, shaking his core. Sweat beaded on his nose. Fear pooled in his stomach, but anger filled his arms. He listened to his hands, and both of his hands listened to him. His rattles began to buzz.

Guns pointed at the sky, Sam Miracle stepped out into the sun.

Doc Holliday saw it all, and he wasn't the only one. When the Poncho Kid had ducked into the shop, the whole situation had gone from street standoff to full-on war in no time. But only because there were plenty of cowboys in Tombstone who wanted to see the end of the Earp brothers and their gambling dentist friend. Word had gone out quick that the Tinman was in town. If anyone could take down Doc, it was the Tinman.

Rattles had followed the boy. Red had ridden his horse around the block toward the back of the buildings. The Tinman stayed in the middle of the street. Seven cowboys had come out of the alleys and taken up positions behind rain barrels and stairs and benches. One with a shotgun, two with rifles, four with revolvers, all with smiles.

In Tombstone, Arizona, this was better than Christmas.

Morgan Earp pinched his mustache with his lower lip and raised his weapon to his shoulder, quickly swinging it from target to target. Tall, jowly Virgil drew his guns and stepped closer to his brother. But Doc and the Tinman simply stared at each other.

And then a sharp whistle rolled down the street behind Doc. A familiar voice followed.

"You having a party, Doc? Why wasn't I invited?"

Wyatt had arrived on horseback. The most famous Earp. The legend. The man with the stubbornest jaw and the scrawniest neck and the widest curled handlebar mustache in all of Tombstone. And pinned to his chest, a shiny piece of badge tin that Tiny would prize above all his other tin trophies.

"Now, Wyatt, you know better than that," Doc said. "You're always invited, and I've already filled up your dance card."

Wyatt wasn't one for chatter. He slid off his horse, slapped its rump, and then pulled his long coat behind his back, freeing up his gun hand, and immediately drew his pearl-handled Colt.

But three Earp brothers and one gunslinging dentist were not enough.

Bullets began to fly. Doc dove toward a horse trough

in front of a stable, but a bullet caught him in the thigh. The Tinman put Wyatt on his back, and with both guns drawn, he walked forward at an angle, winging Morgan in the shoulder and sending Virgil scurrying. The elongated man in the tight suit and bowler hat dropped his guns when they were empty and stepped behind the corner of a building to pull two backups.

From there it was all crawling and kicking dust and splintering wood. But the Earp brothers were done. Doc knew it. Every cowboy there knew it. The Tinman had nine men fighting for him, and Doc and the Earps were already hit and fighting back from the dirt.

The lawdog legends of the west had found their final page.

Until the boy stepped out of the general store.

He had shrugged his poncho up onto his shoulders so his lean, scarred, sun-brown arms were bare. And he had the most detailed tattoos that Doc had ever seen—snakes that ran the lengths of his arms. Only . . .

Glory had tried to stop him. She'd begged and bossed and grabbed his poncho, but Sam had given her a look that hit harder than a punch to the face. As she watched him leave the store, she was sure that she was seeing the end of Sam Miracle. The Vulture would have his way with whatever parts of the world he might want, and she . . . she would be in Tombstone. Alone. Ducking low against the front wall, Glory watched out of an already broken window.

SAM MIRACLE CROSSED THE WOODEN SIDEWALK AND STEPPED out into the dirt street. Cindy and Speck were so tight and excited, his arms felt like electric stone. For a split second, the gunfire paused as all eyes focused on him. And then Sam started firing.

Doc's gun shot out of his hand at the same time as Wyatt's, and the boy threw away his empty weapon and pulled a new one. His arms blurred and snapped like whips, and his gunfire was more like rolling thunder than separate pops. Virgil lost both of his guns, Morgan lost his rifle and his backup at the same time that Wyatt lost his.

And the boy hadn't even looked in their direction. Doc stayed low and kept his second gun well out of sight.

On the other end of the street, bodies were dropping. A cowboy fell off stairs, another from behind a barrel, a third, and then the kid's left hand changed revolvers so fast that Doc only knew because the empty one hit the dirt at the boy's feet. Red Beard reappeared with guns raised, but dropped before he could even set down his first step. A holy hush spread out around Sam as the echoes died. The guns were silent and the street was as still as a funeral. In less than five seconds, one kid had silenced the biggest fight Tombstone had ever seen.

S<small>AM EXHALED AND TOOK HIS FIRST BREATH</small>. H<small>E GLANCED</small>
around, assessing the living and the dead. It wasn't over,
despite the silence. He ignored Speck, but sweat was pouring off him as he fought to control Cindy. She was trained
on the corner of the building where Tiny had taken cover.
But Sam could feel her distraction. There were other living things in the street that she could strike while she was
waiting for the tall stretched one.

Obey.

He tensed his arm to keep her from swinging around
on the Earp brothers. It wasn't easy. Especially now that
the Earps were coming out from their cover and trying
to stand. But they weren't threatening him, and Speck
would take care of them if they did.

"Tiny!" Sam shouted. He licked salty lips. "You want
me? Well, here I am. Take me to the Vulture and let's get
this over with."

Wyatt Earp cleared his throat. Half of his mustache
was drooping. "Son, you aren't going anywhere. Nobody
fires on a deputy in my town without saying hello to a
judge."

"Mr. Earp!" Sam shouted, anger still rumbling
through him. "Sir! I just saved your life, so leave me be.
Tiny! How about it? I want El Buitre and El Buitre wants
me. Show me the way."

"Now, why would I do a thing like that?" Tiny asked. Only the very tip of his boot was visible.

"Your other choice is dying," Sam said. "Come on out."

"With your hands up," Wyatt added.

"Or down," Sam said. "Or with your guns pointed right at me. I don't care. You know you're not fast enough."

Cindy was aiming at about chest height. But Sam brought Speck around and tried to focus him on the shifting toe of Tiny's motorcycle boot.

Glory slipped out of the store and crossed the wooden sidewalk, hurrying toward Sam. She grabbed the back of his poncho and looked around the street. "I can't believe you're alive," she said quietly. "I could hug you right now. Or kick you for being so stupid selfish. Now, come on. Let's go. Right now. While we still can."

"I'm working on it," Sam said.

Speck fired and the tip of Tiny's boot exploded. The outlaw yelped and the boot disappeared.

Wyatt limped forward, pulling a fresh gun from inside his coat and pointing it at Sam.

"That one's empty, Poncho, and you only got one round in the other. Use it on me and the Tinman over there kills you. But use it on him, and I've got you. I'm not letting an outlaw with your type o' condition roam free."

"Seriously?" Sam looked at the famous lawman in disbelief. "I just saved you and both your brothers and your dentist. And I'm not an outlaw."

"Son," Wyatt said. "You fired on me and you fired on my deputies."

"Now, Wyatt," Doc said, climbing to his feet. "We'd all be counting the knotholes in our coffins tonight if it weren't for the boy. And he's hunting the right game." He tossed his second gun through the air toward Sam. Speck dropped his empty one and snatched Doc's, immediately covering Tiny's corner again.

"Kid," Doc said, removing his hat and bowing painfully. His pale-mushroom skin glistened with sweat. "Poncho, allow me to apologize for my obstruction and for the obstruction of my simple, law-loving friends here. Yours is clearly a unique situation. We wish you victory and Godspeed."

Wyatt sniffed, saying nothing. Finally, he holstered his gun, tugged his drooping mustache up, and nodded.

"Great," Glory said. "Come on, Sam. We shouldn't be alive, but we are. If we want to stay that way we need to move, like, *now*. He knows exactly where we are."

"Not without Tiny." Sam looked back where Speck was still pointing Doc's revolver. "I'm going to need help sneaking up on a Vulture when he's already hunting me." He glanced at Wyatt. "Can I borrow handcuffs?" he asked. "Have those been invented yet?"

~ 11 ~

The Road through Darkness

MILLIE WAS ASLEEP. IN HER DREAMS, SHE WAS IN WEST VIR-ginia, watching Sam snore in the hayloft of the barn where they had hidden for the night. Moonlight from the pigeon roost lit her brother's bony back, and he looked no more alive than a lumpy sack in the straw. Like the priest had told her, they had stayed hidden in the day, and had moved only after sunset for the last week—ever since they'd put both their parents in the ground.

But they needed to find food soon. Millie had been pretending to divide what they had evenly, but the truth was that Sam was eating all of it and Millie was starving.

She hadn't had a bite in three days. Her stomach felt like it had twisted up into a knot that would never untie and her head felt like it was trying to shrink in on itself. Her vision never seemed to quite—

A shadow sliced through the moonlight on Sam, and Millie flinched. A large pair of wings flared in the roost above them. Something grazed her cheek. A feather? She brushed at it but there was nothing there. It grazed her again and she brushed at it again. The big bird was looking down at her from the roost. An owl? If it was, she hoped it would drop its rabbit or mouse or whatever it might have caught. She was that hungry.

The bird spread its wide shadowy wings. And it dove at her.

Millie screamed and jerked away, and as she did, she woke.

She was still in her chair with her ankles and hands tied.

The Vulture was looming over the chessboard, lowering a long-fingered hand from her cheek. His wavy black hair practically dripped with darkness. His eyes sparkled anger in the lamplight, and he was forcing a wide gleaming smile above his pointed beard. His gums were more gray than pink.

Millie leaned as far back in her chair as she could. "What are you doing?" she asked.

The Vulture sat back in a large armchair that hadn't been there when Millie was last awake. The darkness behind him stretched out thin tendrils of shadow, groping for him, brushing his arms, his shoulders, his hair. He seemed to feel its touch and watched it, amused.

"It always seeks me," he said quietly. "I have walked its boundaries with the world of light perhaps more than any other man. It would like me to dwell forever in its nothingness as many will and many do."

Millie said nothing. El Buitre tented his fingers at his mouth and stared at the chessboard. The darkness clung to his hair, smoothing it back.

And then Millie heard the ticking. First one watch, and then another slid out of the Vulture's vest and floated slowly around him. With no noise to compete, the sound of the tiny gears and ticking hands grew into a chaotic clatter—seven watches marking seven different flows of time.

With the watches in the air, the darkness retreated.

"You could live here forever if you like," the Vulture said, finally moving a piece. "Because there is no time. The outer darkness retreats from time just as it retreats from light."

"I'd like you to let me go," Millie said. "My brother needs me."

The Vulture reached across the board and moved a

piece from Millie's side. He was playing himself.

"Your brother . . . ," the Vulture said, and his teeth ground together even louder than the ticking. He began moving pieces more quickly. "Your brother has changed. Something was done to him in that cave that I do not understand, and there's nothing about it in the book." He looked up suddenly into Millie's eyes. "What was the priest's plan this time?"

Millie shook her head. "I don't know what you're talking about."

The Vulture's eyes darted over the board as he moved pieces on his side with his right hand and pieces on Millie's side with his left. "I have been as patient as the mountains, climbing into the sky. As patient as the sea, eating cliffs." Chess pieces began to die quickly. He threw them all on the floor as he took them and his voice rose almost to a yell as he spoke. "And now . . . my . . . patience . . . is . . . running . . . out!"

He swiped the board clear with his left arm, kicked the whole table away, and flopped backward in his chair, breathing hard.

Watches floated and ticked. Millie stared into the man's eyes. He was clearly insane, but he was the only one who could set her free.

"If you let me go," Millie said, "I'll tell my brother to leave you alone. I promise."

257

"Leave me alone?" The Vulture began to laugh. "I just spent three years and many, many people building a grand and glorious trap for your brother in the desert. It was perfect. I opened a doorway for him into the darkness. I would have brought him to you here, but the girl he is with destroyed it with one of the priest's toys. A toy that does not belong in the hands of children." El Buitre re-tented his fingers over his mouth. "I have put lifetimes into this match. I want your brother dead. I want to smell his blood pooling on the ground. I want to feel the cool breeze of his spirit departing from the world for good. I have no desire for him to leave me alone." He stared at Millie over his fingertips. "What has the priest changed about him and how?"

"I beg your pardon?" Millie asked.

"If you do not answer, I will kill you now," the Vulture said.

Millie sat up straight and squared her shoulders, thrusting out her jaw.

"Then kill me," she said. "I don't know, I don't understand, and if I did, I still wouldn't say."

The Vulture didn't move. His eyes stayed on hers. Finally, he pointed at her.

"If Sam Miracle was bound in your seat, if I had him here and you were the one I was hunting, your brother would not be so loyal."

Millie imagined Sam, tied up and stuck sitting in the dark. And she couldn't stop a smile.

"He'd likely enjoy the quiet," she said. "Everywhere he goes, he gets distracted. He can't focus on serious things. He's happiest when he's imagining his stories, and I don't think you could bind his imagination. I've tried."

The Vulture sneered. "Of course. Imagining his stories." He plucked a watch out of the air and examined it. "And now all of his stories—real and imagined—must end."

El Buitre stood up slowly, his head entering the darkness just above the lantern.

"I have finished with grand and glorious. The time has come for ruthless brutality. You shall see your brother's body soon, Millicent Miracle. If not in whole, at least in part."

While Millie watched, El Buitre turned and walked away, trailing seven chains. The darkness opened wide to receive him, and then swallowed.

Millie bit her lip and blinked away tears as she twisted her wrists against the ropes until the raw skin screamed. Then she jerked her ankles against their bonds as she had done already hundreds of times. Nothing budged but her own bones and her own flesh.

"If you hurt him . . . ," Millie said quietly. "If you do anything . . ."

But she had always been honest. Always. And she knew that nothing she might threaten could possibly come true.

Millie Miracle swallowed down a sob and shut her eyes. She went looking for the West Virginia sun, the smell of pies, her father's laugh, and her mother's smile.

SAM AND GLORY FORCED TINY—TALL, SLENDER, AND ashamed—to sit on a bench between them at the sun-bleached and sagging train station. The Earp brothers had loaned them a pair of shackles, not handcuffs, but only Doc had bothered to come to see the two kids and their captive leave town. Which Sam appreciated, because a whole lot of locals were sure that a new western legend had just been born in Tombstone, and they were just as sure that they needed to get a good look at the Poncho Kid before the legend moved farther west.

It only took a look from Doc and people touched their hats and hustled off. As a result, the train platform remained fairly clear.

Tiny had tried to escape, but his bloody toe trail had been easy to track. Glory had insisted on leaving without him, and then—when she'd been ignored and Tiny had been caught—she had wanted to leave right away. But there were only so many trains through Tombstone. While they'd waited, Glory had picked out some boy clothes that fit her in the general store and then filled her backpack with food and loaded a couple of canteens. She also picked out a shirt for Sam. But he refused to wear gloves.

Or the snakes did.

Sam had his eyes shut, listening to Tiny grumble and Doc hustle people off and appreciating the feel of an actual shirt against his skin. Glory rose from her side of Tiny and dropped back down beside him.

Sam opened his eyes.

"Doc," Glory said. "What's the local newspaper called?"

Doc spat, nodded some people back off the platform, and looked at her.

"*The Epitaph*," he said. "Every Tombstone needs one."

Glory had *The Legend of Poncho* open and she held it out to Sam.

"There's a copy of a news story, Sam." She tapped a page. "With pictures. It just showed up."

The story was dated October 26, 1881, and it had a cover photo of the clerk of the general store standing behind his bullet-puckered counter with his thumbs under his suspenders.

The headline was: "Goodness Snakes! Eight Men Hurled Into Eternity in the Duration of a Moment."

Sam couldn't help but smile.

In his interview, the clerk swore that he would never fix the bullet holes. He also swore that Poncho had tattoos of snakes in his arms that came alive. And his arms had moved like snakes when he'd been fighting. Faster, even. They were, perhaps, possessed by snake demons. A fat fortune-teller from Omaha confirmed that possibility. But every fool knew that the boy couldn't have had real snakes in his arms.

The editor had then described every detail of the fight in the street, next to a grainy photo of a row of coffins propped up, with the now peaceful cowboys inside all dressed up with their hands flat against their chests. It was a little grisly and Sam didn't like it. He skipped on quickly.

The editor had asked Wyatt Earp for his opinion. "The boy has a condition," was all he would say. "I'll thank him never to set foot in my jurisdiction again."

Doc Holliday said simply that the Poncho Kid had the fastest hands that he—or any man—had ever seen.

But while Sam was reading, the pages began to change. The ink was crystalizing and cracking off the paper. The photos, the headline, and every single word of the newspaper story turned into sand, slid down the page, and rained out of the book onto Sam's feet.

Sam looked at Glory. Her eyes were wide with worry.

"What just happened?" she asked.

"Nothing good," said Sam.

A flood of sand spilled out of Glory's backpack and flowed down around her legs and off the bench.

Tiny, with iron shackles on his wrists, nudged Sam with a pointy elbow and grinned. His one blue eye was sparkling in his elongated and scarred face. There was dislike in that eye, and even loathing. But the amusement was far more worrisome to Sam. Tiny's mouth was coiled up in a minuscule smile, and his stare iced the air in the train car with confidence.

Glory slung her backpack down onto the ground and dug out the sand-spewing hourglass.

"We'll be fine," she said. "We did this before, we'll be fine."

Tiny's eye stayed on Sam.

"Kid," Tiny said. "How much do you remember? Every time that priest bounced your soul back and forth it must've done wonders."

Sam didn't answer. His memories were much sharper than he would have liked. He still felt sick from the gunfight. Like a heavy black blanket of skunk smell and queasiness had been thrown over him. Guilt was a strange pain, worse than anything physical, and he wanted it gone. He couldn't let himself feel guilty for the bodies that had been dropped in the dirt street of Tombstone. Those men had made their own choices. He felt guilty for all the bodies that had chosen to lie down for him, for all the people who had believed that he was worth more than they were.

He turned away from Tiny's stare, scanning the town around them for any sign of El Buitre's rewriting.

Glory stood up, holding the hourglass away from her body, trampling in a pile of sand as she tried to look in every direction.

"Sam remembers more than enough," Glory said.

"The very beginning?" Tiny asked, and his smirk grew. "Where you're from? Before Arizona and West Virginia?"

"Baltimore," Sam said.

Glory looked at him, surprised.

"Good," Tiny said. "Baltimore. But your mind is pointed backward. It's hard to point memory forward. Just isn't designed for it. You don't know where you're from, do you?" He laughed. "You don't even know *when* you're from."

Sam didn't answer. In the distance, a train was approaching, dragging a steam plume behind it.

"Me," Tiny said. "I was born in Licking, Ohio, in the year 2014." He smiled. "That's A.D."

Sam knew the man wanted to confuse him, wanted Sam to ask how that was possible. And so he didn't.

But Glory couldn't resist. "When was Sam born?" she asked.

Doc's nods had stopped working on the crowd. They were accumulating quickly now, but they weren't looking at Sam. They were watching Glory and the sand.

"What's going on?" Doc asked.

Sam stood up beside Glory and flexed his fingers. He could feel his rattles shivering against his skin. And then sand stopped draining.

Glory was breathing hard, waiting. Sam braced himself for the whirlwind.

The first explosion was on the other end of town, and it threw an entire hotel into the sky. Women screamed. The thunderous echoes died as timber rubble clattered to the ground in the distance. Faint shouts and cries for help followed. A bell began ringing wildly. And then another. Most of the townspeople on the train platform retreated. Only a few of the men raced toward the wreckage.

"I have to get down there." Glory took a step forward, holding her hourglass like a weapon. But it wasn't swirling yet, and Sam grabbed her shoulder, holding her back.

The second blast was close enough that Sam felt it like a kick in the stomach. Another building had been obliterated.

Doc raged on the platform beside Sam. He wheeled on Tiny, his eyes on fire and his sunken cheeks more skull than face. "They're blowing the mines! Who is doing this?"

Tiny began rocking in place, his smile gone.

"Answer me!" Doc shouted.

"The Vulture," Sam said quietly. "He's hunting me."

"Then get out of here and away from our people," Doc said. "Out of town. Now!" And he limped quickly toward the smoke.

As Doc loped down into the street, the entire center of Tombstone went straight up in a pillar of fire. Flames and smoke and dust climbed higher than the distant mesas, higher than the circling vultures, up to where the air was cold, and only then did the pillar flatten. The concussion knocked Sam and Glory backward, and a slow-rolling wave of rock and soil expanded outward from the explosion in a ring, heaving every building off its foundations and bucking and rolling them into splinters and rubble as it went.

Sam scrambled to his feet. Houses and hotels and saloons were rolling toward them in a wave of jutting timbers and snapping walls.

Sam grabbed Glory by the arm and pulled her to her feet. "Hurry! Use the glass!"

A whirlwind was already stretching out of the hourglass, sucking up all the sand off the platform. Glory's lip was bleeding, and she stumbled against Sam, hanging on to him as she raised her storm like a whip.

Tiny's long leg kicked up past Sam's face. His big

motorcycle boot smacked into Glory's hand and the hourglass flipped away behind them and landed, spinning and swirling, on the plank platform.

Sam let go of Glory and spun around. Tiny was already sliding after it, already rising up beside it and raising a heavy boot. Sam took two quick steps and dove for the glass. But Tiny's bloody boot slammed down before his fingers reached it, and broken shards sprayed across the scaled backs of Sam's hands.

The whirlwind died. The sand grew still. Tiny, hands still shackled, turned and raced away with a long loping limp.

"Run!" Glory screamed, tugging at Sam's back. The roar of the rolling demolition behind was growing fast. He didn't have time to hate Tiny. Right now, he had to survive.

Sam jumped to his feet and Glory pulled him into a sprint. As the wave heaved up the train platform behind them, Sam dragged Glory to the side, and they both leapt down onto the tracks.

The steel rails began to whine and shriek beside them. The metal twisted and arched, flinging hundreds of heavy spikes into the air, tumbling tarred timbers on their heels.

Sam Miracle knew what it felt like to die. It felt like this. His body still strained, his legs churned, but his mind was calming, finding peace, taking note of every little thing as if time had stopped and nothing mattered.

"Sam!" Glory shrieked as a heavy steel rail whipped beneath their feet and then swung up over their heads and back down again before springing away to the side. Sam leapt after Glory, barely clearing the whining, lashing rail. It was the deadliest game of jump rope he would ever play, but it felt simple. And quiet. He was just a page torn from a story, floating on a breeze through no effort of his own.

"Sam!" Glory screamed again. He was beginning to fall behind. "Sam! He's here!"

Up ahead on the tracks, a white-haired Father Tiempo faced them with his arms raised. A train was steaming toward him from behind, toward Tombstone and its own destruction. The priest was too far away. They would never beat the wave. They would never beat the train. They were dead and he was dead.

"You run, Sam Miracle!" Glory yelled. Her face was on fire with anger. "Right now! You're losing to a girl!"

The train whistled desperately. The brakes screamed on the rails, but it wasn't going to stop in time. Father Tiempo was as still as a statue, but sand was swirling around his feet. Glory was somehow accelerating, and she had managed to lurch Sam's mind back into full roaring speed. His jaw was tense to the point of pain. His strides grew.

Chased by rolling wreckage, Sam and Glory raced headlong toward the man who stood between them and the shrieking, steaming train.

The train was too close and coming too fast. Thirty yards. Twenty. Sam slipped. Glory staggered. Father Tiempo would be crushed before they reached him.

And then the earth heaved beneath Sam's feet. It lifted him up, and he was suddenly running downhill with Glory beside him. The moving hill snapped, flinging them forward with tarred timbers and gravel.

Sam and Glory flew toward the priest. They hit the ground, tumbling to his feet just between the screaming train and the roiling wave of wreckage.

Father Tiempo dropped his hands.

Sam felt himself dissolving into sand, and the train blasted through him like a hot wind. He saw it, ghosting around him, launching up the bucking ground and twisting off the tracks. Faintly, he saw the train sliding to a stop in the flattened remains of Tombstone, and then it was gone.

Daylight had vanished. Sam and Glory were tangled up on asphalt, beneath a clear night sky.

"Ow," Glory said. "What just happened?"

The priest was still on his feet above them.

The asphalt was warm on Sam's back. He gasped, breathing heavily, staring up at the stars that swarmed above him. Every inch of his body throbbed. He was going to need a minute before he could speak. He had just been in a collision between a train and a Vulture-made earthquake. In his game of hide-and-seek through the centuries, El Buitre had just destroyed an entire town trying to catch him.

His heart was kicking hard, almost cramping. Sam was alive, but he didn't feel like he had escaped. Escape should have brought relief. Instead, an enormous heaviness pressed down on Sam, and his stomach twisted like the ground beneath Tombstone.

From his back, Sam looked up at the white-haired priest. Even seeing Father Tiempo alive again couldn't offset the weight of what had just happened. And clearly, the old man felt the same. While Sam watched, Father Tiempo shut wet eyes and lifted his face toward the stars. His lips moved with a whispered prayer.

Sam would have gladly remained motionless, but Speck began twisting his right arm into a coil on the asphalt, enjoying the warmth. Cindy tugged Sam's body to the left, trying to sidewind him off the road an inch at a time.

Glory jumped to her feet and threw her arms around the priest.

"I'm so glad you're here!"

Father Tiempo rocked back a step, and then hooked

an arm around her shoulder and gently peeled Glory off.

"We got your note in Tombstone." Glory shook her head. "Sam didn't hurt the Earps, but oh, that was so awful. And Tiny stomped on your hourglass."

Sam wanted to sleep. Or daydream. Anything to shake the memory of what had just happened. But he could hear a radio playing faintly. And an engine running. Slowly, he pulled his arms back in, sat up, and looked behind him. The vast scene of rubble and destruction had vanished, and he was in the middle of an intersection. Two old-fashioned cars were crumpled around each other in a terrible accident. The headlights were still on. The radio was playing inside one of them. Less than a mile away, streetlights glowed over a modern Tombstone, Arizona.

Glory had refocused her attention on the cars, and she was moving carefully toward them. "What happened?" She glanced back at the priest. "We have to help them!"

"They are beyond help," Father Tiempo said. "Grievous, but that's why I chose this place and this moment. I am weary and must ration my strength. Death leaves the easiest doorways through time."

Sam stared at the cars. It was awful, but nowhere near as awful as what he had just seen. "Old Tombstone," he said. "The Earps?"

"Dead," the priest said. "And destroyed. Seven thousand souls made that place their home. Only a few hundred survived. The Vulture grows desperate, and now the future has been horribly marred. It cannot be undone if El Buitre lives, and perhaps not even if he is killed. Now stand up."

"Nice to see you, too." Sam stood, wincing. He'd banged both knees and an elbow on the road. Cindy lifted his left hand and stared at the priest. Speck tugged his right hand straight down. He liked the ground.

"When is this?" Glory asked. She was still staring at the accident. "That's so sad. You're sure we can't do anything?"

"Nineteen fifty-four." Father Tiempo limped toward the side of the road. "And I am sure. But you will not be here long. We are waiting for your friends, and they are late." He looked back at Glory. "From here, I am sending you to 1969. A big year, and with an earthquake exactly where we need one. Do either of you know how to ride a motorcycle?"

"Not really," Glory said. "But I can ride a four-wheeler."

"I have no idea," Sam said. He looked at the cars, at the shapes inside the cars, and then he shut his eyes. But then all he saw was the rolling wave of destruction shattering Tombstone. He heard the screams. He saw the ghostly train tumbling through the ruins, flinging people from the windows, and he opened his eyes again quickly.

His heart was still pounding.

When he spoke, his voice was flat, but only so he wouldn't throw up.

"Why are we here?"

Father Tiempo met Sam's gaze. "Because you have never been in this moment before and there is no reason for you to be in this moment now. From here, you go elsewhere." The priest moved down the shoulder of the road into the ditch. "In the book, do you remember El Buitre's seven hidden gardens?"

"Listen to me," Sam said. "I don't want to hide. I don't want to run. I just ran, and you just saved me, but thousands of people died. And I don't care about the book. I care about my sister. So why will you be sending me to 1969? She'll have been dead for almost a century, right? Send me back to when she's still alive so I can at least try and save her! Everyone gets hurt around me. Just let me save her, and then I promise I'll face the Vulture and he can do what he wants and stop smashing towns."

Father Tiempo paused in the ditch and looked up at Sam. His white hair shone. His dark eyes swallowed the starlight. "Do you want to *win*?" he asked. "Because I want to win, Sam. Not for me. Not for you. I desire the defeat of this evil. I want to stop this man from destroying every life centuries in both directions. And that is why I am going to go die for you in this desert. That is why I am going to stand over your body after El Buitre has destroyed your arms, and I am going to lay down my life years at a time, shortening my very existence, keeping you alive. The years I lay down, I will never get back."

"I never asked you to do that for me," Sam said quietly. "I wouldn't."

Father Tiempo smiled. "Of course you wouldn't ask me to. But you need me to. And, more importantly, the thousands who died in the annihilation of Tombstone need me to. And so do the many thousands who live in every city the Vulture will choose to eliminate in the same way. Samuel Miracle," the priest said, "when I die for you, I am also dying for millions. And you know that I will die, because in your life, I already have. You are here, alive, eager to save your sister. You have survived, you have been . . . *equipped*. And now you are ready to strike."

"Equipped?" Sam splayed his fingers and studied his arms. Cindy's horns threw strange shadows across his hands.

"Yes," the priest nodded. "Equipped. Protected. Surrounded with friends and allies. All that remained was to find the right time. And I have found it."

"Allies?" Sam asked. "What allies?"

Headlights crested a hill coming toward them from outside of town. Sam heard gears grind and squeal from a mile away.

"Late allies," Father Tiempo said. "Allies who cannot be trusted to arrive on time, but allies all the same."

Glory and Sam stood next to each other on the shoulder of the road and watched a short white bus bounce to a stop beside the car wreck.

"SADDYR" was painted in black letters on the side.

Broad-shouldered Drew was behind the wheel, and he threw the door open.

"Sorry, Pete!" he yelled at Father Tiempo. "Engine trouble. We got here as fast as we could." He pointed at the car wreck. "Anything we can do?"

"Not this time," the priest said. "Sadly."

Sam moved toward the bus door. He looked from Drew to the priest.

"Pete?" Sam asked. "Are you Peter?"

"I am," the priest said, smiling slightly. "Peter Atsa Eagle Ignatius Tiempo. Your Ranch Brother. And these"—he gestured at the bus—"are the other men who gave up their childhoods to be your brothers, to be with you, to support you, and to surround you as you healed."

Sam's jaw fell open and his eyes grew hot as the boys tumbled out, slapped his shoulders, and examined his hands and arms. They laughed at Speck and whistled in disbelief at Cindy's horns and devil eyes, and when she tensed Sam's arm and began to rattle, they laughed some more and backed away.

Drew Dill, missing a finger. Flip the Lip. Barto with his wired-together glasses. The brawling redheads, Jimmy Z and Johnny Z. The blond game-players, Matt Cat with his lumpy biscuit face and Sir T with his nose and chin as sharp as creased paper. The hunters, Tiago Lopez with his Mohawk and Simon Zeal with his thick permanent bed-head. Tiago and Simon were the only ones brave enough to touch Sam's hands and trace the scales up his arms. And finally, smiling Jude with his sharp eyes and curly hair, and a thick notebook under his arm.

The priest smiled. "We are proud to be your brothers, and I am proud to give you my life."

Sam was stunned. Surrounded by his Ranch Brothers, memories flashed through his mind. Laughing in the Commons, working on the land. Pillow fighting in the Bunk House. But most of all, the faces of the boys as they saved him. All the times they had found him lost in the desert. The times they carried him home. Peter pouring water over his sun-blistered lips.

Sam faced the old priest. "You do look like Peter," he said, slowly. "But different. Did you really burn down a gas station, or was it all a lie?"

"I hid my appearance a little," the priest said. "But it was all true. I've burned down a lot more than one gas station. But those stories, and the stories of all our Ranch

Brothers, can wait." The priest grabbed a large clump of dead sagebrush and threw it away. A little motorcycle with a sidecar had been hidden beneath it.

"It is time for our final moves."

"Are we going back into the past?" Glory asked. "We have to. Sam can't leave his sister. And the Vulture—"

Father Tiempo climbed onto the motorcycle. He turned a key, and kick-started the engine. Exhaust flowed and the roar drowned out Glory's angry yelling.

The priest bounced the motorcycle up onto the road. "Triumph" was painted on the side of the gas tank. It was all wrong for the moment. The priest twisted the key back off and the motorcycle died.

"Thank you," Glory said. She glared at the priest and eyed all the boys. "So are we saving Sam's sister or not?"

"We hope to," the priest said. "And so much more. I asked if you remembered the Vulture's seven hidden gardens."

"Yes," Glory said, glancing at Sam. Sam nodded. How could he forget? It had been one of the creepiest parts of the whole book—seven gardens where the Vulture buried his victims so he could always visit them.

The priest gestured at Matt Cat and Sir T, and the blond boys stepped forward.

Matt spoke first. "It took awhile to figure out how the

Vulture's system works, but Pete gave us a lot of the pieces and spent hours explaining the geography of time to us. From there we just puzzled it out. There had to be seven gardens."

"It's a lunar thing," Sir T said.

"Right," said Matt. "Anyway, they're all walled and hidden, but they all open onto the dark outside of time. The Vulture can move between them through the outer darkness, and from them, he can step out of the gardens into any moment in history he might choose."

"He built a prison around us in the desert," Sam said. "And then he came out of the bottom of a tower."

"I told you," Sir T said. His sharp eyebrows rose almost to his hairline and he pointed at Matt. "I told you. From the outside, he has the ability to open—"

Father Tiempo cleared his throat. "I told you both. I've seen him do that hundreds of times. Please continue and stay focused."

Matt saluted. "So from any of his gardens he can travel back to his tower nest and his favorite month in San Francisco. I expect the top of the tower has a doorway into the dark edge of time, as well."

"Or the bottom," Sir T interrupted.

"Sure," Matt said. "A basement is technically possible, but it wouldn't match his alter ego. He's a bird."

Sir T shrugged. "Either way, he has seven sun- and

moondials," Sir T said. "One in each garden. And seven watches in his vest."

Barto leaned forward, adjusting his glasses and speaking for the first time. "Likely chained to his heart."

"You're just guessing and that's not important," Matt said. "What's important is that he enters the gardens from any time, and they open onto the darkness which has no time and from there he can get back to his roost in the 1880s. And in that place, your sister may still be alive."

"Maybe," Sir T said.

Matt shrugged. "So if that's where he kept Millie, then you can reach her through the gardens just as easily right now as one hundred years ago. So 1969 is just as good as any year, but better, because Pete picked a day when a quake should open those garden walls right up."

"Maybe," Sir T said.

Matt shrugged again.

Tiago stepped forward, rubbing his Mohawk, glancing from Sam to Glory and down at Sam's hands. His voice was almost too quiet to be heard over the bus engine, even from three feet away.

"It was our job to find one of the gardens." He stared into Cindy's eyes and his voice trailed off.

Sam tucked Cindy under his poncho and Tiago blinked.

"And we did," he said, backing away. "Simon?"

Bed-head Simon stepped forward and handed Sam a map of San Francisco with a route and location marked in black.

"That's where we hit him," Simon said. Tiago nodded.

"We?" Sam asked. That little word sent his hopes rising quickly.

Father Tiempo looked around the group of boys.

"I cannot," the priest said. He was still straddling the silent motorcycle. "I must get to where I need to be to save your life, Sam. And after I have, there will be fewer of my moments available."

"Understatement," Drew said. "We have to get this done ourselves, Sam. Young Pete will come when he can. The plan is simple. These boys and I will hit the garden loud and hard in this year—1954—while you and Glory try to get into the garden in a different time completely. Hopefully, we'll get his attention and hold it until it's too late."

"Too late for who?" Glory asked.

"For whom." The correction came from Jude, standing in the back of the group beside the redheads.

"Whatever," Glory said. "Do you have any idea what this guy can do? He just wiped out an entire city from end to end, and we only survived because of Father Tiempo. If you get the Vulture's attention, and he isn't there, I don't think we'll ever see each other again."

The boys were all silent.

Father Tiempo shifted his weight on the motorcycle seat. Springs squeaked beneath him. "My brothers know what they are attempting, Glory. They know the possible cost. They know the possible reward. We all do. If William Sharon survives, then the city you saw destroyed will be only one of hundreds like it. With him, it takes only the smallest irritant to provoke annihilation." The priest looked around as the boys nodded. Drew rolled his thick neck. Jude scribbled in his notebook. "And now we must go. The boys will force El Buitre to defend his lair in 1954. I will set Sam and Glory on a path to strike in 1969. Understood?"

"You're just sacrificing them," Sam said, shaking his head. "I don't like it. Isn't there some, I don't know, magical way to change things? Just get Jude to write the story different. He's right here."

Jude lowered his notebook, surprised.

"No one has to like it," the priest said. "But we choose to do it. Even with all that I have seen and known, there is only one way to change history. By living. By dying. We take the risks we must take to be the men and boys we are meant to be." He smiled at Glory. "And women. Someday, if he survives, Jude will write the story of our living now. But if this goes badly, then he won't be writing anything at all. Now, if I don't get to where I need to be to save your life . . ."

"Then I'll disappear or something?" Sam asked. He sniffed and crossed his arms.

"Of course not. Your soul will be plucked from you and your body will crumple to the ground where you stand. Now say your good-byes and get on the motorcycle."

"Promise me that this is the best way to save my sister, not just the best way to kill El Buitre," Sam said.

"I do not know of a better way," the priest said. "Now get on this motorcycle before you die."

Flashing red lights were approaching through Tombstone. An ambulance.

"Boys, go!" Father Tiempo commanded. "You know your moment."

The boys piled back into the bus with nods and slaps and various quiet farewells.

Matt Cat hesitated beside Glory. "So . . . you've kept our boy alive. After all this is over, I'd love to share a meal and some conversation."

Glory flinched in surprise, and then shoved him away with a sneer. "Get on your bus."

The boys on board all whooped and laughed.

Drew shut the bus door and smashed the engine into gear.

"Oh, hey!" Glory yelled, cupping her hands around her mouth. "Jude! Grammar Boy!"

Jude's face appeared in the window.

"Whenever it is that you write *The Legend of Sam Miracle*, if I'm still alive, you run it by me. Got that? I will not let you screw it up."

Jude smiled. Drew cranked the bus away from them, bounced it on the shoulder as he turned around, and rumbled quickly away.

Father Tiempo stared at Sam, and Sam stared right back. He still hadn't gotten on the motorcycle.

"I know you just want me to think about saving the world," Sam said. "And to you Millie isn't as important. And I understand. After Tombstone, I do."

"No!" Glory crossed her arms. "Sam, if you don't do your best to save her, it's a terrible story. I read it. I liked Poncho, and I still wanted him to die."

The priest shook his head. "Glory, this isn't about living a story that you like. This is about the entire world. And if I don't get where I need to be . . ."

"Why can't I do both?" Sam asked. "I don't want to let my sister die."

"She already did," the priest said quietly. "So many times. There is a graveyard filled with the bodies her soul has possessed. And with yours, Sam." He looked deep in Sam's eyes, searching. "Sam, so much has gone right this time. So much. I was willing to give my life just for this chance. Your arms, your resolve . . . if you would only trust me, this is the moment when El Buitre could finally

283

fall. This could all end. You could fulfill your purpose. It's what your sister would want. It's what she worked for. It's what I've worked for."

"Last chance," Sam said. His voice was ice and the rattles quivered against his shoulders beneath his shirt. "What's the best way for my sister?"

"Sam." Father Peter Atsa Tiempo closed his eyes, and his voice wavered as he spoke. "I'm sorry. There is no best way for Millie. All ways are bad."

MILLIE MIRACLE THOUGHT THE ELEVATOR HAD STOPPED descending. The brass cage door wasn't rattling anymore. She couldn't hear the whining of the cable or distant hum of the motor. The floor wasn't shaking beneath her feet. But it was swaying slightly. Rocking as if they were on water.

She rubbed her raw wrists and looked at the tall man in the elevator with her. He was in a much better mood than when she had last seen him. His thumbs were in his belt and he was smirking above his oil-dark pointed beard. At least his seven gold-and-pearl watch chains were tight to his vest instead of floating all around. The space was too small for that.

"I always wonder how much you remember," the man said. "Do you even know who I am?"

Millie nodded. "You're the Vulture."

"Oh, please," the man said. "We're old friends now. You can call me . . ." He thought for a moment. "Fate. Destiny. Doom. Whatever feels right." He shrugged and twitched a quick smile. "How does God sound?"

"You destroy things," Millie said. "You don't create. You and God have nothing in common."

"Smart girl. Call me Mr. Sharon. Or William. That's how this body was first christened, and it has been one of my favorites." He nodded at the door. "Open the cage whenever you like."

Millie assessed the brass accordion door. Gripping the handle, she slid it open, and then staggered back in surprising light. They were thousands of feet up, and outside the elevator, stars were whirling. The sun looked like a throbbing white-gold symbol, coiling around itself in a loosely braided sphere. Below her, mountains rippled like fields of grass crawling in the wind. Forests spilled across the land like dark liquid. But the ocean was as hard and motionless as a smooth sapphire.

Millie couldn't pull her eyes away.

"I'm a bit of an ancient nomad," Mr. Sharon said. "Not much younger than this world, actually. But I'm only just beginning to enjoy myself. When I've finally dealt with your brother in a permanent way, the fun will truly begin."

"Sam will kill you," Millie said. "That's what everyone

says. That's why we ran and why the priest hid us."

"Oh ho!" El Buitre sneered at her. "You think your memory is sharp? Let me show you something you won't remember."

The Vulture slammed the door shut, pulled out a watch, adjusted it, and then threw the door back open. Millie blinked again. She was looking out at a small walled garden—a graveyard—beneath the night sky. A yellow shard of moon hung low, between two hulking trees that loomed over the wall. The moonlight was just bright enough to throw shadows behind the headstones, and the grass was just long enough to bend smooth backs.

In the center of the graveyard, there was a stone bench with the seat worn smooth. A narrow dirt footpath led straight to it through the grass. Behind the bench, there was what looked like an old stone sundial. A gold clock floated above it, leashed down to the dial face with a heavy gold chain stretched taut.

"One of my thinking spots," Mr. Sharon said. He stepped out of the elevator. "Where I contemplate time and mortality and your frustrating brother. Although it isn't really his fault that he's frustrating. It's all that horrible priest."

Millie moved out into the graveyard and the air was sharp in her lungs. Each breath had glass edges.

The priest. Millie had a picture in her mind. Black

hair, dark skin, obsidian eyes. His name . . .

"Father Tiempo," she said.

Mr. Sharon dragged his hands over headstones as he walked toward the bench. "Yes," he said. "Father Time. Can you understand why he doesn't like me?"

Millie didn't move. Mr. Sharon turned and sat on the bench. He extended his legs, crossing his booted feet at his ankles. Moonlight crawled across his watch chains.

"Well," Mr. Sharon said. "I don't like him either. He's a poor loser." He spread his arms, rippling his long fingers as if he were testing the texture of the air. "Do you like this garden? I do hope so. If you don't help me, you're going to stay here forever. I will personally dig yet another hole in my Miracle garden, and you will go into it very much alive, screaming, until I've shoveled enough earth on your face to silence you."

Millie took a quick step back, but there was nowhere to run. And the man wasn't coming toward her. He was pointing at the headstones.

For the first time, Millie looked at the names. To her right every stone was the same. Dozens of them.

Millicent Miracle

She turned left, and her eyes bounced from stone to stone. They were all her brother's.

287

Samuel Miracle

Millie's heart went cold in her chest, cold and heavy. She opened her mouth to speak, but her voice was frozen. First the darkness and then this. She didn't understand, but she'd seen too much to doubt the headstones. She was living in a nightmare. Her heart sank low, and she followed it down, landing on her knees in the cool grass.

Her eyes settled on a pale marble slab beside Mr. Sharon's bench.

Gloria Spalding

Mr. Sharon followed her look with his own.

"Stubborn girl," he said. "Smart, but not as smart as she thought. Tiny—you remember Tiny?—shot dear Gloria with Sam in Arizona. Doesn't matter. What matters is you." William Sharon raised his nose to the air. "Would you like this to be your final resting place, or shall we leave all your old exoskeletons here and move on?"

Suddenly, he leaned forward, staring straight into her eyes. "Join me, and I can give you the world—every moment of it. Be more than bait on a hook, always devoured. Why should you have to die? Why should Sam? Help me take him alive. Without a fight. I have won by spilling blood often enough already. You'll be saving him as well as yourself. And then I can show you anything, take you anywhere, grant any wish, help you live forever, choosing lives for yourself, choosing cities and nations and eons. I'll have Mrs. Dervish make you a queen. Would you like a Chinese dynasty? I can give you one. Would you like to burn kings and make soap from the ash? Is there someone you hate? Anyone? I will teach you to peel their entire life apart, second by second. Maybe you'd like to see the great sea serpents of forgotten time or rewrite the golden age of Europe? The past is my back garden. I only need one thing in return." He smiled. "Sam Miracle. How many times have you died for him? And all your dying has accomplished nothing. Nothing but these stones around you, and the lifeless bodies beneath them. This time, live."

Millie swallowed. She licked her lips. Her last memory was of Sam being shot in the train wreck while she screamed into a gag. He hadn't even seen her. Then she had been knocked out. She didn't understand how he could have survived, but clearly he had. The Vulture had raged angrily over the chessboard and had stormed off to destroy him. And he had obviously failed again, or he wouldn't be asking for her help now.

The villain had tried to terrify her, but she had been terrified already. He had tried to entice her, but he had used nothing but lies. But, almost accidentally, he had given her something she badly needed. Something beautiful. A spark that she could cling to.

He had given her hope. And hope could burn anything.

Millie filled her lungs and her voice thawed. She stared the Vulture right in the eyes.

"When Sam comes," she said, "where will they bury you?"

THE PRIEST HAS PRACTICALLY FLOWN THROUGH THE DESERT on the motorcycle, bouncing against rocks harder than a jackhammer. Sam could still taste the blood in his mouth from biting his lip in the sidecar; Glory was massaging her nose after smacking it into the priest's back.

Old Father Tiempo had jumped them into 1969. The extra effort seemed to have drained him a little, but Sam was grateful not to be immediately greeted with bodies from a fresh tragedy. Then the priest had said a quick good-bye and dissolved himself away. It was strange to think that the old man was traveling to the smoking train wreck to stand over Sam with his shattered arms, to lay down his life just to keep Sam breathing. Sam had been relieved to see the priest alive again, but he knew the relief was false. In the priest's time line, he simply hadn't died yet.

"Well," Glory said. "You're still alive, so he must have made it."

Sam stretched in the moonlight and tried to stop thinking about it. But he couldn't. He wondered if he would see the old priest again, maybe years from now, but still before he had died for Sam. Or maybe all of those moments had been used up already. Father Tiempo had said that he lived in a straight line, but that his straight line was different from their straight lines. Sam didn't understand. But he didn't need to. Something else the priest had said . . .

Glory was watching him. The motorcycle was lifeless on the rough desert horse-track the priest had chosen to get them back toward the canyon where the blown bridge and the train wreck had begun Sam's journey toward new arms. Metal was still ticking in the motorcycle engine from the heat of its exertion. Sam's arms kept sliding under his poncho and winding tight around his torso. Speck and Cindy didn't care for the night air. They preferred body heat.

"I could have kissed you back there," Glory said. "Even if we die, we need to try and save your sister. The story is so much better."

"I'm glad you didn't kiss me," Sam said.

"I'm not even your sister," said Glory, "and I wouldn't want you to leave me to die just to save the world. Which is how I know I'm way too selfish."

"Selfish?" Sam shook his head. "Don't be stupid. You

didn't have to come. And you didn't have to stay with me in the desert." After a moment, he looked over at Glory. "What if I really do have to choose? What if I die saving Millie, and then the Vulture gets to do whatever he wants to millions of people? Is it wrong to want to save my sister more than all those people in Tombstone?"

Glory didn't answer.

Sam sighed and continued, now talking up at the sky. "I don't know. It all makes me feel sick. And I really don't like this plan. I don't want all those guys to die. And they will."

Glory tucked her hair behind her ears. "So. What do you want to do?"

"I want to move faster. I don't want to wait for any distractions. I want to hit first. I don't want to have to choose between saving my sister and saving everything else."

Something feline sent a yowl rolling over the rocks.

"Do you think he was lying?" Sam asked.

"About it being more than thirteen hours to San Francisco?" Glory shrugged. "I don't know why he would lie about that."

"About Millie. You think she doesn't have much chance no matter what I do?"

"She has a brother with snake arms who is willing to do absolutely everything he can to save her or die trying."

"Yeah," Sam said. "But even if we follow the map

perfectly and find this graveyard, and we wait for the earthquake Father Tiempo said would happen, and the guys beat us there and have him distracted, we still have to get into the outer darkness—whatever that is—and then through it into the Vulture's tower, just hoping that he hasn't killed Millie yet." He faced Glory. "Feels kinda like we're about to die trying. And if I die and the Vulture lives, what was all this for? What then?"

Glory slapped the motorcycle. "We have exactly one way to find out."

"Well, I know we can make better time to San Francisco than that bus," Sam said. "At least if you can really run this thing."

Glory threw her leg over the seat, turned the key, and kick-started the engine hard. Exhaust ghosted off into the night as she revved the engine.

"You don't need a driver's license to dirt-bike in the desert!" She smiled. "Saddle up, Poncho."

~12~

The Vulture's Wings

SAM GROANED. THE SUN WAS BRIGHT BUT LOW. AND HE could hear voices. His knees and arms were tucked up under his poncho, and his cheek ached where it was resting on the edge of the sidecar.

He had no idea how long he had been asleep.

Yawning, Sam sat up. The motorcycle was parked on top of a hill, in long grass beside a road. Below Sam, San Francisco was curled up on its own hills running down to the bay. The city looked like a colony of slow-rolling ant mounds, clothed with trees and then dotted with houses and finally crowned with towers, all of it leashed together with taut and slack and tangled roads. If Sam didn't know that he'd been to San Francisco countless times, he would have said he'd never seen a city like it. In the morning light, whether he was in 1969 or in 2069, it looked to him like it belonged in another world.

About ten feet away, Glory was facedown in the grass.

Two shaggy men stood above her. One nudged her with his bare foot.

"Bro! Don't wake her up," the other man said. "She'll just make a scene."

"Scene either way, my brother. At least if we take the bike."

"We're taking the bike for sure. Nice bike and they're just kids. You know they stole it. The universe wants us to have it."

Sam whistled, and as both men spun around, Speck pulled his revolver and Sam's right arm slithered out from under the poncho.

"I don't care what the universe wants," Sam said. "You're not stealing anything."

"Whoa!"

"Bro!"

Both men retreated back through the grass. And then one of them began to laugh.

"You know, little brother, for a second, I thought you had a snake pointing a gun at me."

"I do." Sam cocked the hammer and both men broke into a run, jumping through the long grass back toward a wall of trees.

Sam holstered his weapon and tried to stand up. His legs were heavier than concrete and he couldn't feel his right foot at all. He slipped sideways, banged his shin on the lip of the sidecar, and fell out into the grass.

Glory rolled over and sat up. "What are you doing?"

"I'm falling," Sam said. "Is this San Francisco? You drove the whole way?"

"I did. And you slept the whole way. Which is ridiculous. Even when I stopped for gas. You're like a dog, the way you sleep. Just flop you anywhere and you're out."

"I had to sleep just so I wouldn't notice how uncomfortable I was," Sam said. "How much farther?"

"If your Mohawk brother's map is right, it's just at the bottom of this hill. But it was creepy down there in the dark, and I didn't feel like hunting around with you still snoring."

Sam stood up and winced at the tingling in his foot as blood returned.

"Want me to drive?" he asked. "I can. If you teach me."

"Ha," Glory said. "Funny, funny, Miracle boy. Let's walk."

Sam didn't move. He stood, feeling the sun. Smelling

the wind. Watching the grass bend in the breeze toward the swaying trees and the distant white lines marking foam on the bay.

Glory stood beside him.

"Any reason to wait?" she asked.

Sam shook his head. "No. Not really. It's just . . ." He took in a long slow breath, and told himself that the knot in his stomach was hunger.

"While I'm still right here," he finally said. "This still might go well."

"I get it," Glory said. "Whenever you're ready."

Sam and Glory walked down the hill. They hopped a fence and moved through a goat pasture. They rounded a small slumping house and then a collapsing barn. Finally, they entered a grove of ancient trees.

The trees were cedar, with massive sinewy trunks rising up in dozens of different positions, each one a tree unto itself. The earth beneath them was soft and bare, but ferns grew in thick flocks wherever enough light reached the ground.

At the center of the grove, Sam and Glory stepped into a wide clearing. In the center of the clearing, high stone walls were wedged inside two of the largest trees yet, enclosing what had to be one of the seven hidden gardens. A little stone building the size of a backyard veranda guarded the far side with a tarnished copper weather vane perched on its peak. Beyond the building, a narrow road wound away into the trees.

"See what I mean?" Glory said. "No way I was sleeping down here."

As Sam and Glory walked around the walls, Sam's eyes traced the muscled branches of the trees. They hugged the stone, bending around the corners, interlacing with one another, forming a wooden web of protection. Or maybe it was a posture of attack. He couldn't tell, but if trees that strong wanted to attack, he was pretty sure the walls of the garden would have been long gone.

Cindy was on edge the entire time, thrust out from Sam's body and as rigid as one of the tree branches. Speck, however, badly wanted Sam to let him down in the grass, and he wouldn't stop tugging his right arm straight down.

On the road side of the garden, Sam and Glory stopped in front of the building. There was no door. Sam walked all the way around the walls and back again.

Nothing.

"So, if you've decided to stick to Father Tiempo's plan, we wait all day until the earthquake shakes things up and knocks walls over," Glory said. "Although I think the priest might have had some bad info. I can't see these trees letting the walls fall down for us even if the earth does start shaking."

"You know we're not waiting," Sam said. "I'm not

letting ten guys get themselves killed as a distraction. I'm the first one in, and if I survive, I'll be the last one out." He gave Glory a tight smile. "Thanks for everything. You've been amazing. Really."

"Oh, heck no," Glory said. "I'm not sitting out here by myself. Do we climb? Shouldn't be hard with these trees."

Sam looked at the heavy wooden arms, coiled and tensed around the stone. They seemed oddly intentional, like set traps, ready to crush a skull or shatter bones. He didn't feel like climbing them. But he would. They weren't any creepier than his own arms.

Glory walked to the wall, hopped up, and grabbed the lowest branch. Scrambling against the stone wall, she grabbed the next branch.

Sam heard the stone groan. The ground shivered under his feet.

"Glory?"

But Glory ignored him. She climbed higher. Above her, the upper branches of the tree gently swayed. Sam held his breath. What else could he do? He could feel his snakes tightening, his rattles beginning to whisper. But he couldn't shoot a tree.

Glory jumped and managed to grab the very top of the wall. Shoes scraping on stone, she hoisted herself up, and then froze.

"Oh . . ."

The giant tree rocked above her, but she didn't notice. She stood up on the wall slowly, still looking down inside.

"Sam," she said. "I . . . I don't understand. It's like my whole life in a pool. Like time is—" She broke off suddenly. "Mom? Mom! Look at me!"

The tree branches tightened. The stone wall heaved. And Glory fell.

Sam raced forward, but the earth shivered beneath him and a ripple of turf threw him to the ground. All the trees were shaking now. The earthquake was coming.

Sam jumped up and attacked the swaying wall. Desperate, while the branches tensed and heaved, he climbed faster than he ever would have on a ladder. At the top, he threw one leg over the wall, and sat on the uneasy stone like a horse.

And he forgot the quaking earth around him.

He was looking down into a pool of time—crystal clear, as clear as spirit, swirling just below his boot. At the bottom of the pool, he saw the world. He was looking into the garden of everything. And then, slowly at first, it became the garden of every*him*.

Tiny trains crashing into tiny canyons. Miniature mountains and forests surrounding a miniature white house in West Virginia. Miniature ships at the docks in Baltimore, and a miniature Sam in the arms of a miniature old man who had been his grandfather.

But it wasn't miniature. The pool was just so very, very deep and so very, very clear and so very, very fast. The scenes at the bottom slid away faster than Sam could recognize them. He leaned down toward the surface, hoping for a glimpse of his oldest past, for a flash of where he truly belonged.

The tip of his boot touched the surface, and in a flash of cold, it disappeared. Sam jerked his leg back up. The boot tip was gone. Sliced cleaner than any blade could ever achieve.

"Glory?" Sam said out loud. What had happened to her? He searched the pool, but everywhere he looked, his miniature selves were busy dying. He grabbed a branch above his head and leaned further over, lowering a fingertip toward the surface.

Cold pain shot up his arm and he flinched away. The skin on his fingertip and a slice of his nail were completely gone. There was no blood. No wound. Perfectly flat, perfectly smooth skin where part of him had just been erased.

Sam looked up at the two dark trees swaying above him, bent and flapping at the sky—like a massive vulture's wings. He looked back at the weather vane. A vulture. Spinning.

Sam took one big breath. And then a second. His stomach heaved like the ground.

What else was he supposed to do?

Holding his breath, he tumbled into the perfect cold.

Sam slammed onto his back, knocking the wind all the way out of him. Gasping in pain, he rolled onto his side, gripping cool grass.

The air was rippling. The grass was writhing, twitching and lashing its blades with insect quickness. Rows of tombstones marched from one wall to the other. There was a stone bench near the center. Behind it, something was flashing in the dim light. Sam sat up. A gold clock like a large pocket watch was spinning through the air, swinging in an orbit at the end of a gold chain anchored to a sundial.

Sam drew his right gun and shot the clock. It skidded to the ground in an explosion of gears and springs. As the echo of the gunshot died, the air stopped rippling and the grass stopped its itching. The moment had settled.

Sam rose to his feet and looked around.

"Glory?"

Nothing.

He looked up at the trees above him—great wings now stretching high and quietly into a hazy sky.

"Glory!" Sam moved quickly toward the bench. As he went, he saw the names on all the headstones, and he immediately slowed. He had found the bodies that went with his daydreams. The bodies that had lived his jumbled memories. All around him. Beneath the thick turf. And every stone marked a different version of his story.

Metal rattled behind him, and Sam spun, gun raised, letting Speck guide his aim. Cindy twitched toward hers, but Sam managed to keep her still.

A brass accordion door clattered open in the small building.

William Sharon, hatless and coatless, stepped into the light and stopped when he saw Sam with his gun already drawn and pointing. Seven gold watch chains glittered against his vest. Perfect pearl-handled revolvers hugged his narrow hips.

"Well," he said. "Well, well. You came. And alone. No priest? No earnest young posse? I expected you at the hotel and assumed that you would show a little more . . . *effort*. I don't know whether I should be thrilled or furious." He pointed at the wreckage of the clock behind Sam. "That mattered."

Speck cocked the hammer. "I'm here for my sister."

Mr. Sharon rubbed his loose neck and smiled. "Peruse her many graves. Leave a flower. Or thirty. Is that all? Your sister? After all that you've achieved, and all that you've escaped, and all the priest has sacrificed? Surely there was some kind of plan. Amazing."

"What's so amazing about it?" Sam asked. "Tell me where she is."

"What's amazing," Mr. Sharon said, "is how hard that fool of a priest has worked to make you something other than what you are. You are the same fish hitting the same hook for the same bait every single cast. Poor Tiempo, all that effort, all that dying, and you're still just you." He waved his hand at Millie's graves. "You've already found her. I told you. Here she is."

"I want her alive," Sam growled. "And you dead."

The Vulture laughed and the grass rippled. "Of course you do. But that will be difficult," he said. "On both counts. I'm not afraid of you, which means your threat does nothing to motivate me to give her to you."

"Oh, you're afraid of me," Sam said. "How much time have you spent hunting me? How much of your own effort? How much worrying? Flattening an entire city? Sending Tiny after me when I was just daydreaming at a youth ranch? I scare the Vulture. And I should. I have a gun pointed at you right now. I am the plan. These arms are the plan. And if you can't give me my sister, why shouldn't I just shoot?"

Speck was steady, but Sam let Cindy slither out away from his body, and he watched the Vulture's eyes as she did. He showed no interest. No fear. No surprise.

Anger and worry surged through Sam, and Cindy's rattling grew. Should he have followed the plan? Should he have let Father Tiempo measure all the risks?

Mr. Sharon pulled out a gold watch. It had shattered. He tapped gears and glass out into the grass, and then pulled out another, winding it. And then another. And another. Carefully tucking each one back into its own pocket. When he spoke, his voice was hushed and hard.

"You are holding that gun in your right hand, Samuel Miracle. I have heard about your right hand. It won't shoot me. But even if it tried, before you pull that trigger, I could put six more bullets in each of your ghoulish arms."

"Try," Sam said. "My hands are faster now."

"I am El Buitre," Mr. Sharon snarled. "My hands are faster than time."

Sam knew that was true. He'd seen it. He doubted if even Cindy was fast enough. He knew for sure that Speck wouldn't finish the fight. And if he'd been unsure of his choices before, he was absolutely certain now—the Vulture had to die. Now. Here. No matter what. But how?

El Buitre and Poncho stared at each other in a grave-yard full of Miracles. Sam's rattles hummed. El Buitre cracked his knuckles.

Sam had been unexpected. That was his only advantage. He had to stay unexpected. And crazy.

Sam lowered his gun and holstered it. Both of his arms crackled with anger, but he just managed to control them. Cindy was pure fury, tightening his arm until

Sam's broken joints screamed with pain. She went deathly silent, her rattle still, but Speck grew louder.

Just wait, Sam thought. *Be ready.*

Sam showed the Vulture his palms. "What if I surrender? Kill me or don't. Take my heart if you have to, or just keep me. Just let my sister go and this thing between us is over right now. Once she's free, you can pick your ending."

William Sharon's eyes were hungry. "You want me to release her. But it isn't that simple. When? Into what time?"

"Wherever she wants," Sam said. "Whenever she wants. Deal?"

The Vulture stepped to one side, and three men emerged from the building, led by Tiny. All three had guns raised.

That changed things. Sam bit his lip, frustrated, but he was in it now.

"You're lying," El Buitre said. "You have to be."

Sam fought to extend his rigid arms out from his sides and then slumped to his knees. He shut his eyes tight.

"Do what you have to do. But be quick," he said. "Please."

Breathing slowly, Sam tried to quiet his pounding heart. He wanted to feel what his hands felt. He wanted to ignore his own eyes and sense what they sensed.

"Knock him out," the Vulture said. "And then bring him."

FIGHT flooded up his right arm.

KILL roared up his left.

YES, Sam thought. *Attack! Strike!* But he locked his own muscles as tight as he could, holding the snakes back.

SAM'S HANDS WATCHED THE THREE MEN MOVING TOWARD him through the graveyard. He couldn't see the men, but he could locate their warm outlines, even with his eyes shut. They were right in front of him.

And then a pistol butt cracked him on the skull, and sensation vanished.

SAM MIRACLE WAS UNCONSCIOUS IN THAT MOMENT IN THE garden. But his soul knew many moments. And it was praying in all of them.

His hands weren't unconscious at all.

Tiny drew a long knife, and with a snarling smile he bent cautiously over Sam. He nudged the tip through Sam's poncho, through his shirt, and into the boy's chest.

No response.

William Sharon stood with his arms crossed, watching with a suspicious smile.

Tiny looked back at him. "Best champagne tonight, Boss." And then he crouched to pick Sam up.

In a flash, Cindy whipped Sam's gun out and his arm up. The barrel thumped against Tiny's heart as she fired. Before the big man even had time to fall, she had dropped the next man, and the next.

Speck pulled Sam's other gun.

But El Buitre was fast.

Cindy and Speck flopped Sam's body forward onto his belly, hiding behind Tiny.

Cindy missed the blurry cold shape of the Vulture with three rounds, dropped her gun at the first click, and then darted under Tiny's coat for the dead outlaw's gun. She emptied it through the back of his coat at the cold retreating man shape.

She missed.

But Speck didn't. Aiming for the Vulture's gun, Speck hit thigh and then grazed shoulder before the outlaw disappeared.

The graveyard was quiet.

Cindy buzzed her rattle just in case, but nothing moved. Speck dragged Sam's limp fingers beneath her, nuzzling Sam's face with her cold rosy scales, but his eyelids didn't even flutter.

The two snakes wriggled forward, grabbed turf with Sam's fingers, and then dragged his body facedown through the grass. Speck moved nose and knuckles first. Cindy tossed Sam's elbow out, sidewinding.

They were following the cold man, dragging Sam one slow foot at a time.

They were both still tugging him forward when Sam opened his eyes. His head felt like a bear-swatted beehive.

"Did it work?" he asked. He looked back over his shoulder. Three bodies. But no El Buitre. It had worked. But not well enough.

He grabbed the grass and slid himself forward. Grabbed and slid. Grabbed and . . . what was he doing?

Sam stood up quickly and then blinked as his brain blood swam behind his eyes.

El Buitre was gone and he was still missing his sister. And Glory.

Grabbing two still-loaded guns from one of the dead outlaws, Sam ran through the doorway into the little building. Something was missing. An elevator? A mining cart? The building was small, but the space inside was massive and timeless. The door was a gateway into pure dark confusion.

Twenty steps in, Sam was lost. The darkness was heavy one moment and light the next. He felt like he was floating, teetering, slipping, and then suddenly pushed down. It was like sinking through a floor or falling off a building or being thrown up into the sky by the sky. He was dizzy. Tripping. Turning in place, he couldn't even see light from the door he had entered.

This wasn't darkness; this was nothingness. Sam shut his eyes tight and immediately felt a little better. Eyelids aren't much of a view, but they're something.

Cindy and Speck both tugged him in the same direction.

Glory, Sam told them. *You know Glory. Can you find her?*

Both snakes veered to his left immediately. Sam walked where they led and they pulled harder. Faster. Still with his eyes clamped shut, he ran.

One hundred yards. Two. Or maybe the distance was six months. Or seven yesterdays. But suddenly, a cloud of warmth flashed in front of his feet, and he tripped over something and fell. With nothing else in the world to sense, the heat image the snakes gave him was perfectly clear. It was Glory. She was curled up in a ball and crying.

Glory screamed and Sam yelled. Cindy tried to pull a gun.

Sam managed to stand, and then tried to pull Glory to her feet.

"Sam?" Glory laughed and sobbed at the same time. "If we have to die in here, I'm glad we'll die together."

"Stop being so cheerful," Sam said. "We're not dying. I'm pretty sure this is the kind of place where things get stuck not dying forever. Shut your eyes and grab on."

Glory twisted her hands into the back of Sam's poncho.

Sam shut his eyes, held out his hands, and waited. He didn't have to wait long.

The cold one, Sam thought. *Find the cold man.*

Cindy went left. Speck went right.

Sam hesitated. Without Cindy, Sam would be dead. And he knew she only had one violent interest in life. He liked Speck, but the young snake was just as likely to be chasing a butterfly. Not that there were butterflies in the outer darkness.

"Okay, Cindy," Sam said out loud. "You steer."

Sam ran, and Glory eventually managed to match his stride. They veered right and left, they climbed slow slopes and staggered back down. The darkness was uneven and soft, sometimes sucking silently at their shoes, and sometimes jagged and sharp, nicking ankles and stubbing toes.

In places, the air was thick and foul, in others thin and weak and gaspy, but Cindy never doubted where she was going, not even when shapes slid quickly away from them, strange shapes that Sam would only have believed in his nightmares.

"Are we lost?" Glory asked.

"No," Sam said. "Not at all." He could feel the tickle of Cindy's tongue, wriggling beneath the skin of his hand, trying to flick between his knuckles.

That was new. He tried not to think about it.

And then, finally, when his legs were burning, Cindy reached down and pulled his gun.

"Hold on," Sam said, and then he exploded into light.

Chess pieces slid across the floor. A lantern was suspended above a small broken table and a splintered chessboard. There were two empty chairs and a spiral stairwell set into the floor behind one of them.

"What is this place?" Glory asked.

But Sam didn't answer. Screaming echoed up the stairwell. Sam raced to the twisting stairs and tumbled down into a round, opulent room completely lined with windows. There were map shelves and telescopes and tables crowded with globes and chains and strange brass instruments. Sam didn't give any of it much of a look, and Glory was right behind him. The room was empty and the screaming was coming from below.

Cindy tugged Sam toward wide marble steps recessed into the floor. Sam jumped down them and slid out into a bedroom with a massive black bed in the center. Vultures were carved pretty much everywhere.

Millie was barely conscious on the floor. William Sharon, bloody and limping, was dragging her by the hair toward a large open chest. His guns were holstered, but he had a long knife in his free hand. Six watches floated around him. The seventh had a smashed face and dangled limply from his vest. His eyes jumped when he saw Sam.

"How?" he asked. "The dark is pathless."

"Hello, Sam," Millie mumbled the words quietly, and smiling, she shut her eyes.

Cindy began to fire, but everything in the room seemed to suddenly slow down. Everything except the Vulture.

The man slipped left and then twisted right. His watches lashed the air faster than Sam's eyes could track. As Cindy's bullets missed, windows exploded behind her swirling target. A storm of shattered glass floated slowly down while Speck aimed. And aimed.

In the blur, Sam saw the Vulture draw one gun. He saw the barrel spit fire. Twice.

Heat ripped across the left side of Sam's neck and he staggered backward. The second bullet sliced through his shoulder just above the collarbone, and he slipped, falling into Glory. She tried to hold him up, but he dragged her with him to the ground.

The Vulture was suddenly still, knife in one hand, gun in the other. The watches dropped out of the air, bouncing around him on their chains. Glass shards hit the floor all at once, skittering to a stop.

Millie was crying. Cold wind hummed through the open windows. Sam was on his back, shocked and gasping. His left arm should have been useless, overwhelmed by pain. But the arm was no longer his. Cindy was still pointing, cocking, and pulling the trigger on her empty gun, ignoring the brutal pain roaring in Sam's shoulder.

Click.

Click.

Click.

Smiling grimly, William Sharon moved over Millie, and then spun the knife in his hand.

"Don't," Sam gasped. "Please."

The Vulture's blade flashed down. Glory screamed.

Sam's right arm jerked.

Speck fired once. Twice.

The Vulture's knife spun away across the room and his gun sparked as it jumped from his hand. Fury boiled in the outlaw's eyes.

"I will end you, Miracle," El Buitre snarled. "I will flatten every city you enter, I will kill your every friend. If you ever close your eyes, expect me."

His watches rose in the air around him.

Sam wanted to cry. He wanted to sleep. He wanted Cindy to stop pulling at the pain in his shoulder. He wanted to hoe a garden with his sister in West Virginia and hear her laugh while they chased fireflies, finally unafraid. But most of all, he wanted the storm of evil that had swept them both up to stop its swirling and set them down. Anywhere. Anytime. Alive. Together.

"Kill him, Speck," Sam whispered. His throat felt smaller than a straw. "Please."

Speck fired again and a gold watch chain jumped, broken almost completely through.

William Sharon spun around, ran for the shattered windows, and leapt out into the hissing wind. The watches snapped up around him like wings, slowing the moment as he hung in the air. Twisting around, the outlaw pulled his remaining gun.

Glory grabbed Sam and rolled them both behind the massive bed. Six quick bullets kicked clouds of feathers from the mattress. As the echoes died, Sam struggled to his feet, clenching his jaw against the pain, and then staggered to the window, pointing Speck out and down. He had to finish this. The stories, the memories, the chaos in his mind had to end.

The Vulture was gone.

"Your shoulder," Glory said. "You need a doctor."

"I'm fine," Sam grunted. "I have Cindy."

"Sam," Millie said from the floor. Her eyes were wide with horror. "Your hands . . ."

"Fast, right?" Glory said quickly. She was trembling, and her voice shook. "I love you, by the way. In the book. Supercool to meet you."

Sam holstered his weapons and dropped down

beside his sister. She winced with sympathy, touching his bleeding shoulder. Together, brother and sister stood. Then Millie traced the two scaled heads on the backs of Sam's hands. She said nothing. Not until she slid her arms gently around her brother's neck, avoiding his left shoulder.

"After the train," Millie said. "I just . . ." She let him go and looked at him. "It feels like I've been having nightmares for years and years. I was sure you were dead."

Sam nodded. "I know what you mean." He tried to smile and then wiped his eyes quickly. It wasn't over. He knew it wasn't. But his sister was alive.

"Your hands," Millie said again. She lifted them both up and looked from Speck's eyes to Cindy's.

"Best thing that could have happened to me," Sam said. "I promise. Ask Glory. She saw my arms before."

"This is another dream, isn't it?" Millie finally faced Glory.

Cindy began to rattle. Or she tried. Sam could feel her quivering, but there was no noise.

"Not another dream," Sam said. "This is what all those other dreams were about. They were like . . . practice."

Millie nodded. "Real practice," she said. "I saw this graveyard, Sam . . . I don't know how much you remember." She shivered. While Millie's eyes nervously followed

316

his hands, Sam Miracle winced and cautiously hugged his sister with twisting arms.

"Thank you," she whispered. "Dad would be proud."

Sam blinked and pulled away, almost smiling. He looked around the room.

"How do we get out of here?"

"He took me all around in an elevator," Millie said. "But I have no idea how it's controlled."

Glory picked up something bloody off the floor and held it out to Sam.

"You're forgetting something," she said. "Shot off."

She had the tip of Cindy's tail and her knobby old rattle pinched between her fingers.

If the Vulture had been killed, Sam would have laughed, even with the throbbing agony in his shoulder. But what Sam was feeling was far from joy.

Millie was safe.

But so was El Buitre.

For now.

THE THREE OF THEM LEFT THE VULTURE'S TOWER IN DISARray and filed into the elevator with the brass cage door. Millie slid it shut and latched it. There were little levers and a crank on the side. She asked Glory for help, but Glory shrugged.

"I only know buttons."

Millie flipped two levers and nothing happened. She spun the crank, and the cage began to descend.

"Mill," Sam said, and the nickname surprised him. He had forgotten it until after it was out of his mouth.

His sister looked at him, eyes still darting to his hands.

"I'm sorry," he said. "For all the times I didn't come for you." The pain in his shoulder and his anger at the Vulture's escape and his relief at saving his sister were all making a real mess of how he felt. "And I'm sorry for failing again."

Glory bit her lip and pressed herself back in the elevator.

"What do you mean?" Millie blinked quickly, and then shook her head, surprised. "I'm . . . I . . . Sam, you didn't fail."

"It's okay," Sam said. "I'll figure it out. I won't give up."

Millie focused on Glory. "Do you know what he's talking about?"

"The Vulture," Glory said. "Until the Vulture is dead, you aren't really safe. No one is."

The cage rattled to a stop. For a moment, the three of them stared at the door.

And then Millie threw it open.

Green light poured in. Sam stepped out into a hotel lobby completely overgrown with trees and brush. The massive skylight several floors up was missing most of its glass.

"Stay here for a second," Sam said. Cradling Cindy against his stomach to take the weight of his arm off his wounded shoulder, he jogged across the lobby and out the front doors into what had once been a busy crossroad.

The hilltop hotel was now perched on an island. The streets dove away from Sam's feet and ended in water a few hundred yards away in both directions. Thick cedar trees had grown up in between ruined buildings, toppling walls with their branches and tearing up cobblestones with their roots.

Crusty foam lines in the street marked how high the tide could come.

The hotel wasn't the only island. It was one among hundreds. Only the hilltops of San Francisco were now above water, crowned with trees and the bones of buildings.

Sam saw no one, but the glint of gold caught his eye. A pocket watch with a broken chain and a cracked face lay on a bed of green moss between two stones in the road.

Sam picked it up and listened. It still ticked. He turned in a slow circle but saw no other sign of his enemy.

Quietly and quickly, he reloaded Speck's gun, and then handed it to Cindy.

The Vulture couldn't be far. Sam didn't have to fail.

He could end everything right now. Or he could walk into an ambush and be killed. How long would Glory and Millie wait for him before they gave up? Would they be kidnapped or would they be killed straightaway? Or maybe they would find themselves trapped forever in the wrong time.

Sam picked his direction and began to walk, both hands out, letting them scan the shadows, still trusting Cindy with the gun.

A sharp whistle darted off a rooftop and Sam froze. Cindy began to shake Sam's wound as fast as she could while Speck buzzed his rattle. Two of the nearest cedar trees bent and shook as a pair of massive hairy shapes pushed past their trunks and lumbered into the street.

Sam stumbled backward as the animals rose slowly up onto their hind legs, taller than twin houses, with claws as long as Sam's legs and huge slobbering tongues. They weren't bears. They were something Sam had never even dreamed before, and both of them were rumbling drumbeat growls inside chests the size of cars.

"If you're hunting that dirty time-stopper, he's gone! Stole my bird, too." The voice was a man's and it came from above the street. "Now I have to ask you to drop your guns and set down that gold trinket you found in the street before I let Earl and Wayne here have a little taste of fresh meat."

Sam didn't wait. He spun around, ducking, expecting gunfire from above, and he ran for the hotel. The drumbeat growls erupted into thunder and the ground shook as the animals slammed back down onto all fours.

But from above, there came only laughter.

Sliding back inside the hotel, Sam sprinted to the elevator, slammed the cage door shut, and began slapping levers. When the elevator jerked upward, he slumped against the back and let himself breathe.

"No good," he panted. "He's gone and we have to get out of here."

"Where?" Millie asked.

"Back to the garden," Sam said. "Hopefully in this elevator, but through the darkness if we have to."

"When was it out there?" Glory asked. She reached up and touched the bloody patch on Sam's shoulder.

"I have no idea," said Sam. "But a long while after something awful."

13

Pizza

PETER TIEMPO SAT ON A TRIUMPH MOTORCYCLE IN THE grass, watching two huge trees sway above high stone walls like wings. Their lowest branches gripped the stone like roots. The moon was up, but weak. Peter kept his headlight pointed at the walls.

Nineteen fifty-four had been a complete waste. He had met the boys on the road, but when they'd arrived, they hadn't been able to draw out any kind of opposition.

It had been hard for him—given how unrefined his abilities still were—but he had finally been able to move the bus full of boys to the right afternoon in 1969. He was still sweating from the effort. There hadn't been any mass deaths close enough, and he still wasn't comfortable using that kind of opportunity even if there had been. He would get comfortable with it eventually. He knew that. Just like he would get comfortable with people calling him *Father*. Right now, that just seemed ridiculous.

It was annoying how other people got to talk to his older self, but he never could. He knew that much already. Run into yourself and one of you had to drop dead.

Sam and Glory had made it to the garden, because they had left the motorcycle. But they were already gone, the biggest of the day's shocks hadn't even rolled in yet. The walls were still standing.

"What happened, Sam?" he said out loud.

The ground shivered under his feet.

He whooped loudly, and ten boys jogged back through the shadows from around the walls toward the white bus behind the motorcycle.

"See?" Peter said. "Earthquake. Right on time."

Drew nodded.

The earth heaved. The motorcycle bounced. The bus bucked and the trees shook and hopped, suddenly weak. The boys ran. The continent groaned, grinding its teeth miles deep. The forest stampeded in place. And then both of the big trees fell straight out—doomed, slow, moaning giants. Their branches pulled the walls down. Their roots flung Miracle headstones high in the air.

Pooled time flooded out, pouring across the meadow grass.

And then, apart from a few shivers in the ground, the grove was still.

On the other side of the toppled garden walls, two shapes slowly stood up in the light from the motorcycle. A third was curled up on the ground.

"Hey!" Glory yelled. "I'm glad you guys are finally here. Sam's pretty much passed out, he needs stitches, and we all really need something to eat."

Laughing, Peter throttled the motorcycle forward between the fallen trees.

SAM MIRACLE LOOKED DOWN THE LONG TABLE, ACROSS THE steaming pizzas to where Peter Tiempo sat at the foot of the table in front of the old-fashioned arcade games. Peter was still pale and sweating from the effort of moving everyone again, but he was eating like a funnel cloud and the waitress couldn't replace his Cokes fast enough. On Sam's right, Millie nibbled at her pizza, unsure of what it was, but clearly happy and a little nervous. She caught Sam's eye and smiled. He understood the confusion she was feeling. The fog of uncertainty about what might be real, and what would turn out to be imagination. Or memory. Or nightmare. She wouldn't be herself for a little while. If ever.

He hoped that the world would be better off with her alive. That he hadn't ruined everything.

Glory sat on Sam's left, and she had taken it upon herself to explain every single thing about the modern world to Millie.

And then there were the boys. Sam's Ranch Brothers. The ones who had kept him alive. The ones who had been willing to leave their own lives behind to help Sam live his. Sam wondered if he would ever be half as generous to anyone as all of them had been to him. Even biscuit-faced Matt Cat.

"You know," Glory said, leaning toward Sam. "When you're stuck hungry in 1969, it helps to have a friend like Peter who can get your whole bus to a pizza place in 2016." She smiled. "Even if he does grow up into a crazy priest who totally ruins your life."

"He saved it, too," Sam said. "Just not as often."

At the far end of the table, Peter raised a glass bottle of Coke and whistled for everyone's attention.

"To Sam," Peter said. "Who's only just getting started!"

Sam didn't like how that sounded, but he forced a smile as everyone else raised their drinks, because he was alive, and so was his sister, and he had friends. Real ones. As real as they come.

Which was a lot better than nothing. But maybe not enough.

Sam pushed back from the table and stood, wincing at the freshly stitched pain in his shoulder. It was bad enough that he didn't even feel the bullet burn on his neck.

He waved off assistance and acted like he was heading for the bathroom. Instead, he pushed out the swinging glass door and moved out into the potholed parking lot.

The white bus and the white moon were keeping each other company.

Dew hung in the cool air, and even under his poncho, Sam shivered.

Speck and Cindy were both at full alert, creeping out from Sam's sides, tasting the air.

Father Tiempo, older than Sam had ever seen him, hobbled out from behind the bus and approached Sam, leaning on a cane.

"I'm sorry," Sam said. And he was. More than he could say. Not that he had changed the priest's plan. Not that he had saved his sister. He was sorry for the next Tombstone. And the one after that. He was sorry that his sister might not stay saved. He was sorry that he still felt fear and the fear made him sick and the sickness made him angry. He was sorry Father Tiempo had spent himself on him. Looking at the priest, Sam knew the time-wandering old his fingers tight around the golden watch on its broken chain.

The metal was colder than it should have been.

Sam could feel the ticking in his palm.

GRATITUDE

Katherine, Claudia, and Alex for making me find Glory (and so much more)

Heather Linn for sharing the first sweaty dream

Rory, Lucia, Ameera, Seamus, and Marisol for loving Speck and Cindy before they were real

Aaron Rench for battles past, present, and future perfect

Jim Thomas for betting